'I actually **loved** Blood Crazy. No__j... ---
it.' – Mark Morris

'*Blood Crazy* is a truly terrifying look at the generation gap.
This is cutting edge dystopian horror at its finest! Simon
Clark is a horror legend. His work is essential reading for
fans of the genre!' – Paul Kane

'*Blood Crazy* is a seminal work that transcends genre and
provides an original, fresh, and chilling take on the post-
apocalyptic theme. A compulsive page-turner and required
reading. One of my all-time favourites!'
– Brian Keene

'The first part of *Blood Crazy* depicts the horror, the second
the isolated communities of survivors, the third part,
revelation, explanation and resolution...It's very persuasive
and justifies the horror that comes before it. Not that it
needs to be justified, but it's even more satisfying when the
experience of horror is put to a purpose and not just used
for sensationalism.' – Noel Megahey

'Simon Clark has been a vibrant stalwart of the British
horror scene for the best part of 25 years. His work is,
nevertheless, consistently fresh, urgent and powerful,
informed by a broad knowledge of and affection for the
classic genre touchstones.' – Conrad Williams

'The horror in a Simon Clark book is never where you
expect it to be; it's subtle and disarming...it'll creep up on
you, politely tap you on the shoulder, then grab you by the
throat, squeeze tight and won't let go until it's finished with
you...A distinctive, respected, uniquely British voice in the
horror genre – Simon Clark is a dark master of his art.'
– David Moody

Simon Clark's novels, include *Blood Crazy, Vampyrrhic, Darkness Demands, Stranger, Whitby Vampyrrhic, Secrets of the Dead,* and the British Fantasy award-winning *The Night of the Triffids,* which was broadcast as a five-part drama series by BBC radio.

Weird House Press have recently issued Simon's new collection, *Sherlock Holmes: A Casebook of Nightmares and Monsters,* and a novel, *Sherlock Holmes: Lord of Damnation.*

He has also scripted audio dramas for Big Finish, including for their reboot of the apocalyptic drama, *Survivors.* Simon lives in Yorkshire, England, where he can be seen roaming this legend-haunted landscape with a black and white Border Collie by the name of Mylo.

Website: nailedbytheheart.com

Twitter: hotelmidnight

BLOOD CRAZY:
ATEN IN ABSENTIA

BLOOD CRAZY SERIES
BOOK TWO

Also by Simon Clark

BLOOD & GRIT
NAILED BY THE HEART
BLOOD CRAZY
DARKER
ON DEADLY GROUND –
(formerly KING BLOOD)
VAMPYRRHIC
THE FALL
JUDAS TREE
DARKNESS DEMANDS
NIGHT OF THE TRIFFIDS
STRANGER
VAMPYRRHIC RITES
THE DALEK FACTOR
IN THIS SKIN
THE TOWER
LONDON UNDER MIDNIGHT
DEATH'S DOMINION
THIS RAGE OF ECHOES
LUCIFER'S ARK
COLOUR OF ECHOES: A VAN GOGH MYSTERY –
(formerly THE MIDNIGHT MAN)
VENGEANCE CHILD
GHOST MONSTER
WHITBY VAMPYRRHIC
HIS VAMPYRRHIC BRIDE
HER VAMPYRRHIC HEART
INSPECTOR ABBERLINE & THE GODS OF ROME
SECRETS OF THE DEAD
INSPECTOR ABBERLINE & THE JUST KING
RAGE MASTER
SHERLOCK HOLMES: LORD OF DAMNATION
COLD LEGION

BLOOD CRAZY:
ATEN IN ABSENTIA

BLOOD CRAZY SERIES
BOOK TWO

SIMON CLARK

Darkness Visible

First published in Great Britain in 2023
by Darkness Visible Publishing

www.dv-publishing.com

ISBN 978-1-9998516-1-3

Get this message into your head.
You, too, have a monster to kill.
– And this book just might save your life.

CHAPTER ONE

IT'S A BLOODY START

'Gorron? What happened? Why is everyone lying out in the snow?'

Gorron looked up at me from where he sat on a tree stump. His eyes were not eyes anymore. They were open wounds.

Open wounds of sheer fucking horror.

Gorron spoke in a voice that was so tired. Absolute exhaustion stopped the words coming from his lips properly. 'I...they... they...last week. When you...were away.'

Slipping off my rucksack, I crouched beside him, my knees touching a mound of milk-white snow that was speckled crimson. Gorron's nose was bleeding. He sniffed up, spat out. A dab of red appeared on the snow. The dab steamed in the cold air.

Gently, I put my hand on Gorron's shoulder, but I wanted to shake the guy hard, while saying over and over: *Tell me what happened! Why are our friends crawling through the snow? Open your fucking mouth – tell me!* But Gorron only mumbled now, as he stared at the red lick of blood marking the snowdrift beneath his face. His head hung forward. It was low and somehow heavy looking. Like his skull was made of iron. And it was so heavy he couldn't raise it to look at me. Those eyes of his were nothing more than raw, open wounds. No, his eyes weren't injured, or cut, or punched until they looked like that. No, it was something else. The whites of his eyes were red. They were watery. Sore-looking. Dazed and out of focus, too. Gorron was so tired he sagged. His arms were hanging down. He was ready to fall asleep at any second.

I glanced back at the houses where us sorry little bunch of survivors had made our homes. We'd settled there after the adults had gone crazy all those years ago, and had started murdering the young – especially their own children.

'What happened here?' I kept banging out the same question. I wanted information. I needed words that would explain why the doors of our homes all lay open, and everyone who lived in them now crawled belly-down through the snow, away from the houses, and out across the fields – a strange, slow-motion exodus. *Dear God, some of them aren't even wearing any clothes.* 'What happened? Gorron, can you hear me?'

Gorron managed the smallest of nods. Then he took a deep breath and began speaking. He was taking care to shape the words with his lips in such a way I could understand them. Even so, he barely spoke above a whisper. 'Jack. I'm sorry.'

'What have you to be sorry about?'

'We got lazy. We stopped boiling water from the well. Everyone became sick.'

'Sick? In what way sick?'

'Some bug...it makes everyone tired. People just sleep all the time...we can hardly walk. Even...even talking is...so hard.'

'But why has everyone left their homes? It's freezing out here.'

Gorron sagged. Exhaustion was draining him of every molecule of strength. 'Boil water, Jack...gotta boil water before...drinking... boil it before even washing your hands. That's what we should...uh, I'm sorry, Jack.'

Gorron's a big guy of nineteen, strong as Zeus, but right then he looked as if he had difficulty lifting his own eyelids. Exhaustion made his lips go slack. Speaking became as hard as galloping a marathon.

'Gorron. Tell me why everyone left their houses.' Yep. Still persisted...burning with the need for my questions to be answered. My mouth felt much too wet – a sure sign of vomit chugging its way up from my stomach. The sight of my friends squirming like knackered snakes through the snow made me feel sick. I hated seeing what they had been reduced to. Because three weeks ago (when I saw them last), they had been teenagers, erupting with health and vitality – with teenage preoccupations on their mind – that being having a great time, drinking homemade hooch, laughing loads, and blazing with sexual energy (yeah, older teenagers, right? Our group, our commune if you prefer, were seventeen, eighteen, nineteen years of age). Now they slithered through the white stuff. Some wearing indoor clothes, some just bare skin against freezing snow. And where's Dane? My girlfriend, Dane. Eighteen. Pretty as sunrise and sunset rolled into one. By now, my mind had locked itself into a spin. My heart pounded. Thoughts were just a yelling Bedlam inside my head. *Calm down, think clearly. Focus. Find out what happened. Then find Dane. If she's out here in the snow, she won't survive for much longer...*

I gently gripped Gorron by the shoulder. 'I'll get you indoors, otherwise you'll freeze to death out here.'

My friend shook that heavy-as-pig-iron skull of his. 'Can't...can't go back inside.'

'Whyever not?'

'Because...' He took a deep breath. 'Because they are in there.'

'Who are?'

'Mr Creosote.'

2

With a surge of something that felt like frozen blood ramming through my heart, I turned to stare in horror at the houses.

Dear God. There they are. Gorron's right.

Mr Creosote stood in the doorway of every house. Mr Creosote? Yeah. The silly, jokey name we'd given to something so dreadful that a more accurately descriptive tag would be too horrifying... utterly violating your mouth. 'Mr Creosote', or just plain 'Creosote'. That's what we called the adults who went crazy and murdered their own children. But I hadn't seen Creosotes in months.

Now they were back. Not only that – they came out of the houses. Running toward where Gorron sat. Running toward where all those teenagers struggled through the snow, teenagers that were sick with a disease that caused chronic fatigue to the point they couldn't even walk.

The adults approached. Their homicidal, blazing eyes told me that they had one thing occupying their rage-crazy minds.

'Gorron. Run!'

Beaten down by exhaustion, he shook his head. 'Can't.'

'I'll fucking well carry you, then!'

I grabbed hold, hoisted him to his feet, then after putting an arm around his waist and holding his right arm over my shoulders, I began to move as quickly as I could from the mob of five hundred or so Creosotes flooding from the houses.

As I hauled Gorron away, I asked myself how I could save all those sick teenagers in the field.

I know the answer to that one, don't I? I fucking well know...

CHAPTER TWO

FIRST THE PAIN, THEN THE DYING

The answer was: *I can save* **none** *of them.*

There were perhaps ninety teenagers. They were either lying there or crawling on their bellies across the snow-covered field. They knew full well that the Creosotes were coming, Creosote eyes were locking onto the objects of their bloodlust. Their mouths were chomping at cold air in a bizarrely disturbing way. And those friends of mine knew they could not even stand up on their own two feet, let alone outrun the invaders. Those young people knew that this was the day they died. And that their deaths would be violent, and that they'd live a nightmare of pain and terror until they either bled out or a merciful blow would shatter the bone that enclosed the delicate structure of their brain. Imagine what they felt at that moment. The terror. The helplessness.

Gorron muttered stuff about me leaving him. He knew that he slowed me down, making it likely the homicidal Creosotes would catch up with us. He didn't want me to sacrifice my own life for him.

'No way, Gorron.' I was huffing out big clouds of white vapour into bitterly cold air. 'No way. You saved my neck in the past, now I'm going to fucking well save yours.'

'Jack...leave me. They'll kill you.'

'Run...that's it, use your feet. Faster...faster!'

The big man managed to run a dozen paces then exhaustion ripped whatever remained of his strength right out of him. He slumped, legs going limp. Then I had to drag the big, loveable brute – all muscle and bone, he was.

My boots kicked through drifts, blasting up fountains of white. Repeatedly, I glanced back to see the Creosotes. They were a wild-looking bunch. They had manes of shaggy hair that hadn't been cut in years. And they possessed mad eyes that stared from filthy faces. Their mouths were chewing the air (a rage thing? An instinctive urge to bite flesh? Who knows?). Hundreds of adults targeted us. They were aged anything from twenties, right up to white-haired grandmas and granddads. All of them, with murderous intent

4

boiling in their veins. Their murder trigger had been pulled: they craved to rip us to pieces...then (if the mood took them that way) stick our heads on the ends of branches, and trot along roads with our bloody, ripped-up, messed-up skulls held up high – skewered lollipop-style on those branches that would be scarlet and oh-so wet with our blood.

By this time, I howled at my mates, most of whom were squirming belly-down, crawling as slow as turtles.

'Move!' I was going frantic with absolute terror because I knew what dreadful things would happen in the next twenty seconds. 'Get to your feet. Run. Run!'

All those faces I recognised – *damn it* – all those faces that I had come to love. Because we had survived against the odds to get this far. They turned wearily to look at me.

'Jack,' croaked Mary. 'Jack, I can't walk. Help me.'

'Mary, you've got to run! And now! Run for your life!'

Others called out to me. I knew them all: Jason, Sasha, Mo, Suzie, Josh-oh, Tanya, Pix, Alan, Fatima, Christine, Dazzer, Rebecca, Yasmin...I shouted their names, begged them to stand, to run, to hide...to live...because DEATH prowled across the field toward them.

'You must get to your feet,' I yelled. By this time, the muscles in my arms and back were on fire. They absolutely fucking hurt. Nothing less than torture. I wasn't just supporting Gorron's weight, I was carrying every single ounce of the man.

I yelled at my friends: 'Come on, you can do it! Run!'

Some did. Yasmin, she of the long black hair, and marathon runner's legs, managed to stand. With a huge effort, she sprinted twenty paces then...all her strength...just gone. Her legs turned boneless as exhaustion overwhelmed her. Down she went. Sprawling. Face down.

I staggered forward in a zigzag way. Heading toward Pix – she with the snub nose and one eye; the right one was lost after a fight with a bulldog that'd gone feral. For ten seconds I ranted, just going frantic: *'Pix! Get up. Get to your fucking feet. Fucking run. Fucking survive. Don't be killed in front of me. Please don't get killed...'*

Pix lay there, waving me on, gesturing for me to keep moving. To leave her.

Then *zig* off to the next teenager to beg them to run. Then *zag* to the next, and more pleading from me. *Zigzag, zig-fucking-zag...* some manged to get upright, then jog a few steps. But whatever disease had got its hooks into their blood soon dropped them back into the snow again.

Meanwhile, Gorron muttered, 'Leave me here, Jack. Don't let them kill you.'

He'd clearly seen the Creosotes moving across the field. They were getting excited now, getting the bloodlust pumping through their veins. They tracked their prey. They wanted to punch, and kick, and rip – and feel eyes pop under their hooking fingers, enjoying the slippery lubricant that was their victims' blood upon their flesh.

What could I do? I could not pick up ninety of my friends, and pop them into my pocket, then run to safety. Just carrying Gorron was torture. Even so, I did entertain the notion of trying to pick up Suzie. She was one of the lightest. But that would be madness to even try. I'd barely get ten paces with her on my back and Gorron under one arm. Even now I grunted noisily as I tried to suck in enough oxygen to keep going. My heart pounded. Sweat was a river flowing down my back.

And all those Creosotes streamed across that meadow of pristine whiteness. Soon, they'd reach me. Then they'd tear me apart as I screamed and convulsed in agony.

But you know something? In the end, my friends saved me.

They saved me by dying. The Creosotes launched their attack: biting, punching, kicking, ripping off faces with their bare hands. For a few moments, which were more precious than gold, the monsters were too busy killing the people I'd lived with, and doing all that friendship stuff of eating together, laughing at one another's jokes – heck, I'd even shared my bed with Yasmin for six months.

Now...these events, which were taking place in the meadow, seemed so remote and were nothing to do with me. It was like I was merely watching black and white footage from a hundred years ago (yes, I was physically there – boots planted in the snow, my back itching from the sweat trickling down, but I also seemed to be seeing the tragedy unfold from far, far away – a distant observer, mentally – though my flesh, blood, heart, eyes, and brain were in that fucking godawful field). I watched as a white-haired grandma tore a hole in Yasmin's slender neck with her fingers. Blood fountained upward – a red plume – a spray of scarlet that went up and up before falling back down onto the snow. Red tears, or so it seemed to me. Tears for the doomed teenagers that died here.

As **DEATH** danced away with the lives of those young men and women, I shouted my girlfriend's name: 'Dane! Dane!' Then I yelled at Gorron. 'Where's Dane?'

He muttered a reply. I couldn't make out what he said.

A hand swiped at my back. Mr Creosote wanted to rinse his fingers in my blood. I kicked out, smashing his kneecap with my boot. With a strange laugh, he toppled sideways and fell into the snow.

'Jack, time to go...' I directed these words inwards at myself. 'You can't save them.'

6

Tanya reached up to me from where she sat on the ground. She was so tired; she could barely raise her hand. 'Jack. Take me with you.'

I could not even say 'Sorry', because I was so choked with the sheer horror of what was happening. Yes, I'd seen death plenty. But that seemed a long time ago, when everyone over the age of nineteen went crazy and civilization collapsed overnight. Now, here in this field, these deaths were so raw, so immediate, so sheer *noisy*. Okay, granted, the virus that had infected these teenagers had robbed them of their ability to run. But, oh boy, could they scream.

I focussed on moving now. Just running. Just getting away from there. I lugged Gorron toward where the black fringe of the woods started, hoping to hide there. But get this: more Creosotes were flowing out of the trees toward me. Creosotes in front, Creosotes behind me. I was trapped.

In desperation, I staggered to where a river formed a dark line between two white-shrouded banks. Creosotes came charging toward me, their eyes bright with rage. Their shaggy hair was flecked with snow. Bloody hands were hooking into claws as they reached out, getting ready to peel the living flesh from my face.

'Sorry,' I panted to Gorron, 'this is the only thing I can think of.'

I hauled him toward the riverbank. To where the ground angled steeply downward in the direction of icy water that was as black as the pupil of your eye.

Creosotes were already grasping my clothes, and my hair, and my throat when I kicked myself forward, hauling Gorron with me. Then we were tumbling down the steep slope. Before I could even suck in a lungful of life-preserving air I crashed into black water. Down, down, down I went, until daylight vanished. And I found myself sinking through liquid darkness.

Every so often in life, you reach a threshold where you cross over into an entirely new kind of existence. That was the moment when it happened to me. Because I was sinking deeper and deeper toward the bottom of the river...where the eels and slimy things live. Far from the light of day.

CHAPTER THREE

WHO THE HELL IS JACK RANZIC?

Okay, when you're telling people what happened to you, it's best to tell them something about your history. Who you are, where you came from, and, perhaps, where you hope to end up.

For obvious reasons, ever since civilization rolled over and died on us, it's not easy to make long-term plans. Certainly, I'll never receive a pension, and you can forget a peaceful retirement by the sea.

My name is Jack Ranzic. I'm nineteen years old. I like steak dinners, barbecues, kicking a ball around with my friends. Once, long ago, I loved listening to music. Though I can't enjoy music these days. I just can't. It's like the music file in my brain is corrupted. It must've happened back when I had to spend every minute of every day either running from danger, searching for food, or fighting for my life. Nowadays, if I hear music on a battery-powered device, it's just noise. An awful, headache-provoking noise at that.

Okay, this is where I confess the thing that I promised my mother I would never mention to another living soul. Well...my mother's no longer around, so here is where I reveal my secret. And here is that big reveal: **my father tried to kill me.** In the light of what happened three years ago, when adults (every single one of them) went berserk and tried to wipe out their own children, that's hardly a unique statement. All over the world, billions of parents began to slaughter their own young. Those without sons and daughters, slaughtered the nearest kid they could find.

But my story is different. My father tried to kill my mother, my sisters and me years before the madness epidemic tore our lives apart. Dad wasn't a bank robber or a drug dealer or prone to violent outbursts. He worked quietly in an insurance office, paid his bills, drove his car to the supermarket once a week, with all us kids loaded onboard, who were squabbling, farting, and complaining that we were being dragged to the supermarket when we wanted to watch television or do the fun things that kids like to do. Once at the supermarket, he and my mother would buy baked beans, potatoes, toothpaste, and stuff. All the normal kind of things that families need. Then one day, the police arrested Dad on suspicion of diverting some of the insurance company's money into his own secret bank account. He was charged, and then went through the long process of meeting defence lawyers, preparing statements – the whole legal fandango. This went on for twelve months, then the case went to court and Dad was found...

...suspenseful pause...**NOT GUILTY**.

The week following the court case, he flipped. Late one night, I awoke to my father yelling, my mother screaming, my eight-year-old twin sisters were sobbing and shouting. Then my mother suddenly went quiet. My sisters ran into my bedroom in their pjs, tears were running down their faces, and they were yelling, 'Jack, he's going to kill us! He killed Piper!'

Piper was our dog, a Border Collie, with a limp in his back left leg, caused by a previous owner who had thought it cool and brave to kick his own dog.

I struggled to take it all in. 'Piper's dead?'

My twin sisters wailed, 'Dad killed him! He's going to kill us!'

Though I was only ten years of age, those words blazed through my ears and into my brain, and I saw, in my mind's eye, Dad strangling each of us in turn – making our eyes bulge, and our tongues push out through our lips and turn black. I saw all this in a heartbeat...and I saw myself lying in a coffin. And my grandparents standing beside that long box – sobbing so hard, their hearts breaking.

As those horrific images blasted through my head, my sisters were shouting, 'What are we going to do?' And: 'Jack, you've got to stop him!'

But how does a young boy stop their parent from hurting them? How can a little kid prevent Dad from punching them in the face, or gripping them by the throat?

I heard the thump-thump-thump of footsteps coming up the stairs. He didn't shout anything that was (what's the word?) *resonant*, or *piquant*, or *witty*. Nothing like, 'Daddy's going to tuck you up, all nice and cosy, and then give you a good night kiss with this dirty great hammer.'

No. All I heard was the thump-thump-thump of his feet getting closer as he came upstairs to murder his own flesh and blood, which he had always appeared to love with all his heart. Heck, the guy even dressed as Santa Claus on Christmas Eve. He gave presents to our dog, and beamed with delight when two-year-old Piper wagged his fluffy black and white tail and started to pull at the wrapping paper with his teeth.

Then my father did speak. Just twice...a strange, roughened up voice, as if he'd swallowed acid that burned his throat. 'I've had it with you.' Thump-thump-thump. Closer and closer. He was on the landing now – the floorboards were creaking. 'I've had it with you three. Take, take, take – never giving anything back.'

9

The doorhandle dipped downwards. Mustering all my strength, my ten-year-old body did what it could. I shoved a chest of drawers right up to the door. Of course, what I needed was a block of concrete, weighing a ton, because my weedy little barricade wouldn't keep out a grown man. But when he pushed open the door, the chest of drawers toppled, the top of it jamming up against the end of my bed, so simply shoving the door open now, and moving the chest of drawers wouldn't be easy for Dad. My sisters became deathly quiet. In fact, they had the cold light of death in their eyes, as if they had given up and were preparing themselves for the end of their young lives.

Right at that moment, I transformed into a kind of whirling tornado of arms and legs. I was shouting and shoving and pushing, as I chivvied them to the window, which I opened, then I scrambled out onto the adjoining garage roof. That done, I held up my hands and got my sisters out of what would have become the murder room.

After that, it was all a bit of a blur. Me, lowering my sisters down onto the path. Me, jumping down and hurting my ankle. Then they were helping me limp to the house next door, where my memories dissolve into faces looming out through doorways. Our neighbours' eyes wide with horror. Then came the flashing lights of police cars.

A police officer drove me and my sisters to my grandparents – the cop kept saying over and over: 'You saved your sisters' lives, Jack. In my book, you are a hero. You should get a medal for bravery.'

Dad went to prison for eighteen months (no, I never did understand why the judge gave him such a lenient sentence; mitigating circumstances, perhaps?). The day they let Dad out of prison he came home, eager to kill his wife and children. He never found us. My mother had recovered from the fractured skull he'd inflicted upon her with a bottle. We were placed in an official protection scheme and sent to live in rooms over a pizza takeaway. My mother chose the name 'Ranzic'. So, I went to a new school as 'Jack Ranzic'. I can remember my old surname (which was my father's surname, as was the practice back then), but I'll never say it, write it, or even piss on it (if such an action was even possible). The one time I did say Dad's surname again, just after I started at the new school (and only then by accident), I threw up so hard that I blacked out.

Later, my mother told me that Piper hadn't been killed, and that she had sent him to live with one of her friends, where he enjoyed lots of walks in the park and wore a bright red collar. What's more, even his sore leg (caused by his previous owner's kick) never bothered him now, and he could run and play with the other dogs. Back then, as a child, I believed her of course. But now I wonder if Piper hadn't really survived that awful night when Dad flipped, and my lovely dog is resting in a quiet corner of my grandparents' back garden.

Then, a few years later, it happened: the thing we now call 'The Day'. This is The Day when adults became angry with their own children. Angry to such a degree they attacked them. Strangely, deep down, I'd been expecting this to happen. After all, it had happened to me when I was ten, so it seemed perfectly natural that fathers would eventually turn on their children and try and snuff out their lives.

The Day occurred when I was working in a warehouse at night. The first I knew that our world had been viciously ripped inside out was when I saw my boss beating a seventeen-year-old order picker to death with a steel shelf. Other guys came running to help. Help kill the kid, that is. After that, they tried to kill me. However, I got away, running off into the dark. So...what about my mother and sisters? After leaving the warehouse, I made my way home to find the rooms where we lived above the pizza takeaway were burning as bright as a monster firework, chucking out sparks, flames – then there were explosions as gas pipes burst. The stench of burning dug itself into my skin...burrowed so fucking deep...I could still smell it on my hands a month later. Or at least I believed I could. No...I didn't answer my own question back there, did I? What did happen to my mother and my sisters? I just don't know. I never saw them again. Except in nightmares...I don't want to recall those night-mares for you...they are bad. Very bad.

Lately, I often wonder if my own father trying to kill me prepared me for what happened when The Day came, and civilization shattered into a billion fragments. I think I not only survived but prospered to a certain extent. After all, for me there was a normality in what happened. A parent attacking children? I'd already been through that particular trauma, hadn't I? And survived. That made me feel stronger inside, and better able to cope with the murderous tidal wave that engulfed the world when the adults when crazy.

Of course, millions of young people weren't fortunate enough to survive. Nevertheless, I met up with a group of teenagers and we went to live in an abandoned village, which we called New Home (nobody liked the village's real name, Midge-Low – that's sort of insectile, makes the skin itch every time you utter 'Midge-Low', doesn't it?). We were happy there, considering the circumstances. But then a new sickness came, causing fatigue. With the sickness came the Creosotes – you know that, of course, because I have just described what happened.

Okay. Now, you're up-to-date with my personal history...more or less anyway. Right up to the point where Gorron and I ended up in the river. There we are – underwater, not able to breathe. Which brings me right up to what happens next...

CHAPTER FOUR

COLDER THAN A RIVER IN THE LAND OF THE DEAD

My head split the surface of the river. I breathed again. I could feel Gorron's mop of hair against the side of my face as I trod water. The water smelt stale, a sort of a fungal stench. Old mushrooms past their best-before date. And the river was as cold as Death's everlasting kiss. Flowing water sounds echoed back at me. I saw nothing. Absolutely nothing. And even though my head was above the surface, all that flooded over my eyes was darkness, total darkness.

'Gorron.' My voice rebounded back at me. It was a tunnel echo – a repeating *Gorron* slowly died away, all ghostly and eerie, into the distance. 'Gorron, are you still alive?'

*Gorron, are you still alive...still alive...*The echoes repeated my words until they were finally swallowed up by darkness and the deathly cold.

Gorron made no answer. His body was limp. I had to use the side of my face to push his face clear of the water as I clung onto him with one arm and paddled forwards with the other. Soft things stroked my face – rats' tails? Cobwebs? The caressing fingers of the crazy adults who were teasing us before they ripped off our heads? I could not tell, but my heart almost exploded from my chest with the shock of being touched by those things. When it happened again, I reached up, grabbed one, while bellowing, 'You don't scare me!' Of course, I was scared, but bravado was my only weapon.

What my fingers did grasp there in the darkness were shreds of what (I guessed) were polythene, hanging down from what must be a tunnel roof. I reached up again, higher this time. Yep. Hardness. Brick or concrete. The river had carried us into a tunnel. A very dark tunnel because I saw nothing. I didn't even know if I floated along holding the corpse of my friend, or whether his heart was still beating inside his body.

'Gorron. Can you – uh!' Yep, the river poured in over my lips to hit the back of my throat. I coughed out a gob full of water. Disgusting. I pictured all the things that must have peed in the river

12

(rats, foxes, humans), and I'd just gone and taken a dirty great bite out of that cold and absolutely vile brew of mucky liquid.

'Shit!'

My predicament made me angry now. And that anger put some fire into my veins. I thought: *Time to stop drifting...time to start doing some fucking thing that will get us out of here.* I knew that the river flowed past New Home before entering a tunnel that carried it beneath the site of a huge factory. Though I didn't know if the river ran underground for such a long distance that we'd die of hypothermia before we could get out, or whether the water-course returned to the surface again at some point soon.

As I wondered what I should do, I glimpsed a grey patch ahead. Fortunately, I didn't need to swim in that direction, as the current carried us to a segment of tunnel that was open to sky. Maybe some kind of inspection point. Now I could see that over the years lots and lots of polythene – bags, plastic sheets, all that kind of crap – had been washed downstream where it had caught on steelwork that helped support the tunnel's roof. The roof, therefore, resembled the 'hairy' belly of a polythene monster – from the roof hung thousands of limp strands of plastic. It was these that I had felt touching my face as I'd drifted along.

The current suddenly quickened, boosting us along the tunnel. I noticed the section that was open to the sky had a steel ladder bolted to the wall. As it approached, I swam one handed, while kicking my legs, sometimes kicking Gorron in the process, but I had to reach that ladder. If I failed, we'd be carried back into that evil subterranean darkness again. Every minute counted now. The cold would kill us for sure in the next hour or so.

As I swam, hauling Gorron (an unconscious, Gorron), I grabbed a rung of the ladder, and hung on.

Then came the really hard part. Climbing out.

Mainly, I remember the foulest of swear words rocketing from my lips. That and the pain in my arms, shoulders and back. Because I had to lift Gorron out of the water as I scaled the ladder. What helped, was when I managed to fashion a support harness by threading my belt through his belt. I then wore mine, bandolier-style, over my right shoulder. Now I didn't have to rely on using just one hand to pull him fully clear of the water. Somehow, helped by that torrent of swear words, while grunting, and grimacing like the ugliest Notre-Dame gargoyle you've ever seen, I made it to the top of the ladder. Finally, I hauled us both out onto the snow-covered earth.

By some miracle, we had made it into the huge factory complex. Of course, the site was abandoned now. There were no people here. Well, I hoped not, because if there were, they were likely to be Creosotes. For a long time, I sat there, trying to catch my breath, while dripping river water, and gazing at those bleak structures, which consisted mainly of steel skeletons that were linked to all that factory hardware. And I pictured the ghosts of dead workers still toiling over machines that pumped toxic chemicals through pipes that wormed their way across the landscape here.

Gorron was lying beside me. And I did not know whether my friend was alive or dead.

CHAPTER FIVE

SUGAR ISLAND. DANGER.
DO NOT GO THERE

We arrived sopping wet.

I was still carrying Gorron, our belts hitched together. As I pushed the door shut behind me, I manage to gasp out the words: 'Gorron...take your clothes off. You've got to dry yourself. Or...the cold will fucking kill you.'

Gorron muttered something.

I stared at him in amazement. 'You're alive? I'd begun to have my doubts.'

'Yeah...I'm alive...but I feel like a hippopotamus just crapped me out of its arsehole.'

Not the most picturesque phrase I've ever heard, yet I felt a surge of relief. That was more like the old Gorron I knew. He was a striking looking teenager, with a massive dandelion clock of hair standing out from his skull. He possessed dark eyes that could be so expressive, and the man was, as another picturesque phrase goes, built like a brick shithouse.

'Sit down.' I manoeuvred him to an armchair in the corner of the room. 'You're soaking wet. So, you've got to get your kit off...then you've got to dry yourself.'

Water poured off my clothes, too. That awful stinking river water. Nevertheless, I needed to get my friend dry and warm again. Slowly, he began to strip, but that disease, which inflicted extreme fatigue on its victims, made his movements clumsy and slow. He stood up to try and unbutton his shirt. His legs wobbled, his head drooped, his hands were shaking. Dear God, though he was nineteen, he looked to have aged a hundred years since I last saw him three weeks ago.

'I'll help,' I told him. 'Raise your arms.'

He didn't protest as I lifted the shirt up and over his head. After flinging the sopping garment aside, I stripped off his other clothes before pulling off his socks.

I said: 'Good thing we're mates. I wouldn't do this for anyone else, you know?'

'Not even Dane?' He spoke before realizing that Dane might be lying out there in the snow, ripped into quarters, into tenths, fuck knows what. 'Sorry, Jack.'

'What happened to Dane? Was she lying out there in the snow with everyone else?'

'I don't know. I saw her yesterday morning. That's the last time...' He groaned.

The groan might have been a groan of regret that he couldn't tell me more, or maybe he was in pain. His eyelids drooped. That sickness had robbed all the strength from him, sending him back to sleep.

The building we'd entered had SECURITY written on the door, and it was some distance away from the other factory buildings, and the big steel tanks that contained whatever dangerous chemical brew they had concocted here. The room we occupied must have been where security guards took their rest breaks. There were armchairs, a sofa, a table with cutlery set out as if dinner was just about to be served. Of course, the building had been abandoned years ago. Thick dust made all the hard surfaces of the table and plastic dining chairs soft-looking, almost as if the furniture had sprouted feathers. There was also a gas fire, a gas cooker, microwave oven, sink, shelves with plates, cups. A fridge stood by the door. A toaster had popped up toast a long time ago, maybe just moments before all the adults in the world went berserk. The toast had fossilized...is that the right word? Or should that be ossified? Or petrified? Well, whatever, the toast was as hard as a bathroom tile after all this time. There were rolls of paper towels on a shelf. Grabbing a roll, I blew off the dust then did my best to dry Gorron. I used handfuls of tissue, rubbing the scrunched-up paper over his back, chest, stomach, and that big mop of hair of his. Drying him was a matter of life and death. As well as the illness, there was a real danger he'd be killed by hypothermia. Even now, cold blood might be returning along veins to his vital organs. A rush of cold blood into his chest might stop his heart, which would kill him as suddenly as a shotgun blast.

So, I scraped away at his skin with big handfuls of tissue. As soon as the paper was mushy, I tossed it and pulled more off the roll. Water still dripped from me, of course, though I guessed all that strenuous movement, while carrying Gorron, had heated my blood up, thus sparing me from the worst effects of the cold.

Being a survivor in that busted up world, where only a few thousand (yeah, maybe as low as that) *sane* young people clung to life, always prompts me to instantly assess any new surroundings I find myself in – whether that be a road, field, forest, or building. Immediately, I'd ask myself questions: *Is it safe here? Is there anything I can take that will help me survive? Is there food? Is there clean water?*

16

As Gorron began to snore in the armchair, I tugged a little plastic box from my pocket: a watertight one where I kept plasters for cuts, needles, thread (not just to mend clothes but to stitch up gashes in flesh, if need be); there were blister packs of painkillers, as well as a precious cigarette lighter (matches and lighters are scarce on Apocalypse Earth). Quickly, I checked the gas stove, not expecting it to work – but, lo and behold, a miracle – one of the gas rings popped into life the instant I'd turned a knob and held the flame of the cigarette lighter to the burner. That was the first time I'd seen a gas-powered appliance do what it was supposed to do in years. Despite the novelty of it all, I only stood there marvelling at the sight of that beautiful ring of blue flame for three or four seconds. I had to get to work fast. Another requirement of a survivor is to be efficient. To do a heck of a lot quickly.

So, I got moving. I then lit the gas fire. Brilliant! The gas ignited with a pop. For a moment, smoke gushed out – just accumulated dust being burned off, and, yep, it did stink of burning, too. But that thing blasted out heat, glorious heat. The armchair Gorron snoozed in was on castors, so I wheeled him closer to the fire, so he'd benefit from its warmth. But how could there still be gas in the mains network after all these years? Gas was no longer being pumped from the ground. The pipes that carried it were no longer maintained. A quick look out of the window provided the answer.

'Gas bottles.' I nodded. 'Finally, something breaks our way.'

Another survival technique: reccy your new location. Who knows if there's a gang of smackheads in the next room with guns? Sincerely, I hoped not. Nor was there any indication that anyone had been in here for years. The dusty floor only revealed our wet footprints. The door had been shut – not locked. Windows were intact.

At a run, I went upstairs, going from room to room. In one, a bank of CCTV monitors. Not working, of course, as no electricity had flowed through the power lines since The Day. Other rooms upstairs were offices, complete with desks and computers. Downstairs, I found a storeroom that had shelves of T-shirts and sweatshirts – all new, wrapped in cellophane, and all black with the word SECURITY printed on them in big white letters. So, the guards were provided with uniforms. Excellent. I opened a couple of these cellophane-wrapped packages to find dry garments that didn't even smell fusty.

Still moving at high-speed, I gathered up a bunch of security guard clothing and manged to get them onto Gorron. Then I peeled off my own clothes, dried myself, before pulling on several T-shirts and a couple of sweatshirts. Adding plenty of layers certainly makes you warmer. The gas fire had heated the room as well. It was lovely and toastie. Another search revealed a room with boots on racks, and waterproofs on pegs, including coats, hats, trousers. I pulled on a pair of waterproof trousers, then I donned a coat, again with SECURITY printed on the back. Gathering up more coats, I piled these over Gorron. They'd serve as blankets.

Then everything eased down into domestic mode. I carried pans outside, filled them with snow, the cleanest snow I could find. Nothing with droppings, and avoiding snow that was a shade of yellow or green, for obvious reasons. Thereafter, I put pans of snow on the stove, melting the white stuff to water, which I then boiled good and hard. Our bodies would need liquids soon, and no way did I want any microbes turning my gut into their new home.

With Gorron asleep in the armchair, snoring softly under the coats, I decided to take a walk around outside, just in case any Creosotes had made it into the factory complex. All being well, they wouldn't succeed in breaching the formidable security fences, which I knew enclosed the massive site.

The factory wasn't at all far from New Home. In the early days, we'd foraged for supplies here, though it appeared as if none of our people had ever been into the security guards' building, which lay some distance from the main complex. We'd called the place 'Sugar Island' on account of the rivers and canals cutting it off from the outside world. The only way in an out for vehicles was by a road bridge. The 'Sugar' part of the name came about when chemicals started leaking from overhead pipework that ran for miles around the place. There were also huge metal spheres that contained more of the witch's brew (as we named it). Those chemicals smelt incredibly sweet, hence 'Sugar Island.' For a while, this factory appeared to be very useful indeed. We scavenged bucket-sized cans of vegetables, stew, soup and meat from the canteen kitchen. However, one day, a scavenging group of eight from our community came here, hunting for provisions, when one of the leaking storage tanks detonated. I mean it really **DETONATED**. The explosion ripped apart the storage tank and knocked the walls down of a nearby building. Three of the scavenging team were reduced to something that resembled smears of tomato ketchup on the ground.

After that, we decided foraging on Sugar Island was too risky. A decision proved right when we were startled awake many a night by frequent explosions, as the witch's brew of chemicals detonated in pipes and other storage tanks. Sometimes we'd see flickers of green and blue light over Sugar Island as chemicals spontaneously ignited. On one occasion, chemicals leaked out to float on a canal. Even in pouring rain, the chemicals erupted into flame for no obvious reason we could figure out. The canal turned into a river of fire.

So: Sugar Island. **DANGER. DO NOT GO THERE**. However,

fate had brought me to this place, so I decided to scout the area. Those waterproofs, and a pair of rigger boots that I'd found, fitted me just right. I closed the door after me before heading out across thick snow, hearing the crunch of it under my boots.

Finally – after the mayhem, and the accidental but fortuitous river journey – I had time to take stock, thinking about what Gorron had told me about the disease striking down my people. As I walked alongside a canal that formed one of the site boundaries, I touched my forehead, checking for fever, and then prodded at the glands in my neck, wondering if I'd get that sleeping sickness, too. There were no symptoms that I could detect. Therefore, I judged myself to be fully fit and bug-free.

As I explored, I worked out the chain of events in my own head, starting with the time when a group of us had arrived in a village called Midge-Low three years ago. Its houses were all abandoned, and it looked a good place to stay. Thereafter, we moved in, and voted 'New Home' would be name we called the village. As I've previously mentioned, 'Midge-Low' didn't sound good on the ear to us. Ever since civilization had gone belly-up, we were forced to grow our own food as well as scavenge provisions from other abandoned towns and villages. We tended to keep away from cities as that's where Creosotes gathered in large groups. As time went on, we basically quarried out supplies from nearby supermarkets and villages. The downside to that being we were in competition for food from other groups of kids who had survived The Day – consequently, supplies were drying up. That chain of events took me to scouting up on Moor Top, ten miles from New Home, trying to find houses that hadn't already been picked clean of food. I'd taken a tent with me, together with a water filter and portable alcohol stove. So, I had been habitually filtering water from streams before boiling it for ten minutes. No doubt that had killed the Sleeping Sickness bug, which seems to have contaminated water supplies of late. Therefore, I returned from Moor Top in perfect health to find my friends at New Home in the grip of an illness that fatigued them so much they could barely walk. When the Creosotes had arrived, my friends had tried to flee, only they'd been so weak they had ended up crawling across the ground on their bellies. I tried not to recall the mass-murder of my friends and neighbours. Instead, I wished there had been enough time to grab a rifle and ammo from my house. But, no, there hadn't been enough time...all I could do was fucking run and leave the people I loved to be torn apart.

My face burned with anger, despite snowflakes now streaming from the sky.

'Bastard!' I exploded a snowdrift with my boot. 'Bastard! Bastard!' I hated myself for running away, but how could I have

19

saved all my friends? How could I have fought five hundred blood crazy Creosotes, and defeated them all? 'Bastard!' The anger I felt was directed inwards – at me for not thinking up some shrewd plan to save everyone.

I'd been stomping along, fists clenched, eyes glaring downward, not noticing what was around me. However...that little red light that is nature's danger detector began to flash inside my head.

Suddenly, I stopped and looked across the canal. On the other side, there they were. Creosotes. Hundreds of them. That grim legion consisted of men and women, dressed in rags, most without footwear. They'd not washed in years, not cut their hair. They were brute creatures – not entirely human now. For some reason, on The Day, everyone over the age of nineteen was affected: parts of their minds had burned out, reducing their intellect. Yet whatever had burned away a chunk of their IQ also welded murderous rage onto their minds. They were not zombies (even though some children called them that), they weren't possessed by demons (at least, I don't believe they were), and they hadn't undergone some mind control process that had been inflicted by aliens from outer space (though who knows?). I tended to think of them as being mutants. Mind mutants. Their minds had mutated into something strange and dangerous. What caused the mind mutation? A virus? A solar flare burning away minds with radiation? Or even that microwave stuff leaking from microwave ovens? Was electromagnetic radiation mucking about with the biology of their brains? Okay, okay, I'm digressing. Ultimately, my belief is that the mind mutation, which affected everyone over the age of nineteen, had been lurking in human brains for thousands of years. A dormant volcano, if you like. Something that slumbered for generations...which abruptly erupted three years ago and caused such utter chaos and slaughter.

The Creosotes stared at me. They did not move. They had no expressions on their faces. Then I noticed that lots of them were carrying objects. That's when I lost my own mind.

'Monsters. Fucking monsters.' There were stones near the path where the ground remained free of snow. I began flinging the stones at those men and women. 'Fucking monsters! Why couldn't you leave them alone? They weren't hurting you! They couldn't even walk!'

I kept hurling stones at the men and women, who silently watched me through their shaggy, overhanging fringes that hadn't felt the touch of a comb or hairbrush in years. One of the stones cracked into the shoulder of a behemoth with a huge red beard. He didn't even flinch – he just kept watching me, as I screamed and swore and flung rocks in the stupid belief I could hurt that swarm of murderers.

My rage-driven voice burned my throat. 'I had a girlfriend. What have you done to Dane?' Tears gushed out of my eyes now. 'She was the best thing that happened to me. I loved her. When my own father tried to kill me, he did kill part of me. In here.' I jabbed my finger against my forehead. 'For years I trusted no-one. I thought everyone would turn on me one day and fucking hurt me. Dane brought that part of my head back to life. I started to trust again. For the first time since my father tried to murder me, I could relax and feel safe – properly safe. Dane loved me. She would have given her own life for me...but you...you monsters killed her. Just look at yourselves. Look at what you're carrying!'

The Creosotes had collected trophies after their murder spree. I saw faces hanging limp in their hands...along with heads, hearts, lungs, flannel-sized pieces of skin. All torn from my friends who had died, screaming in agony.

My face was burning. Tears were running down my face. My throat was sore with shouting, and I felt like shit inside. The next thing I knew, I was running back through the snow, toward the security guards' building. The Creosotes were on the other side of a security fence, on the far side of the canal – so it was unlikely they would invade Sugar Island anytime soon. However, I needed to get ready to move out.

As I ran through a clump of bushes, a figure stepped out, just in front of me.

Tears blurred my eyes, I couldn't see clearly, nevertheless I bellowed, 'Creosote!'

I bunched my fists, getting ready to fight for my life.

The figure pulled a hood back from its head, revealing a round face with a broad smile. 'You're Jack.'

'What?' I stared at him with what must have an expression of gormless surprise. *Where has this guy sprung from?*

The stranger put a clenched fist on his heart in greeting. 'Pleased to meet you, Jack.' Then he told me his name in such a grand way that he clearly expected it to mean something to me, like he was famous. 'My name,' he said, 'is Martin Del-Coffey.'

CHAPTER SIX

DEL-COFFEY, THAT'S WHO

Martin Del-Coffey trudged alongside me. He was late teens, I guess, a good bit shorter than me, and dressed in winter survival gear – big boots, big coat, big fur hat that might have been mink, then again, it might have been faux fur. He carried a green rucksack on his back. And he had the highest forehead I have ever seen. I mean, one of those foreheads that, once noticed, draws your eye back to that white cliff-face of smooth skin – a massive forehead. Heck, you could bounce a ball off that, or take a felt-tip pen and draw pictures of cats and dogs on that broad, blank canvas.

I tried not to stare.

Wisps of blonde hair curled out from the fur hat to dangle down a forehead that stretched down to blond eyebrows. What was that I told myself NOT to do? NOT stare at his humongous forehead. But I did stare. If he lay down on his back, you could land a helicopter on that prodigious acreage of head skin.

Oh, another thing. Del-Coffey could talk...he kept talking, didn't pause for breath – yabber, yabber, yabber.

As we walked across the snow toward the security HQ building, he said peculiar stuff like this: 'Jack. Do you know how to trigger a dog to attack a dead rat?'

'No.'

'Roll the dead rat onto its stomach. The dog will think the rat's alive again and will attack it. The second you roll the rat onto its side the dog loses interest.'

'Right...I didn't know that...but why are you telling me stuff about dead rats?'

Del-Coffey ran his fingers over that helipad of a forehead of his and sighed as if he suspected I was an idiot, and now I had just gone and asked a stupid question that proved his suspicion was correct.

He then explained, with a definite smear of impatience in his tone, 'Nature programmed dogs to attack only live rats – and, to a dog, a live rat is one that is upright, with its two eyes arranged on a horizontal line. If the rat lies on its side, the two eyes form a vertical line. That vertical arrangement of the rat's eyes will not

22

trigger an attack response in the canine brain. Equally, a dog's attack instinct is not triggered if the dog perceives the rat to be belly-up. *Ergo:* dead.'

'Yeah...what's so important about dead rats?'

'Why Creosotes don't always attack us has a reason akin to dog-rat attack instincts. I've just walked along the canal now, by hundreds of Creosotes, and they didn't even show much interest in me, let alone chose to attack.'

'Yeah, but there's a canal and a high fence between you and the bad guys.'

'But an obstacle between us and the Creosotes doesn't always result in a non-aggressive response from them. When the urge to attack erupts in the Creosote mind, they would run through a burning building to attack children and teenagers.'

'Oh, right.'

'Look, Jack. Don't you understand what is so important about what I'm telling you?'

'Frankly, no.'

Martin Del-Coffey's face turned red, which had to be due to a mixture of frustration and anger. I'm sure I was hitting his infuriation button. 'Jack. If we can discover what triggers the Creosotes to attack us, we might be able to develop a technique where we can avoid pulling their rage trigger.'

'Then they stop killing us?'

'*Yessss.*' He spoke the word in a long, hissing gush, as if relieved I'd finally understood the gist of what he was explaining.

'A pity our people hadn't discovered that trigger earlier – if we had, then my friends wouldn't have been slaughtered today.' Coldly, I gestured for him to go first. 'After you.'

Del-Coffey pushed open the door to the security guards' building. After doing that, he went in, stomping the slush off his boots. Gorron had woken up by now and had dressed himself in the security guard uniform that I'd left on the table. The big man stood at the stove, where he used a plastic spoon to stir the contents of a pan.

Gorron still looked dog weary. Even so, he nodded at Del-Coffey, taking the appearance of a stranger in his stride.

'Gorron. This is Martin Del-Coffey. Del-Coffey, this is Gorron.'

'Pleased to meet you.' Gorron licked the spoon. 'I'm making fruit punch.'

Del-Coffey nodded his approval. 'Where did you source the in-gredients?'

'There's a stack of blackcurrant juice cartons in the cupboard. Don't worry, the sell-by date hasn't expired yet. And I found a bottle of vodka in a cabinet back there. There were bundles of money as well, along with dealer bags and electronic weighing

scales. One of the security guards had been doing some moonlight-
ing.'

Del-Coffey sniffed. 'That actually smells pleasantly fruity.'

'You're welcome to have some.' Gorron began pouring out the
purple liquid into mugs. His punch did smell good, and I realized
how thirsty I was.

Del-Coffey shrugged off the rucksack. 'And a gas fire, too. You've
certainly made yourselves comfortable. Hmm, that punch really
does smell sweet. Syrupy sweet.'

Of course, I had to point out an important fact. 'That isn't just
the punch you're smelling. This factory has been leaking chemicals
for years. They give off a really, *really* sweet smell. Trouble is, the
chemicals are extremely volatile. Every so often...boom.' I raised
my hands in such a way to suggest I was miming an explosion.

Gorron made a throaty groaning sound. 'Ugh, that bug's kicking
in again. I feel weak as...ugh.'

I caught hold of him as he swayed. Gently, I guided him to the
sofa. 'Here, sit down. I'll get you a drink.'

Del-Coffey pulled off his fur hat and pressed it to his nose and
mouth, shielding himself. 'Nothing catching, I hope?'

'*No.*' I pretty much shouted the word. Del-Coffey had started to
irritate me. 'Our settlement went down with a kind of sleeping
sickness.'

'Ah,' murmured Del-Coffey in such a way that he could have
been a doctor recognising a patient's symptoms.

Gorron yawned. 'Uh, we're sure it came from the water. I think
it was—'

'A water-borne infection,' interrupted Del-Coffey. 'Yes, that's my
conclusion. Of course, it is absolutely essential to boil all water
before use. Whether for drinking, washing, even wiping down
tables and the like. For several weeks, there has been a virus
spreading through this part of the country, which has been causing
extreme fatigue. The virus doesn't occur in moving water, but
prefers wells and pools fed by springs. Possibly insects or birds
carried the virus to these water sources. The infection vectors are
so widespread that it suggests this is how the virus is spread.'

'You a fucking scientist, or something?' Gorron stared at Del-
Coffey in amazement.

'No. However, I did have the highest IQ of anyone of school age
in the Doncaster Education Authority's catchment area.'

'Oh. Congratulations.' Did I mean that to sound sarcastic?
Possibly. No...make that 'definitely'. The big-headed gob-shite.

Did I mention that Del-Coffey loved to talk? Yabber, yabber,
yabber.

That motormouth of his hit the gas again, powering his tongue:
'The disease first appeared around three months ago, resulting in

24

extreme fatigue. Yes, indeed a kind of sleeping sickness, where the infected spent most of the day in bed. Fortunately, symptoms disappear after fourteen days or so, and those who contracted the disease appear to suffer no lasting harm.'

'Sleeping Sickness.' Gorron looked very sleepy himself. 'Is that its name?'

'Absolutely not. There is another condition called Sleeping Sickness, which is an insect-borne malady, prevalent in Africa.' Del-Coffey began to walk slowly around the room as he lectured us, his tall forehead gleaming in the light coming in from the window. 'My research reveals that this is likely to be a new strain of virus. I called the infection "Hypnos-Fever". Hypnos being the Greek god of sleep.'

'Wait...' His statement puzzled me. 'Who gave you the authority to name diseases?'

Del-Coffey appeared surprised that I had even asked the question, as if I was irrationally challenging his right to name to every new bug or virus that evolved on the planet. 'Someone's got to do it.' His voice got all lofty and dignified. Stupid prat. 'It's important to allocate a name to a new disease, then we can discuss it without confusion.'

'So,' I said, 'everyone calls this disease Hypnos-Fever?'

'Ah, no.' Del-Coffey looked annoyed. 'My community call it Yipno-Fever.'

'Yipno-Fever?'

He began to look sulky. 'You know what people are like. They shorten place names, give people nicknames. It's like their tongue muscles aren't supple enough to form vowels properly.'

'So, I've got Yipno-Fever. You know, that's a neat name for it.' Gorron's expression became serious. 'And I'll recover? Recover fully?'

'When did you first notice the symptoms?'

'Nine days ago, I guess.'

Del-Coffey nodded, as if he was a medical specialist who'd got the measure of his patient. 'Then, in five days or so from now, symptoms will start to disappear. You'll stop falling asleep constantly, and you will regain your strength.'

'Thank you.' Gorron appeared to be genuinely sincere in his thanks. With that, he lay down on the sofa, took hold of a security guard fleece, and pulled the garment over himself as if it was a blanket. He looked worn out.

Del-Coffey, meanwhile, took a swallow of punch. He was liking it a lot. 'Hmm, that is good, gentlemen.'

Yeah, maybe my brain works slower than the average person's. Or maybe the cold water from the earlier dunking froze a few brain cells, but at last – POW! I suddenly had an important question to ask.

25

'Hey, Del-Coffey. We've never met before.' I found myself staring at the helipad forehead, rather than looking him in the eye. 'So, how do you know my name?'

'Ha. Elementary, my dear sir. Yesterday I met Dane Rivers. Your girlfriend.'

CHAPTER SEVEN

THE REMARABLE THOUGHTS OF MISTER MARTIN DEL-COFFEY

I had been convinced that my girlfriend, Dane, had been killed that morning by the Creosotes, along with most of the population of New Home. Martin Del-Coffey telling me that she was very much alive was such an exhilarating feeling. Joy slashed through me as fiercely and as violently as a blade – a strange comparison, I guess. However, news of her being in the land of the living overwhelmed me.

For a while, we sat in the guards' HQ on Sugar Island, chatting and drinking the vodka-blackcurrant punch that Gorron had made. Del-Coffey explained that he had come across Dane as she stood on a wall that separated the road from a field. Dane told him she was checking out the area, because there'd been an influx of dangerous Creosotes. All that Del-Coffey told me reassured me so much I felt like crying with happiness. He said that five people from New Home accompanied her – they were camping a mile away from where she was at that point. Dane, for some reason or other, hadn't revealed their names. As I sat there, sipping hot punch, these words pulsated so powerfully in my head, over and over: *Dane is alive. Dane is alive...*

Del-Coffey's cream-coloured forehead turned pink, both from the punch and the heat of the gas fire, no doubt. Gorron had drifted off to sleep on the sofa. Soon, Del-Coffey repeatedly began to glance at the window, his gaze either drawn by snowflakes gliding by or, perhaps, he expected to see a frightening face appear at the glass.

'Don't worry,' I said.

'Uh?'

'This factory complex is like a fortress – there are canals, high fences, big steel gates. The enemy are unlikely to get in.'

'That's good to know.' He nodded in the direction of his rucksack. 'I've got a couple of pistols, if any do show up. You got any shooting irons?'

I shook my head.

'Maybe we can do something about providing you with weapons

later,' he told me. 'The reports I have are that Mr and Mrs Creosote are becoming more aggressive again, and more likely to walk considerable distances to find...' He gave a little smile. 'Teenagers like us. You know, I have a theory about why the adults suddenly went crazy and started attacking us. Something similar happened in the Eastern Mediterranean, in the Late Bronze Age about three thousand years ago. Back then, the human mind operated differently. People did not internalize their thoughts, so when they thought about their work or life in general, they'd speak aloud. Just imagine all those people in the streets, or picking apples from trees, all jabbering away to themselves. There is a distinct similarity to this in the way children learn to read. Remember how you used to always read aloud when young?' Without waiting for me to reply, he surged on: 'It's only later that children learn to read inside their heads without vocalizing text. Well, at some point in the Late Bronze Age, ancient people suddenly, and spontaneously, began to internalize their thoughts. This had a tremendous impact on them. It would have seemed as if the gods spoke inside their skulls. The result? An epidemic of madness. Societies collapsed. Towns were abandoned. For a period of time, entire populations became deranged...tormented by the voices inside their heads. Then it all happened again three years ago. There was a transformation in how the adults' minds operated. Strangely, and this is a real mystery in itself, there are people now reaching the age of twenty and they remain completely sane. This suggests that the night when everyone over the age of nineteen became homicidally deranged was a one-off – it was an isolated event that hasn't been repeated. The madness epidemic was more like an explosion. A sudden dramatic psychological event that erupted, then instantly dissipated after reconfiguring the adults' mental structure. It is fascinating to speculate that—'

'I need to check the perimeter fences.' The words shot from my lips. I couldn't bear another lecture from cliff-forehead guy. He was a fellow survivor of the collapse of civilization, like me, so I didn't want to be impolite – after all, he'd been the model of courtesy to me. Even so...there was only so much of his endless jabber I could take. What I didn't need was a speech about human psychology.

What I did need was fresh air.

'Stay here.' I tried to sound friendly. 'Help yourself to more punch. Gorron found some packs of dried noodles in the cupboard next to the sink. The date's good on 'em, if you're hungry?'

'Cheers, Jack.' Del-Coffey didn't seem to pick up on the fact that I badly needed a break from his decidedly intense company. 'I'll warm my flesh in front of your very pleasant fire for a while.'

Earlier, I'd noticed binoculars hanging from a wall peg in the next room, so I collected those. After that, I checked mine and

28

Gorron's clothes that I'd draped over chairs near the fire. They ponged of river water. Fortunately, though, they were almost dry. Meanwhile, Gorron still slept, dead to the world. And so, mercifully, he was spared Del-Coffey's litany of pompous erudition (that might not be good syntax, though I'm sure you understand what I'm getting at).

I said, 'I'll be ten minutes or so.'

Quickly, I pulled on another security guard jacket over the one I already wore, doubling up against the cold, then stepped out into crisp whiteness. By this time, the early January dusk had begun creeping in as I trudged in the direction of the canal. That's where I'd seen Creosotes standing, grim as tombstones. Doing nothing really, but still looking as sinister as hell. Those men and women were each like an explosive device, ticking down to zero and boom time. Whenever I saw Creosotes, I always felt such a sense of danger. Hardly surprising, because they'd tried to kill me before on...what? Twenty-five occasions? Okay, we survivors call our enemy 'Mr and Mrs Creosote' – that sounds almost jokey, as if they aren't really dangerous, and maybe we're suggesting that they are even figures of fun. That's what survivors do, don't they? They try and bleed the danger out of risky situations, or out of menacing individuals, by giving them light-hearted names.

For example, I read somewhere that soldiers in World War One gave joke names to the artillery shells that would, one day, probably kill them. There was one particular kind of shell, that made a loud whizzing sound as it flew toward the troops. A timing fuse caused the shell to explode in the air, inflicting dreadful casualties with shrapnel. That shell was referred to by the troops as a 'Whizz-Bang' – the name almost sounds like a little kid's toy. But the Whizz-Bang did the Grim Reaper's work, killing tens of thousands of young men.

So, there I was, patrolling the edge of the canal, alone with my thoughts, while the silent and absolutely still men and women who had killed my friends that morning watched me from the other side of the water. Those Creosotes seemed deactivated, somehow. Apparently waiting for the spark that would detonate yet another homicidal fury.

I trudged alongside the water's edge. Gusts of white vapour were coming from my lips. Meanwhile, the crunch of snow sounded astonishingly loud as daylight faded. A lot of thoughts vied for space inside my skull, wanting to be heard. The main thought that had hit the repeat button was *Dane is still alive. Dane isn't dead.* Knowing she was alive lifted my heart skyward with sheer relief. Though, I have to say, there were other morbid thoughts with sharp fangs that tried to chew pieces out of the happy knowledge that Dane was safe. And, constantly, those dangerous people stared at

29

me from their side of the canal. Their wild manes of hair were being blown by the breeze, and specked white with flakes of snow.

I found myself imaging the fate of my friends from New Home. Even though I did not want to picture what happened to them, lo and behold, those pictures streamed with vivid horror through my head. When I left New Home, to look for supplies in remote moorland cottages, everyone was fit and well. Then the virus struck. They were so exhausted that, in all likelihood, they couldn't even eat or dress themselves properly. Then, when most of those young people were at their most vulnerable (confined to bed, or napping in chairs like they were ninety or something) that is when the Creosotes came. Imagine the choking horror of knowing you could not move about properly yet realizing that killers were walking across the field toward your home. The sick tried to flee, they really tried – they managed to struggle out into the meadow. Only their feet would have felt like they weighed half a ton each. Within moments, they were too exhausted to walk any further. After that, they dropped down onto their knees and crawled.

Imagine the absolute fear. You know that people are coming to murder you, but you can't run. You try to wriggle through the snow, try to get away, try to yell for help, only you are too exhausted to do anything meaningful to escape or to fight back. Then you hear the crunch of heavy feet approaching. Here comes your enemy. Here comes your death. And you can do nothing about it as you—

Dogs started barking. They were loud enough to drag me away from my morbid thoughts. And there, against a hillside, was a group of dogs – they were just dark specks moving across a mass of white in the distance. Dogs that were once pets had gone feral – they'd formed packs that hunted like their wolf ancestors. They could be dangerous now. No longer the loveable mutt, they'd rip the meat from your bones, given half a chance. The dogs continued barking. And the sound of them carried so well, I could hear the note of excitement in every yap and woof. They must have been on the trail of fresh prey.

What prompted me to do it, I don't know, but I raised the binoculars to my eyes. There they were: ten dogs running across the hillside. They looked to be a mix of terriers, spaniels, Labradors. Then a lone Border Collie, trailing at the back of the pack. A Collie with one side of its head pure white, the other side pure black.

Something like a hand carved from ice gripped my heart.

'No.'

I stared at the dog. Because an impossible event was happening.

The Border Collie stopped running, sniffed at a base of a tree, then it began to walk. Its head was swinging left and right as it trotted. The animal was on a high state of alert. Catching faint scents a human being could never catch. And maybe hearing the heartbeat of a mouse underground.

'What's wrong?'

I jerked my head round. Del-Coffey stood there with a bunch of strangers.

Seeing the dog had knocked the air from my lungs. I had to catch my breath before speaking. 'It's Piper,' I said at last.

'What?'

'That's Piper...over there on the hill...my Piper. I haven't seen him in ten years.'

Del-Coffey glanced back at his companions like I'd gone crazy.

'Piper...my dog, Piper.' Then I did go crazy. I started yelling: 'Piper! It's me – Jack! Piper! Here, boy! Here, boy!'

The strangers stared at me in amazement as I shouted. Then one of the strangers, a tall woman with long black hair, stepped forward from the group – and then she slammed the butt of her rifle into the side of my head.'

CHAPTER EIGHT

'HE PULLED THE TRIGGER'

Shouting woke me up. Lots of shouting. That and boots thumping the floor of the security guards' HQ as people cannoned from room to room in a ferocious meltdown of sheer fucking panic.

I added to the shouting. 'Gorron? What's wrong?'

He lounged there on the sofa, drowsy from the effects of that new disease some were calling 'Yipno-Fever'.

I sat up – that's when I realized I had been sleeping on the floor under a pile of fleece jackets. 'Gorron? What's happening?'

Gorron didn't answer – Del-Coffey, however, did. 'Jack. Didn't you listen to me when I told you how to make a dog attack a dead rat?'

'What the hell are you talking about?'

The man loomed over me. The big cliff of his forehead was pink with anger. 'When you began shouting for your imaginary dog, you triggered the Creosotes.'

'They've got over the fences?'

'Got it in one, you little shit.'

Gorron took greater offence than me at the insult. 'Hey, you can't talk to my mate like that.'

'I'll talk to him how I like. The little shit has put us in imminent danger of getting killed.'

All of a sudden, the room flooded with strangers.

Creosotes. Fucking Creosotes! I jumped up, ready to fight them. Then the pain ripped into the side of my head. Damn it! Someone had clubbed me with a rifle. I remembered now. I'd seen Piper, my Border Collie, out there on the hill. The last time I'd seen my dog was the night Dad tried to kill me. Last night I saw Piper, I'd called his name...

Figures loomed toward me. I bunched my fists, then started swinging, but not hitting anyone. Instantly, I lost my balance because the blow to the head had left me as dizzy as if I'd guzzled a mugful of neat vodka.

Del-Coffey screeched – the same kind of sound a pig would make with its bollocks on fire. 'Stop! Little shit! These are my friends!'

After struggling to regain my balance again, I looked hard at those faces that were glaring at me, like I was enemy number one. Six young people – three female, three male. Definitely not Creosotes. But all of them were angry at me. Not that I understood what I'd done wrong to infuriate them.

'Uh...my fuggin'ed.' That was the most adroit way I could articulate my physical condition at that moment.

One of the women spoke with cool clarity. 'It's okay, Del-Coffey. We got the cars started. What we need to do now, is just get the hell out of here.'

'You're the one that hit me.' I pointed at the woman with long black hair.

She admitted her assault on me with a nod. 'Just to calm your excitable nerves, sunshine. Now, get in the car.'

'Uh? What car? There are no cars anymore. Not working ones...'

'You want explanations, Jack?' She knew my name. Del-Coffey must have been facting her up, to coin a new phrase. 'At a moment like this? With Creosotes trip-trapping across the bridge toward us?'

A big man, with nothing less than a shining beacon of copper-coloured hair frothing around his head, leaned against the door-way, staring in at me. 'Jack. There were two 4x4s in a garage back there. One amazing talent we have, is that we are fucking outstanding at bringing dead machines back to life. We pumped tyres. We recharged car batteries from a generator we found out there. All of which means, we now possess working, viable automo-tive transport...so, for the love of your God, my God, everyone's God, get in the car.'

Everything was then shooting star fast. All Gorron and I had time for was to grab our clothes that had been drying by the fire, then stagger out through the door in our security guard uniforms that we'd harvested from the building.

The universe, I realized, had maliciously decided to attack us poor little bunch of survivors. Hail, as sharp as broken glass, slashed across my face from a dark-as-midnight sky. Even though dawn had broken, Sugar Island had become a gloomy, doom-laden place – a grim domain that evilly whispered this is where I'd leave my bones. To my surprise, there were, indeed, two big cars out there. Battle-tank-sized machines they were. Huge tyres with treads so deep they formed ravines in the rubber. Stencilled on the flank of each car: SECURITY.

'Here they come.' The woman who'd spoken had an automatic rifle slung over her shoulder – military hardware for sure: the kind of gun that comes with a long, curving magazine for ammo, which made the weapon almost glow with menace. She grabbed hold of my arm and began shoving me toward a car. 'My name's Tasmin, by the way, if social niceties help reassure you at a time like this.'

'Thanks a bunch,' I grunted. 'Though what I can't understand is that, when we first met yesterday, instead of shaking hands you bashed me on the skull with your rifle.'

'Sunshine, I thumped your head bone in an attempt to stop you triggering the Creosotes.'

I didn't get chance to demand either a full explanation or an apology from her because she vigorously slung me into one of the cars. Tasmin quickly occupied the driver's seat. Me, I was in the front passenger seat. Del-Coffey and Gorron scrambled into the back. The remaining five of Tasmin's squad occupied the other car.

Meanwhile, four hundred yards away, a big mob of Creosotes powered across the terrain toward us. Not running, but, as the quaint old saying goes: 'walking like they meant it.' That is, to be more explicit, walking like they meant to slaughter us.

There we sat. Waiting.

Then Tasmin turned to Del-Coffey and uttered words that, although understated, were extremely disturbing: 'Where are the car keys?'

Del-Coffey stared at her. His eyes were bulging with shock. 'What?'

'The keys, Del-Coffey. I told you to keep the ignition keys safe while we recced the area.'

'I don't have the keys.'

'Del-Coffey, are you saying you lost the fucking keys?'

The blond-haired man looked like he was going to start crying.

I chipped in with my own decidedly bleak observation. 'You've got five minutes before the Creosotes get here. That's when they'll start murdering us.'

Tasmin reached back, then she plunged her hand between Del-Coffey's legs, grabbing his balls.

'Ow! Tasmin?'

'Del-Coffey, what have you done with the keys?'

'Ouch, stop nipping my goolies!'

'Keys?'

'Ow! Ow! Ow! Stop that!'

The murderous men and women approached through a white fog of hailstones that spat from a furious sky.

'Del-Coffey,' yelled Tasmin. 'Keys! Where are they?'

'Don't know, can't remember. Ow! Ow! Ow! No...don't twist! *Don't twist!*'

I saw her hand powerfully rotate as she twisted his balls. Tears gushed from his eyes. His face went from blazing red to full-blown purple. Del-Coffey was chin-deep in absolute agony.

A guy from the next car ran over and yelled, 'Where is our key?'

Tasmin let go of Del-Coffey's testicles, though she must have given them one last muscular tweak the way he let out a bizarre whoop of pain.

She called out through the window to the guy from the other car: 'Del-Coffey was supposed to be keeping them safe. The idiot lost them.'

Gorron stared through the side window at the approaching mob – he wore the expression of a man feeling the executioner's noose slip over his head to encircle his vulnerable neck. 'You best do something, or those Creosotes are gonna start ripping meat – our meat. Okay?'

'I'll find them.' With those words, I kicked open the car door.

Hailstones blasted my face as I ran back toward the building.

You know, maybe all people (when they are in danger) do this: they utter the mantra, prayer, magic spell, or however you'd describe the message that begs for salvation. Therefore, when the possibility of my own violent death was so close, the following words reverberated inside my skull: *I will not die. I will not die. I am going to live.*

With that promise to survive made, my thoughts abruptly barrelled along a different track. *Now, think! If you were a conceited clever dick, like high and mighty Mr Martin Del-Coffey, where would you put car keys that were entrusted to you for safe keeping?*

I charged into the building, where I slipped on a pool of snowmelt on the floor and landed on my backside. Straight away, I was back on my feet again, knowing all too well that time was running out. The **ENEMY** were coming.

'Think, Jack. Think. Where would it be oh-so clever to put the keys?'

An urgent voice bellowed through the door from outside. 'Hurry, Jack! They're almost here!'

Then the *crack* of a gunshot. Okay, Del-Coffey's buddies had guns, yet they couldn't kill all the Creosotes. Because if they were the same bunch that attacked New Home, there'd be about five hundred, at least. Far too many for a few teenagers with rifles to exterminate. What's more, guns don't intimidate Creosotes. They will keep coming at you, trying to bite your face off. The only sure way to stop a Creosote is to shoot it dead.

Taking a deep breath, I forced myself to slow down...to focus...not to rush. *Think, think, think. Where would you put the car keys?* There were shelves. I checked them. Nope. I yanked drawers, scattering cutlery, searching, searching. No keys.

Voices now clamoured in panic. 'Jack, hurry. We've got to go. They're nearly here!'

There were a few fleeces hung up on pegs, all of the SECURITY variety. I searched pockets.

35

Then I closed my eyes – and took another deep breath. 'Okay,' I murmured. 'There were once people in the world who would ask the ghosts of their ancestors for help in times of crisis. Not asking Dad's ghost, though. The monster tried to kill me. Now...this is Jack Ranzic asking the ghosts of his ancestors this question: where would a quirky guy, who believes he is a genius, find somewhere to keep very important keys safe and sound?'

My eyes snapped open. 'Fridge!'

I dashed toward the refrigerator as Tasmin yelled, 'Hurry up, Jack! They're nearly here! They'll fucking slaughter us!'

Then came an absolute cacophony of people begging me to bloody-well **HURRY**. I ripped open the fridge door. Checked the shelves. Nope. Nothing. Had my ancestors let me down? Didn't those spirits want me to remain in the land of the living? Yeah, weird flippant thoughts, but my mind was in an elevated place that was almost transcendental...maybe the knock on the head with the rifle had mushed my brain a bit?

There were brown lumps on the fridge shelves that had been food a long time ago. *Would Del-Coffey put his soft, clean hands near those? No, Jack, he would not.*

'Ah-ha.'

I saw that the fridge had one of those little plastic covers that, when flipped up, would reveal a compartment to tuck your eggs into a Goldilocks zone that wasn't too cold, wasn't too warm. So, *click!* I flipped the plastic hatch up. There they were.

'Keys! I've got the keys!'

I grabbed the keys, then barrelled out through the door into the snow. A guy of around fifty, with a bald patch at the top of his head, and a kind of wispy grey curtain of soft fluff sprouting out from the back of his skull, lumbered from left to right in front of me, closing in on the car with Tasmin at the wheel. I shoulder charged that hefty mule of a man, knocking him forwards, and off his feet. I heard his jawbone snap as he crashed, face-down, onto frozen muck was as hard as iron.

Everyone in the cars yelled with absolute bellowing joy as I shook the keys above my head as I ran. I flung one key at the driver of the other car.

Did I fling him the right key? I hoped so...because on that bitterly cold morning, when our survival hung in grim balance, it really did seem that my ancestors had helped me get my mitts on those keys. The driver, upon neatly catching the key, raced back to the car, shooting a woman through the heart as he did so with his pistol. Mrs Creosote went down, her hands clawing at her ribcage, like she thought she could pull out the bullet that had just gone and popped her heart.

I thrust the key into Tasmin's hand. Then I flung myself into the

36

passenger seat. Tasmin said nothing. However, she locked eyes with me, nodded, then started the engine.

Bless you, ancestors! They had come through for me. I will have to try that technique again. When you are in the shit, call out to the spirits of those lovely people in your bloodline. You never know your luck. They might just save your life.

Del-Coffey's team had worked their own magic on the cars, which had been standing unused for years – engines were firing into glorious life, wheels were spinning, kicking up snow fountains. Instantly, the machines powered away across the factory complex as those raggedy men and women, with their burned-away minds, suddenly charged forwards, hands clutching for the metalwork, like they believed they could stop those heavyweight 4X4s.

Tasmin powered the car along a roadway, its engine bellowing. She was making for the exit at the far side of Sugar Island.

Del-Coffey had recovered from his nut-pinch, and he began to holler in a high, excited squeal, 'We're going to make it! We're leaving those little shits behind.' Then, after turning around to look out of the rear window, he gave a splendidly vulgar upthrust of his middle finger. 'Guzzle my exhaust! You derelicts!'

'Derelicts?' echoed Gorron, puzzled.

'Their brains,' yelled Del-Coffey. 'Three years ago, their brains were shipwrecked on the deadly reef of madness.'

Yeah, Martin Del-Coffey really does talk like that.

'We're not safe yet,' Tasmin pointed out. Her bright eyes were fixed on dozens of Creosotes that were running between those big steel tanks of chemicals that were a universal feature of the factory complex. 'They're going to block the road.'

Tasmin drove with an assault rifle between her knees, muzzle pointing upwards.

I grabbed the gun.

'Hey, leave that.' She glared at me.

Calmly, I said: 'Stop the car.'

'Are you crazy?'

'See the pool of blue liquid – right around the tanks, where it's melted the snow?'

'See it?' Gorron rubbed the tip of his nose. 'You can smell it. Sweet, like boiled fruit.'

'Tasmin, stop the car.' I pulled the bolt back on the rifle. Safety off. *Click.*

Tasmin looked me in the eye – she saw something there that answered a question forming in her own mind. With a nod, she brought the car to a dead stop.

Dozens of Creosotes waded knee-deep through the blue lagoon – a lagoon as big as a football pitch, which was formed from that

37

witch's brew that had leaked out of a tank full of volatile chemical compounds, which had been bubbling away in there for years.

Del-Coffey had a stark warning. 'If enough Creosotes reach the road, they'll block it. We'll never ram our way through.'

'Del-Coffey.' I spoke in a cool, neutral voice. 'For once...shut up.'

And, for once, he did clam up that yammering trap of his.

I opened the door before standing up on the passenger seat, which allowed me to aim over the roof of the big vehicle. Then I fired.

But not at those shaggy-headed Creosotes, with their mad eyes that blazed with hatred for the young. Instead, my bullet struck one of the metal supports of a massive cannister. Sparks flew when the slug struck the framework at a fiery velocity of three thousand feet per second. Too high, though. The silvery sparks I'd created with the bullet-strike died to nothing before they hit the pool of luminous blue.

Okay. Aim lower.

So, I aimed lower. My next bullet from the automatic rifle struck the metal support just above the blue goo.

Sparks shot downward, kissing the blue in a way that was hot enough to...

...and it did.

The volatile liquid erupted into a ball of yellow flame that was so bright that I flung up my hand to shield my face. Even at this considerable distance from the inferno, the heat stung my skin. The awful stink of singed hair – my hair! – filled my nose.

'Right. Drive.' I pounded my fist down onto the car roof.

I remained standing there, hanging on by clutching the car's roof-mounted searchlight. Tasmin drove the car along the road. The other car followed.

And I watched the calamity I had created. Vapour above the blue lagoon had flashed off in a fireball of such power and heat it had cremated those of our attackers that were nearest to its epicentre. Other Creosotes had been knocked off their feet by the shockwave from the explosion. Even at this distance, maybe two hundred yards from the blast, the high temperature toasted my face. Steam came rolling off my clothes. My lips tingled from the sheer heat of that horrific lake of fire.

My heart thrust my body's hot blood through its chambers – out along arteries – my arms and legs surged with strength. And that's when a wave of euphoria hit me so hard, I opened my mouth and let out my own version of a battle cry – a yell that told the cruel universe that, today, I had won a fantastic victory.

Because in this world, when you reach the end of the day, and you are still alive, that, my friend, is indeed a victory worth celebrating.

CHAPTER NINE

DID YOU SAY, QUESTORS?

'Well done, Jack. You did great back there.'

Tasmin spoke those words as she drove the 4X4 away from the extraordinary Sugar Island factory complex. A factory that now hurled balls of fire into the sky – those leaky old tanks, which contained a madly dangerous mixture of volatile chemicals, were igniting like monster fireworks.

Gorron leaned forwards from the back of the car to cheerfully thump me on the shoulder as I sat in the passenger seat that I'd reoccupied, just moments ago. 'Yep! Well done!' Then he said to the others, 'Jack's a warrior. He is a fucking warrior. In our tribe, he is a legend. He's the kind of guy who achieves the impossible!'

'Thanks, Gorron,' I said, and I meant it.

We looked back at the factory as one of the huge metal spheres exploded. Even though we were a mile away, the force of the explosion rocked the car on its suspension.

Tasmin glanced sideways at me, almost a shy glance; her dark eyes were sparkling. 'You saved us back there, Jack. We owe you our lives.'

Gorron gave a *harrumph*. A note of irony. 'You praise my friend here for saving your necks, but you haven't apologised yet for clunking him on the head with the rifle butt. You could have killed the guy.'

'I'm sorry, Jack,' she said. 'But you were provoking the Creosotes when you were calling the dog.'

'Imaginary dog,' added Del-Coffey with a sniff of contempt. 'Jack could have got us killed.'

Tasmin twisted her head back as she drove, so she could glare at Del-Coffey. 'Don't get too comfy there on the moral high-ground, Mr Del-Coffey. You forgot where you put the car keys.'

'And Jack had to go find them.' This was Gorron again, fighting my corner. 'I thought you were brainy, Del-Coffey. How come you couldn't remember where you put the keys?'

Del-Coffey's face turned an indignant red. His eyes glistened as he held up his hands – the gesture of an oh-so innocent, don't-

39

blame-me kind of person. 'You were all shouting at me. I couldn't hear myself think.'

'Prat,' was Gorron's verdict.

The driver of the car that followed us, with five of Tasmin's squad onboard, began to sound the horn, while flashing its headlights.

One of the guys leaned out of a side window of the car – he was cheering and shouting, 'Jack! You rock, man!'

'Ah...' Del-Coffey sighed. 'Enjoy the approbation, Jack.'

'Approbation.' Gorron scratched his head. 'What the hell does approbation mean?'

Del-Coffey spoke in his refined professor voice. 'Approbation? Meaning praise. Approval. Glorification. They praise your friend, Gorron. They are in adoration of Jack's heroism, inventiveness... and his incontrovertible ability to protect us from danger.'

Gorron pointed at Del-Coffey. 'Is this guy for real?'

'You'll grow to like him,' said Tasmin, though she didn't sound like she believed the words she'd just uttered.

Gorron, however, slapped me on the shoulder again. 'You are the mutt's bollocks. I can't wait to tell everyone that you blasted a bunch of Creosotes to shit. They're going to...uh, crap.' His hand flew to his mouth as the memory slammed into him so hard it knocked the air from his lungs. 'How could I forget that? They're all dead, aren't they? All our friends died yesterday. Shit, how stupid am I? Why did I forget?'

I turned in the seat to put my hand on his arm. An attempt on my part, small though it was, to comfort him. 'Don't be hard on yourself, Gorron. It's a survival mechanism. When something tragic happens, that's what we do. We forget for a while. We shut it out. We carry on like nothing bad's happened. That's what survivors *must* do. Otherwise, grief will kill us.'

Gorron began rubbing his eyes with the heel of each hand.

Tasmin nodded. 'That's true. The people who survived after The Day when millions died, were the ones who had the all-important talent for managing their emotions – not suppressing them, because that can be dangerous, too. No, when you see a friend die, whether it's hunger, disease, Creosote attack, you grab hold of all that grief you're feeling and you shove it into a room in the back of your mind...you close the door, then get on with the business of surviving.' Her eyes were fixed on the road ahead as she navigated past snowdrifts and long-ago abandoned cars – those eyes started to get glossy with moisture. 'I've had three boyfriends die on me in the last eighteen months. So, I put the grief away until I know I am physically safe, then I bring the sadness out. Look at it, talk about it, examine every aspect of that big painful lump of sheer bloody sorrow, then I shout, scream, weep...and I swear until my fucking throat's on fire, and then cry all over again. But I only bring the sadness out into the open when I know it's safe to grieve. Three dead lovers. Sounds like I've got some kind of bad habit, huh?'

I placed what I hoped was a consoling hand on the firm muscle of Tasmin's forearm as she drove. She did not react to the touch of my hand on her arm. Maybe her memories had dragged her away to that place deep inside where grief never fully dies.

For a while we sat in silence, watching houses flow by where no human beings lived. Flakes of white spiralled from a dark and angry-looking sky. We weren't enjoying that tour through the post-apocalyptic scenery. No, we were processing, mentally, what had happened today. The attack by the adults. The drive through the factory complex. Nearly getting trapped, then my trick with the gun to detonate the blue lagoon of what turned out to be something akin to liquid explosive.

At last, Del-Coffey spoke. For some reason, he'd lost the mightier-than-thou pomposity, and his tone was quite soft, almost humble. 'Jack...Gorron. I didn't get around to telling you who my friends are. I have named them the Questors – Questors on account of them embarking on a dangerous quest.'

Tasmin smiled. 'Questors? That's hifalutin.'

Del-Coffey continued: 'You are on a quest, my dear. These people of yours are searching for a group of adults.'

'Careful you don't find them,' retorted Gorron. 'They'll kill you.'

'No, this group of adults aren't teen-killing crazies. These adults are as sane as you and I. And they could be the miracle we have been waiting for – the miracle that will restore the lost light of civilization.'

CHAPTER TEN

BACK TO THE SCENE OF THE CRIME

Finding sane adults? That was a remarkable quest in my estima-
tion. Because, ever since The Day, all adults have been on their own
bloody quest to kill all of us young people. Clearly, the Questors
were doing big, important stuff. But I had important stuff to do as
well.

Our two cars trundled and slithered through thick slush, those
big tyres sometimes spinning fast before the tread regained traction again.

I said, 'I don't want to hold up your quest, though can I ask a
favour?'

'Ask away,' said Tasmin.

'Would you drop Gorron and me off where we live...I mean,
lived? The Creosotes attacked the place yesterday. We need to
check if there are any survivors.'

Tasmin nodded. 'Of course.' She could have added: *But there
will be no one left alive. Creosotes are very thorough when they
do their slaughtering.* She did not say that, of course, and merely
asked me to direct her to where we'd find the scene of yesterday's
massacre.

New Home was silent...absolutely silent. It was a place for the dead
now, but this was no cemetery. The dead, I knew full well, must rest
on the surface, just yards from the houses where we had lived in
relative peace, ever since we decided this was the village where we
could build new lives for ourselves.

I trudged away from the car, my boots kicking through knee-
high drifts. Cold air bit deep into my skin – yet it was bleak, awful
sadness that bit deep into my brain.

Gorron had wanted to come with me, but the flippantly named
Yipno-Fever inflicted exhaustion on him to such a degree he could
only manage to climb out of the car then lean back against its
steelwork, while watching me with such melancholy eyes. Both cars
had parked up by the old church. Tasmin and Del-Coffey had
offered to accompany me. I told them I was grateful for the offer,

but I wanted to go alone. To be alone with my thoughts. To be alone with my grief. Because I could safely grieve now that the danger appeared to have gone. There was no sign of Creosotes, because they tend to move on to find fresh victims after they'd wiped out a community. Though I had expected to see corpses lying on the surface, that wasn't to be. Because a new fall of snow had concealed all evidence of the massacre. It was as if a milk-white tide had flowed over the landscape, covering pathways, gardens, roads, turning the thirty or so houses of New Home into dark blocks that stood out so starkly against the white.

I trudged through thick snow toward the meadow. I saw the paw prints of rabbits. Tree trunks were black against that backdrop of whiteness – their branches formed complex bone-work structures, as if the trees, themselves, were once enclosed by flesh that had been brutally stripped away. *I want to feel disconnected from this place,* I told myself. *I want to be a detached observer, merely here to check the area – to locate any of my friends that survived the attack.*

'Who are you kidding, Jack? None will have survived.' That's what I muttered to myself as I kicked on through the drifts.

Snow crunched loudly under my feet. Hard grains of ice stabbed downward from the sky to unpleasantly prickle my face – no soft flakes today, only cruel hailstones.

In the meadow, there were smooth mounds that could have been snowdrifts, though I knew that some of these mounds had become shrouds that covered the dead.

Be detached. Be a dispassionate observer. And yet I failed to distance myself from this scene of mass-murder, because I knew that the people I loved, those wonderful friends who had become my new family, lay dead under flesh-freezing mounds of white. I wanted to draw my feet up from the ground, to disconnect my body from the Earth. But I couldn't, of course. There was no way I could instantly distance myself from the dreadful reality of what the meadow had become. If the snow somehow magically melted in a second, I'd be viciously assaulted by a ghastly scene of butchered corpses. Friends without heads. Neighbours with bellies ripped open, and intestine and bowel strung out in crimson strands across the ground.

The only evidence of a body I did see was what appeared to be the yellow petals of a flower in the blanket of white. Those 'petals' were the fingers of a hand, just poking above the surface of the snow. The rest of the body lay buried.

Everyone was dead here, of course. Nobody would be alive in their ice tombs. Swiftly, I checked the houses, then went to my home where I stuffed clothes from my bedroom into a rucksack.

After that, I went to Gorron's house, found a holdall, and crammed as many of his clothes into that as I could. Five minutes later, I was collecting our sole remaining rifle from the armoury, together with three automatic pistols, and ammunition for all four weapons. That done, I returned to the car.

Soon we were driving away again – hail stones clattered against the car.

Tasmin said, 'You can travel with us, if you want?'

I turned back to Gorron. 'What do you say?'

The guy looked worn out. Nevertheless, he nodded.

I nodded, too. 'Thanks. We will.'

We drove on. At one point, we caught a glimpse of a dozen figures in the distance. The rucksacks they wore told me they were young people like us, not hostile adults. Part of me wanted to approach them, say hello, swap information, but they had the look of people who had been forced out of their own homes by a Creosote attack. Admittedly, kids like that would be grateful to meet others like themselves. The fact is, however, young people were competing for dwindling resources. Canned and dried food from the old world, when trains still rumbled along their tracks, and televisions still worked, was running out. Strangers you met were gushingly friendly at first. Yet, as so often happened, your new friends turned into perfidious houseguests, who'd sneak away in the middle of the night with your guns, ammo, and food.

So, today at least, we would keep away from strangers. Better safe than sorry, huh?

Gorron moaned for a while, saying he was so tired he ached. Then, mercifully for him, he fell asleep. His mouth was open. He made soft sighing sounds as he gently snored.

Del-Coffey evidently decided to cheer me up. 'Don't worry,' he told me, 'there's no human-to-human transmission of Yipno-Fever. It's only transmitted to humans via contaminated water.'

'I fell in a river yesterday.'

'The virus is only present in still water, such as pools or wells. Don't worry. You won't catch the disease.'

As the saying goes, *Famous last words*.

CHAPTER ELEVEN

FEVER

Yes, okay...I don't know how I caught the disease they call Yipno-Fever. Whether the bug came from Gorron, or if it really did contaminate the river that I'd jumped into, to escape the Creosotes the day they attacked New Home. The thing is, the day after we left Sugar Island I could feel exhaustion creeping through me like some ghost that had evilly sidled through my body to take possession of me. For days after that, I lived life in either a misty, half-awake state, where I hardly had enough strength to sit upright, or I simply slept, dead to the world. Those periods of unconsciousness were so long that entire days could pass by.

Tasmin and her squad, meanwhile, had found a deserted farmhouse, which they decided to use as a base. Every so often, Tasmin would bring food to where I occupied a bedroom at the back of the house. She'd give me bits of information, though sometimes I was so tired I found it hard to grasp what she was saying.

On one occasion she spooned vegetable soup into my mouth as I sat propped up in bed. My arms were so heavy they felt like they'd been glued to the mattress. Fatigue deprived me of the strength to even move my limbs.

As Tasmin fed me the soup, she told me this: 'The farm's on Moor Top. We're keeping a look out for your girlfriend...Dane, that's her name, isn't it? Well...all the houses are deserted up here, not that there are many of them, and most have been picked clean by scavengers. One has a kitchen full of lightbulbs – by that, I mean actually full to the ceiling with thousands of the things. God knows why anyone would want to hoard lightbulbs. After all, there isn't any electricity, is there?' Sometimes I thought she told me all this during one mealtime as she fed me. Then I realized that she wore a different change of clothes. That fatigue was so knackering I'd not realized that entire days had passed between her saying one thing before saying another.

Another occasion she said: 'We've found them. Luckily, this farm was used to breed dogs. There's a kind of warehouse fitted out with cages. We've put them in there.'

45

'You put dogs in there?' I mumbled this question before falling asleep again, while wondering why on Earth they were collecting dogs.

Sometimes Del-Coffey would visit me.

'Perhaps the virus can survive in running water,' he said, before asking me to list symptoms which he noted down in a book, saying, 'Hmmm...Hmmm...' as I spoke.

When Gorron came to see me, he brought vodka. I nearly choked on the stuff when it went down the wrong way.

As he cheerfully pounded me on the back with his fist, he said, 'I'm feeling a lot better. Did Tasmin tell you? We've put them in the cages.'

'The dogs? Yeah, she told me about putting dogs in cages.'

'Dogs? No, mate. Those aren't dogs. They're people. Tasmin found the sane adults. Now they're in the cages and Del-Coffey is studying them. That guy...you know, he's like a mad scientist. Writing down what they do, what they eat, when they pee.'

I just did not know how many days had gone by since I became ill. One night, I managed to get out of bed before walking, as unsteadily as the town's most consummate drunk, to the window and looked out. The moon shone on a bunch of outbuildings. They looked like big tombs out there in the snow – the kind of ancient tombs where they put the coffins inside gloomy chambers, which have pictures of demons painted on the walls, and curses chiselled into stone slabs. *Enter here, and death will come to you at the midnight hour.*

A dog stood out there in the snow, looking up at me as I looked down at him. The dog was a Border Collie – one half of his head was a perfect black, the other half, a perfect white.

I shoved the window open. 'Piper!' I yelled. 'Piper!'

I hadn't seen my dog in ten years. Now, somehow, he had found me. I still shouted Piper's name as Gorron guided me back to bed.

'Gorron.' Tears ran down my face. 'Please bring my dog to me. He's out in the yard.'

'There is no dog, Jack. The yard's empty.'

'Piper's out there.'

'No, he isn't. There, let me cover you up. You've got to keep warm.'

A dog began to bark in the distance.

'There...listen.' I grasped Gorron's arm. 'Piper. Can you hear him? He's barking.'

'No, there's no dog barking. But the adults – the sane ones – they're calling to us from the cages. They want to be let out. They scare me, Jack. They're not like Creosotes. The thing is, they're not like normal people, either.'

'What do you mean?'

'They've changed, Jack. They're no longer human.'

46

CHAPTER TWELVE

THOSE THINGS IN THE CAGES

They took me to see the Creosotes. They were kept in one of the big cages in a cold warehouse of a building at the far side of the farmyard. I remember it was snowing.

Tasmin and her squad were so damn pleased with their captives – their trophies – because they behaved liked they'd found a truck full of gold. That destructive fever made my entire body feel so heavy I could hardly walk, so Gorron held onto my right arm, while the teenager with the copper-red hair gripped my left arm hard enough to make it go numb. Tasmin and her friends talked in excited voices. They had been absolutely determined to get me across the deep snow and into the building, where they could show off their new prize possessions. My legs only moved in a nominal kind of way – a gesture of movement, rather than actively propelling me forward. Gorron and the copper-haired kid basically carried me toward the cages that had once been used to house dogs before civilization went *ka-poww!*

I've seen Creosotes before, of course, thousands and thousands of 'em. These were different, though. They didn't rattle the cage bars, or snarl, or chomp at the air like savage beasts. No, none of that. Instead, they sat there on the concrete floor at the far side of the cage, all clumped together, so they were packed tightly into a group. These ten men and women dressed themselves differently to the usual kind of crazy. Instead of making do with ragged clothes, or no clothes at all, these appeared to have scavenged stuff from other sources, wearing layers of coats or jackets or sweaters. Some wore a boot on one foot and a shoe on the other. What's more, and I guess this is significant, they all wore gloves and scarves as if they felt the cold (whereas the common variety of Creosote didn't seem to care one way or the other about chilly weather). Right then, I would have preferred them to be clattering cage bars, while snarling and wanting to rip us apart, because the odd way they sat on the floor was deeply unsettling. They were leaning against each other, legs straight out in front of them, and saying nothing, and not moving – that body language of theirs seemed absolutely **NOT HUMAN**. And, get this...their eyes were

47

just fucking dreadful. The eyes that stared at me from beneath shaggy curtains of hair were so **KNOWING**. Just a single glance from one of those Creosotes shocked me like a sudden punch to the stomach. What's more, that perturbing gaze of theirs also revealed a sharp intelligence – the eyes darting, assessing me, judging me. Heck, they were fucking evaluating me. Just as Del-Coffey had done when he interrogated me about my symptoms a couple of days ago.

These people in the cages were just so...so fucking weird. They scared me. Maybe I felt more vulnerable because the illness made me so feeble, like I was a hundred years old or something. I'd become weak, all trembly, unable to even stand upright by myself. Yet, undeniably, these creatures were terrifying. I began to shake – almost convulsively shake.

Gorron asked, 'Jack, are you cold?'

'No. I'm terrified. Just look at 'em. Ordinary Creosotes have a big, juicy chunk of intelligence cut away – they are like animals. These are different. They're clever. Very clever. You can tell they're scheming, and planning, and we better watch out or they'll slaughter us.' The speech I made came blasting from the heart. I meant every single word.

Del-Coffey smiled at me – one of his sympathetic smiles that he graciously awarded to those unfortunate souls that were dim of mind. That's how he saw me, sure as eggs are eggs. 'Don't be frightened, Jack. They are locked up in there. See? Tungsten padlocks on the gates. These men and women can't hurt you.'

'They will – just give them time. They're planning something. Look at their faces...sly, conniving monsters.'

Tasmin patted me on the shoulder. Now, that was genuine sympathy. 'There are more of these...evolved...people up on the hills. We are going collect more of them.'

I shook my head. 'Too dangerous. They'll get the better of us. Just you see.'

'No, just *you* see.' Del-Coffey was annoyed. 'I will study these individuals. I shall conduct a critical scientific analysis of their mental state. They will be the key to restoring civilization. Just imagine, if all the Creosotes spontaneously underwent a mental transformation and become these...what shall we call them? Ah...how about Creosote-Plus Iterations? No, on second thoughts, I shall identify them as Creosote-Plus Types.'

I managed to kick the steel bars of the cage, making a terrific clanging sound. The newly monikered Creosote-Plus Types did not even flinch. I yelled at them, 'You don't fool me! I know you are planning to kill us!'

CLANG! I had kicked the cage bars again. Those two kicks and my yelling had hollowed me out – all strength gone, absolutely

48

knackered. I would have fallen onto the floor if the copper-haired guy and Gorron hadn't been holding me up. Meanwhile, the clever-oh-so-devious eyes of the Creosote-Fucking-Plus devils gazed back at me. I thought: *This feels like being stared at by crocodiles. No, they don't move, they don't even look angry. But, my God, you know they are just biding their time before they come lunging at you to bite your head off.* However, these sinister brutes couldn't attack me. Not yet anyway. Padlocks held the cage doors shut.

I noticed bowls of food and bottles of water in one corner of the cage. So, there you go. Mr Martin Del-Coffey had diligently made sure that these murderers-in-waiting were going to be kept alive.

I muttered, 'You should kill them now...before they kill us.'

Del-Coffey shook his head. 'They are here to be studied. They are not the kind of Creosote you are accustomed to. They are placid. They have shown no aggression, nor any inclination to attack.'

Then he did something that, to me, seemed so shocking, especially after all the slaughter we had endured at the hands of the adults. Del-Coffey spoke with absolute politeness to the occupants of the cage. 'We will not harm you. You will continue to be given food and water.'

Then, at last, the things in the cage spoke back. And that did blast nothing less than a shock of terror up my spine – like it was some kind of spectral lightning. A woman of around thirty, clad in what looked like four coats, fixed her eyes on me. Her lips were large, almost swollen – an odd pouting look. Her stare burned right through my face, sizzling deep into my brain – well, that's how it seemed to me.

She spoke these four words in a whisper: 'Let us out of...' Then she stopped.

A man sitting next to her with broken teeth hissed: '...out of here.'

Yeah, at first, it seemed as if the guy simply finished the woman's sentence when she paused. But – get this – they all, every single one of them in the cage, continued speaking in whispery voices. Each, in turn, said a word, or a few words, continuing the thread of the speech. It went something like this (I'll recap what the first two Creosotes said):

'Let us out of...'
'...out of here...'
'...I wish to discuss something...'
'...that is important with you...'
'...I am not...'
'...dangerous...'
'...I will not hurt...'
'...you...'

'...we should look after...'

'...each other...'

Then the first one to speak, the woman with the fleshy, pouty lips finished the speech with these words that I found inexplicably strange – and absolutely frightening. She said: 'Because I don't want my mind to burn again.'

'Weird.' This was Tasmin. 'They talk like they've got one brain that they pass from one to the other...a bit like that story about the three witches who had one eye between them, and they passed it around when they wanted to look at something.'

Del-Coffey's hands actually quivered: he was *that* excited by his biological specimens in the cage. 'Or they have become unified in some way. Ten men and women, ten brains, yet their individual minds have merged into one psychological unit.'

'Or they...they rehearsed all this.' I had to force the words from my lips. That brutal exhaustion was all-but beating me unconscious. This fever was no laughing matter. That bug just smashed the life right out of me. 'And...they are trying to fool you into believing that...that they are peace-loving pussy cats that just want to...cuddle up to us.' My head felt so heavy, my eyelids, too. 'Tasmin. Kill them before they kill us.'

The cold air outside woke me up. Sheer fatigue had caused me to fall asleep on my feet back there in the cage place. Gorron and the other guy carried me across the yard. The toes of my boots were dragging through the snow. My heavier than iron head hung down, so I had a perfect view of snow, footprints, a yellow patch where someone had peed. Charming habits we'd developed since our old world ended, huh? Peeing in public is normal. Anyway, I found myself staring down at the snow passing beneath me, as they hauled me back to the house – hauled gently, I have to say. They weren't angry with me, despite my rant against the Creosote-Plus Types (as Del-Coffey had adroitly named them). More boot prints in the snow. An empty beer bottle. Another patch of yellow snow. Then I saw something that pumped some life back into my body.

'Stop!'

Gorron looked at me, perhaps wondering if I was going to throw-up. 'What's wrong?'

'Let go.'

Shrugging myself out of their grip, I deliberately fell facedown into the snow, so my eyes were just inches from the remarkable thing I had found.

'Look.' I pointed.

'What is it?'

'Pawprints. You see, Gorron? Dog pawprints. I told you I saw Piper.'

'That's impossible. You told me that your mother gave the dog away when you were just a little kid.'

'Yes.' With my bare fingertip, I drew a circle in the snow around the pawprint, creating a frame, as if the print was a valuable picture I wanted to protect. 'That's right. My mother gave Piper to her cousin in North Kirkby. That's not far from Sugar Island where I saw Piper running across the hill. Now Piper has followed me here. A dog can easily cover long distances in one day. Piper has had lots of days to get here. Dogs have this...this amazing sense of smell. Piper can smell me. He knows I'm here.'

Gorron and the copper-haired guy exchanged glances – slightly sad glances, as if to say, *Poor Jack. This disease has affected his mind. He's hallucinating.*

I leaned in closer, studying those rounded depressions in the snow, which had been created by the pads of a dog's paw. 'You see the prints, don't you, Gorron?'

'Of course, I do, Jack. They could be made by any dog.'

'No, Gorron. These are Piper's. I saw him down here when I looked out of the window. After all these years, he's found me again.'

Maybe my mind did wander off into the mist after that. The next thing I knew Gorron was pouring me into bed, pulling my boots off, then covering me with blankets.

He said, 'Jack. Tomorrow, I'm leaving with Tasmin's people. We're going to find more Creosote-Plus Types.'

'They're just regular Creosotes.' I was tired to the bone. 'Somehow they've worked out a way of speaking – it's to trick us into believing they are friendly.'

'If we find anymore, they'll be kept in cages, like the other ones, so they can't attack us.'

'What about Dane?'

'What about her?'

'We should be looking for her...I'm worried about her.'

'Jack.' Gorron sat on the bed and looked me in the eye, his face going all serious. 'You do know she's no longer your girlfriend?'

'We argued before I left to do the recce, that's all.'

'After you left New Home, she told me that the pair of you had split up.'

'I didn't want to split up with her, Gorron.'

'Come on, Jack. If she told you it's over between you, you've got to accept that. I'm telling you this as a friend because I care about you. I don't want you deluding yourself that you've still got a future with Dane.'

'If I see her...I know I can talk her round.'

He looked at me – those big eyes of his were full of genuine sympathy. 'Get some sleep, Jack. And don't worry about those weird characters out there in the shed.' He smiled. 'They are locked up good and tight.'

Just then, I felt like crying...proper sobbing crying, that is. 'I don't want you to leave me, Gorron...I'm scared.' I bit my lip, shook my head, then wiped my eyes with my right fist. 'Sorry for sounding so feeble...but this bug has made me weak...lifeless.'

'It's going to be okay, Jack.' With that hefty boxer's paw of his, he patted me gently on the chest as I lay there on my back, helpless as a capsized tortoise. 'I felt vulnerable, too, when I was ill. Not being able to do anything for yourself is frightening. When it was really bad, I nearly choked on my own spit. Yeah?' He laughed. 'Sounds stupid, eh? But, as I lay there, a gob of spit went down my throat the wrong way. I was so weak I couldn't cough it up. What a way to die. Drowning because of a little bit of saliva. But I survived, of course.' Gorron laughed again. 'Look at me now.' He lifted his arms in a strong man pose. 'Fit and well. You'll be running around and bossing people about in no time.' He winked. 'You might even get jiggy with the beauteous Tasmin. I know she likes you. A lot.'

CHAPTER THIRTEEN

THEN THERE WERE THREE LEFT

So, they went ahead with their stupid plan. Tasmin's squad, along with Gorron, climbed into the two cars, then they drove away through the snow in search of more Creosote-Plus Types, to add to the ones they had already locked-up in the dog cages. Their plan did seem crazy to me. Okay, maybe there were a few Creosotes that had undergone new mental transformations, and they were now different to the old murderous folk that I was familiar with (and who had done their bloody best to slaughter me on several occasions). I just did not believe, though, that the new model of Creosote wanted to be our loving, hug-us-oh-so-gently, friends.

Hell no. They wanted to kill us. I'm sure of that particularly harsh fact. Okay, maybe they'd be more intellectually creative when they ripped the skin from our faces, or cracked our backbones, or gouged out our hearts and lungs. Yep, I confessed to Tasmin and Del-Coffey about my downright alarm at the notion of collecting yet more Creosote-Plus folk.

Smiling, they explained everything would be okay, as they pulled the blankets up to my chin again, while I lay there as inert as a dead fish, my body sapped of every atom of energy by that awful fever.

Anyhow, Tasmin's people headed out to the hills again. They were excited, laughing, and slapping one another on their backs – they were a bunch of friends going on a hunt together. They were loving what they were doing, and my friend Gorron was leaving with them. And, yes, Del-Coffey was bugging me. Yes, he believed that it was his absolute right to personally name everything that the sun shone down upon. The infuriating get. Ah, if you're not familiar with the word 'get' in that context, it's an old insult, meaning (I think) a nasty-minded person who enjoys spoiling things for others. I don't know which country the word 'get' comes from, when it's used in a sneering, insulting way, but just ask Mr Martin Del-Coffey. He will sit you down and explain the etymological origins of 'get' for so long, the bones in your backside will ache.

For the first time in days, the sun blasted down on the snow with an intensity that hurt my eyes as I leaned against the wall next to my bedroom window, my legs all wobbly and weak, staring at the cars as they moved far away across fields of white.

Now, there were just three of us in the farmhouse. Tasmin, Del-Coffey, and me. We had guns to protect ourselves, food for our bellies, and coal burning in the living-room fireplace to keep us warm. So, we were going to be fine, weren't we?

Nah...

Because just you wait and see what happened next.

CHAPTER FOURTEEN

JUST WHEN THINGS WERE STARTING TO GET BETTER

The day after the Creosote hunters headed off in the big 4x4s, I woke up to find the air unusually cold, the house silent, and the time coming up to noon. I lay there, frowning, as I looked up at those delicate crack-lines that decorate ceilings in nearly every home in the world.

Strange...normally, someone would wake me up about nine to make sure that I got plenty of liquid down my throat to keep me hydrated (that was the only treatment we had for the fever: plenty of fluids). I was still so sick with that fucking horrendous bug I didn't have the strength to climb out of bed, so there I lay – listening hard.

Nothing. No sound generated by humans, that is. Only the sound of the cold breeze cruelly imitating the moans and heartbroken sighs of all those young people who, after the collapse of civilization, had been so traumatized by the calamity that they'd just packed themselves off to bed where they eventually died of grief.

See? Being alone, being vulnerable, can do that to you, can't it? Your own thoughts go viciously rogue: they begin to gnaw the inside of your skull. You begin to picture EXACTLY what happened to people you loved, who suffered and died, and who went into the earth to rot, or into the crematorium furnace...into flames that burned hair from head, fingernail from finger, face from bone. Or that moment you put your hand on your chest to feel the *thump-thump-thump* of your heart...and you just know that that rhythm will soon change, the heartbeat will become erratic, then you will be convulsed by a burst of agony inside your chest as your heart abruptly stops – **DEAD**.

Damn it...this is what happens when your thoughts go bad. Normally, if I got all inwardly morbid like that, I'd jump out of bed, then go find someone to talk to. And, after a bit of chat and a joke or two, I'd be back to being happy Jack again.

But I could not get out of the fucking bed.

I could not hear human voices. I only heard the sobbing and

55

crying of storm winds blowing against the house. Hailstones rattled windowpanes – demon claws tapping glass, wanting in. Demons lusting to rip out my beating heart, before devouring that bloody lump of muscle with sharp-toothed jaws.

Damn it. Enough, Jack.

'Del-Coffey...Tasmin.' I'd tried my hardest to yell their names. All I could manage was a feeble croak. 'Del-Coffey, where are you?'

No reply.

They have left me.

Dumped me here.

Abandoned me.

Left me to die here.

Alone.

'Murderers.'

My eyes bulged with the absolute horror of what they had done to me. How could you leave a desperately sick man? I didn't have the strength to dress myself, let alone walk to the bathroom.

'Why did you leave me here to die...what did I do to you that was so bad you did this to me? Pigs. Sadists.' My voice petered out into self-pitying whispers. 'I'll kill you for this. I'll find you. I'll cut off your fucking heads, you bastards. You rotten, filthy scum.'

Then, of sorts, an answer.

Tap...tap...tap...

Such a slow sound – metal on metal, perhaps? With a huge physical effort, I succeeded in rolling out of bed onto the floor. My skull thumped down hard onto the floorboards. *Uh...that bloody-well hurt.*

While rubbing my sore bonce, I muttered to myself, 'Okay...if Creosotes have got in here, just...just lie back, let them get your throat first...make it easy for them, and a quick end for you...don't fight them. Die quick and painless.' I wanted to sob, though I was too exhausted to even produce tears.

Then...when no Creosotes appeared...I slowly...painfully slowly... moved. Crawling on my belly, weary as the oldest man in the world. My breath left my mouth in spurts of white vapour – the air was that cold. What had happened to the fire downstairs, which had warmed the house so beautifully?

Grunting, blurting swearwords to help push myself forwards, I squirmed belly-down along the landing. Outside, black clouds were painting the sky as dark as Death itself. The quickening breeze wove its own grim magic, conjuring up ghostly cries and demon shrieks. Danger – that's what I sensed so powerfully at that moment. The great, flashing red warning light of **DANGER** blazed through every nerve of my body. My heart pounded. Sweat was pouring down my face.

At any moment, vicious Creosotes would hurtle toward me. The intruders would then pounce on me. I was too weak to defend myself, or even to try and escape. They would savagely rip...gouge...claw...until my body was nothing more than a mess of dripping crimson.

Tap...tap...tap...

That unsettling sound again. Maybe that is the Creosote-Plus way? They torment you...before they kill you.

The sheer effort of crawling made me pant as furiously as a horse at the end of its race. Damn it, even steam rose from my arms, because I was putting so much effort into moving forward one oh-so slow inch at a time.

I made it to the next bedroom...slither...crawl...grunting with exhaustion. There was darkness. The curtains were closed.

But someone is in here with me. They're watching me. Getting ready to attack...

Tap...tap...tap...

In the darkness, I saw strange movements...a motion that made no sense. Then my eyes fixed on an object moving slowly...slowly...through the air. A bottle was floating about inside the room.

No, someone is moving a bottle through the air.

Tap...tap...tap...

They were slowly tapping the glass bottle against the metal frame of the bed.

I managed to kneel up.

Tasmin's face gleamed eerily through the darkness. She'd been the one using the bottle to make a tapping sound. Trying to attract my attention because she was too weak to even call out.

She then finally whispered these words. 'I'm not well, Jack...I've got the fever...Del-Coffey...he's got it, too.'

CHAPTER FIFTEEN

SOLE CARER

After Tasmin told me that she and Del-Coffey had the fever, I laboriously crawled out of her bedroom, and back across the landing to Del-Coffey's room. There I found him fast asleep in bed. I had absolutely knackered myself crawling from room to room. Damn it, I was sick myself, though I hoped I'd begun to enter the recovery zone. At least I could move by myself, even if I had to crawl instead of walk. A couple of times, I tried to stand up on my own two feet. I did succeed in standing upright when I clung onto the door to support me. My legs were wobbly, sweat ran down my face, my heart pounded with the sheer effort of it all, but I managed to walk perhaps ten steps before having to sit down as the bug sucked the vitality right out of my muscles, which left me strangely flimsy and empty inside – as if some horror parasite had hollowed me out, leaving a Jack-shaped shell of hair and skin.

I succeeded in bringing bottles of water to Tasmin and Del-Coffey. How I did it, I don't know, considering how ill I was. Even so, I managed to get fluids down their throats, pile more blankets onto their beds to keep them warm, then I achieved what seemed a major victory at the time. Even though I barely had the energy to move my arms, I relit the coal fire in the living-room. The reason the air had felt so bitingly cold in the house was that the fire must have gone out the day before. Then whatever ambient heat had remained in the brickwork must have eventually leaked away into the Arctic-cold air on the other side of the house walls.

Making hot soup for my pair of patients became an epic ordeal in its own right. I burnt my hand on the camping stove, spilt soup on the stairs, forgot the spoon to feed Tasmin and Del-Coffey with – this when I'd just painfully climbed the staircase on all fours. Forgetting the spoon almost had me howling with frustration, But I did it. I crawled back downstairs, and I collected the spoons.

And, hallelujah, I got the pair of them fed.

For a while, I sat on Tasmin's bed speaking to her. Her dark eyes gleamed up at me from the gloom. Her black hair was softly fanned out over the white pillowcase – a beautiful nymph from a dream.

I asked her, 'When will your people be back?'

Her voice floated from the gloom: 'Did they...did they leave yesterday? I've rather...lost track of time.'

I confirmed they left yesterday.

'Then they said they would be back...the day after tomorrow. Uh...I wish there was a...a way to contact them.'

'Just imagine, in the old days we could use a phone. Instant communication. Seems like an impossible miracle now, doesn't it?'

'Jack, your voice is much stronger...you must be getting better.'

'Still a way to go. It feels like my arms and legs are made from lettuce leaves. There's no strength in me at all. Now I know what it's like to be a hundred and three years old.'

'Yeah, I'm nineteen...feeling like ninety...uh, it's a struggle to...keep my eyes open. Just sleepy.'

'Tasmin.' I was feeling closer to her now, and ready to open up emotionally. 'You know something?'

'What is it, Jack?'

'When I woke up today, I thought you and Del-Coffey had left me here alone.'

'I...' Her head sank back into the pillow – exhaustion was winning the fight. 'I...I would never leave you here, Jack. I wouldn't abandon you, because...' Weariness took her voice away into a drowsy slur. A moment later, she was fast asleep.

'Next job,' I murmured to myself. 'Check on the guests.'

Another odyssey presented itself. The arduous journey out to the big shed where the Creosotes bided their time in the cages.

Dressing myself became an interesting challenge in its own right. Just the act of pulling on a couple of fleeces over my sweatshirt made me groan with exhaustion. Even the Jeep hat I tugged onto my head felt so heavy I could have believed it was made from a big lump of dead-weight iron. When I'd done what I could to protect myself against the cold, I did something brave. I went outside.

CHAPTER SIXTEEN

BIG SHED HORROR

I did feel exceptionally brave, leaving the solid protection of the farmhouse, because that ever-present weakness made me so vulnerable. I began to appreciate why elderly people don't like leaving home. That fear of falling. The nagging worry gobby kids will shout insults at them, or even throw a skull-cracking stone or two. Right at that moment, as I hobbled across the yard at such a slow speed it would make a tortoise shake its head in pity for me, my heart pounded because I was so scared of the breeze. Damn it, I was frightened the wind would blow me over. I was scared of falling and breaking a leg bone. Just days ago, I had carried Gorron as I ran across a field before jumping into a river. My God, I was barely strong enough to walk on two legs.

The short distance I needed to navigate gave me heart palpitations. Worse, I felt like whimpering with fear. This wasn't big, brave Jack Ranzic at all. This terrified me as much as that horrendous night a decade ago when my father tried to murder his entire family.

So...out into the brutal cold. Drag your feet through the snow. Head for the grim building. See the door...an entrance to a tomb. That's what it looks like. Darkness pressing in across the fields. Darkness coming to engulf the farmhouse. Darkness to ram its hard fists against my eyes. Hail darting to sting my face. Sharp blades of ice trying to cut my cheeks. Storm winds roaring in from a cold and remote place...from where the God of Death will swoop down to crush my bones. Moving further from the safety of the house. Heading deeper into darkness. Toward that doorway. Toward horror. Through into the grim place of cages. And there I will encounter...

Dizzy with exhaustion, I staggered on...dangerous mind-movies of my own imminent death were blazing inside my skull. Then, **BANG!** I shouldered the door open. Not only men and women were imprisoned here. The cold walls of that giant shed trapped a deeper darkness. A darkness that robbed me of the ability to see properly. *Nevertheless – check our guests. Don't want the monsters breaking out. We all know what would happen to me and my two friends if that happened...*

Yes, this journey had terrified me. But I had to check that those brutes were still there in the cages. I needed to reassure myself that they hadn't escaped.

Oh, they were there alright. Ten men and women lurking at the back of a cage. These individuals smelt of burnt straw. Maybe, before their capture, they had been setting fire to straw bales. Or had they been burning teenagers like me?

Just the sight of those creature was terrifying. Their bright, enigmatic eyes were glinting at me from the gloom. Their faces were almost invisible in the shadows. The Creosotes were shaggy, half-human shapes. If I'd had the strength to scream, I would have howled that blood-red well of my throat raw. Right at that moment, I pictured my weak legs failing...causing me to stagger, lose my balance, so that I grasped the cage bars to support myself. Then they would pounce – hands shooting out between the bars to grab hold of me.

I shook my head, trying to drive those awful images out of my brain.

Even though the gloom created something like a black fog – one that made it so hard to see anything properly in that frightening place – I did shuffle my feet to get me closer to the cage door.

I gasped. 'Padlocks. Where are the padlocks?'

'They'd gone. The monsters had somehow managed to break the locks.

Any second now, they'd rush at the gate. Push it open. Then...

That's when I nearly sobbed with relief. The pair of padlocks fitted through metal loops at the top of the gate and at the bottom. I had expected to find them at the mid-point, near the handle, hence my moment of panic. Those padlocks were tough specimens of metalwork – and they were most definitely intact and strongly holding the gate shut.

The creatures inside had not stirred. Even so, they radiated an air of expectancy, as if something amazing would happen soon. Their eyes sparkled as they watched me.

I glared back at them. 'Good night, sleep well, and...go to hell.'

They were in a cage. So why not insult the creepy dipshits? What could they do to me? Hire lawyers to prosecute me for defamation? Kill me with a perfectly aimed turd?

Shaking my head, I took a step back, ready for the gruelling journey of thirty yards back to the house. That's when they spoke to me. Oh, dear God...the things they said...

CHAPTER SEVENTEEN

THE MONSTERS ARE SPEAKING AGAIN

Throughout the history of human beings, it has so often led to this. The same terrifying situation repeated over and over. And that situation is the necessity to go into the unknown...to go face the UNKNOWN THING in the darkness. There, excitement mates with terror. It breeds a dark electricity that blasts through our bodies, making our hearts pound, our bodies shake and sets a voice shouting inside our heads: ESCAPE! RUN AWAY! The human dilemma is always the same when we approach the UNKNOWN THING which has the power to frighten us. And the questions we ask ourselves at that moment of crisis are always the same, too. *Do I run away? Or do I go forwards to confront the unknown?*

And so that eternal dilemma confronted me inside the shed with the cold metal cage, which imprisoned the Creosote-Plus Types, as Del-Coffey termed them. That's when I asked myself: *Do I run away? Or do I go forwards to confront the unknown?*

My intention had been to walk away from the cage. Before I could do that, however, they had all stood up, as if those men and women were on strings and a giant had pulled his puppets upright to their feet. They stood there in the cage, in their odd assortment of clothing – some wearing three coats, or even two hats, or a boot on one foot, a shoe on the other.

They gazed coldly at me. Their faces were expressionless, yet the blank faces seemed to ooze total menace that drifted through the air, through the bars, and then through my chest to freeze my heart. Even though being in the building with those monsters terrified me, I found myself, once again, asking the age-old questions: *Do I run away? Or do I go forwards to confront the unknown?* Running wasn't possible in my fever-blasted condition. Not that I would have run away because, there and then, I decided to take a decisive step toward the cage and confront the unknown. I've had it with running away. Time to face my fear – a fear that was Creosote-shaped, and which had the power to corrode optimism and destroy our hopes for a happy life. So – back I went, to stand before those figures, to test my own courage, and my determination to stop running away from adults once and for all.

For long moments: silence...just cold, cold silence.

And then they began to speak in what must be their customary way. A way that was absolutely disturbing and inhuman. One beginning the sentence, another supplying a few more words, before a third individual added yet more words, and so on. And, taken as a whole, their fragments of speech formed a rational statement.

A bald man with one eye, and with scars radiating outwards from the empty socket, began the blood-chilling recital in soft murmurs – almost like he was thinking aloud.

'Let me...'

'...out...' added a woman in a red coat.

'...I want to go with...' sayeth a gent with no teeth.

'...you into your house and...' uttered another. You get the picture.

'...I want to warm...' Etcetera...

'...myself.'

'...and tell you something that might...'

'...just save your life.'

'We should look after each other.'

'I don't...'

'...want my mind to die...'

'...only to be reborn again...'

'Just imagine, Jack...'

'...what I had to...'

'...suffer...'

'...endure...'

'...in order to become sane...'

'...again...' This 'again' supplied by the one-eyed man with the scarred face.

I slammed the side of my fist against the bars. *Clang!*

Enough strength returned to my diseased body to allow me to shout, 'How do you know my name?'

'Jack,' announced the woman in the red coat.

'Ah...' I nodded. 'This isn't telepathy or magic. You heard the others use my name when I was here before. I know you're trying to trick my friends into thinking you want to make peace with us. You don't fool me! I know the first chance you get – *you'll slaughter us!'*

I slammed my fists against the bars. **CLANG! CLANG!** '

That did it for me. The strength leaked right out of my body again. I could hardly stand upright. My head felt as heavy as concrete. My eyelids drooped. Fatigue was hollowing me out.

The creatures stared at me – not moving, not saying anything.

Just that murderous stare of theirs revealed their true intentions toward me.

I groaned with exhaustion. 'Stay here,' I muttered. 'You can rot to nothing for all I care.'

The woman in the red coat spoke. Her voice was louder, sharper. 'I know your mother, Jack. She is a...'

'...slut.' This came from the one-eyed man.

The guy with no teeth spoke with obnoxious pleasure. 'A slut...and your slut mother keeps...'

'...her children's heads...'

'...in a grave. And she...'

'...wants your head in...'

'...the grave, too, Jack.'

'...so she can...'

'...have all her family...'

'...with her...'

'Poor Jack.'

'Poor, soon to be...'

'...dead, Jack.'

Their faces were stone, their voices ice. That's when they opened their chapped lips and began to a laugh. One by one they raised their hands to point at me. The laughter grew harsher, echoing back from cold concrete walls.

'Your mother, Jack...'

'...is coming to...'

'...get you.'

'I could not run. I was much too weak for that. My leg were boneless, trembling things. I could barely move my feet, let alone sprint away from that cage full of monstrosities, which were, believe me, no longer human. Nevertheless, I put my hands over my ears to try and keep their taunting laughter out of my brain...because there it would leave oh-so fertile eggs of paranoia that would hatch demons to infest my thoughts.

I shuffled away as quickly as I could. Damn it. Those creatures had messed up my mind. I shouldn't have gone into the building in the first place. I certainly should not have listened to their verbal poison. Two minutes later, I slithered wearily across the yard, leaving twin furrows in the soft, white covering that engulfed the landscape. My eyes were getting blurry. The outbuildings became black tomb shapes. Abandoned farm equipment mimicked the skeletons of long dead creatures. Darkness was sweeping in over the fields. I moved through a cold world of harsh black and icy white.

Then I realized I'd stopped moving. The fever had stolen the last scrap of strength from my body. Slowly, I sank down to my knees. Then, as if lying down on a comfortable bed, I settled down into

64

white softness, feeling its cold touch against my bare cheek as my head went down to the ground.

Snowflakes drifted down from the sky. I knew that to lie out there in deadly sub-zero temperatures was sufficient to push open the doorway, through which I'd step into that eternal silence. Where there is no cold...no feeling...no thought.

I could not move. Fever had closed me down.

Sometime later. Movement...a stumbling, clumsy movement. At last, I managed to get thought flowing again as it should. Senses connecting to nerves. Observations interacting with intelligence.

'Someone is carrying me.' I'd spoken the words out loud.

'Yep, I am. And, dear God, you are heavy.'

'Tasmin?'

'Yep.'

'You found me outside?'

'Yep.'

The woman held me tight as she dragged me upstairs. Her mouth was close to my right ear, and she was panting mightily. Huge gusts of air left her lips to make a roaring sound, her warm breath tickling the sensitive skin of my ear. I knew she was ill, so by what miracle of sheer tenacity she managed to haul me from the yard and upstairs I'll never know. But carry me she did. Her willpower was extraordinary.

I tried moving my legs, to take some of the back-breaking strain off her. However, I was so cold. My entire body was numb. My legs did not work. My arms hung down in such a way they must have resembled soggy noodles – just limp things that swayed from side-to-side as she laboured to get me upstairs.

'Tasmin,' I said. 'You saved my life.'

'Yep.' She grunted with the strain. 'Now...let me...get you...into bed.'

When I was finally in the bedroom, she pulled off my outer layer of clothes that were sodden with snowmelt. Though the woman suffered extreme fatigue, she managed to peel off my wet fleece and jeans. Grunting again with the effort of shifting my unresponsive body, she positioned my torso, head, and limbs in bed, then pulled up the covers.

That done, she removed her wet outer layers of clothing: fleece, hat, jeans, boots. Then she did an amazing thing. Heck, yes, it did amaze me.

She climbed into bed with me. Her arms went around me before she drew me to her chest, hugging me tight. Her hair fell over my face. A soft, warm covering that felt so comfortable, and so lovely. I could smell the heady aroma of the soap she used. Her body felt so deliciously warm against my skin – skin that, to her, must have felt as cold as a gravestone in winter.

'You need to warm up,' she told me. 'This way is the best. Body heat.'

This way is the best?

I whole heartedly agree. And if I had the strength, I would have shouted my full-blown approval from the bedroom window.

CHAPTER EIGHTEEN

DEL-COFFEY...THIS TIME FROM THE HEART

No.

We didn't have sex. Really. Truthfully. We didn't. For one, we were both wiped out by the funkily named Yipno-Fever. Totally exhausted. I've seen livelier pork chops than the pair of us lying together there in bed. Tasmin was holding me tight, using her own body-heat to restore some living warmth into me, gradually ridding my body from the exposure I no doubt suffered after collapsing unconscious outside in that bitterly cold air. I would have put my arms around her; however, they were just not functional. You see, I soon learned that the fever induced bouts of total paralysis. Scary, yeah, because you never know when it's going to strike. What if you're in the bath, and your arms and legs go all floppy and useless, and you slide down deeper into the bath, not able to stop yourself – and you are feeling the water level creeping up over your throat, chin, lips...you get the picture. Frightening, isn't it?

Reason two for no sex. Call me old fashioned, but we weren't in that kind of relationship.

So...no sex.

We lay close, though – very close. Strands of her hair covered my face with a feathery softness – warm, comforting, smelling so pleasantly of shampoo.

The next morning, when I woke to the very grey light of a cold winter morning, I surprised myself by climbing out of bed without any problems. Dare I imagine that my own biological weaponry was murdering the virus? My mind had become clearer. My knees didn't tremble when I stood upright. And, yes, my heart did surge with happiness, I admit it. The disease had scared me. Now, if I were starting to recover, I wouldn't feel so bloody vulnerable.

Tasmin lay fast asleep in bed. She'd only just contracted the virus. Therefore, it would be at least a little while before she started the climb back to full health. Walking with confidence, I left the bedroom to check on Del-Coffey in his room. He was awake but very tired looking.

'Uh, Jack.' He coughed before letting out a long sigh. 'I feel like I've been buried in a tomb for a thousand years. Talk about lifeless...I can hardly lift my arms. How are you?'

'A lot better, thanks. Listen, just try sleeping as much as you can. I'll keep pumping drinks down you and Tasmin. Plenty of fluid helps.'

'Jack...I've been thinking about the Creosote-Plus Types in the cage. What if they do break out? We're in a pretty fragile state here.' His eyes were large and round, and they were shining with something near panic. 'I'm scared, Jack. They could get in here.'

'Don't worry,' I told him. 'I checked the cages yesterday. The padlocks are still in place. Those monsters are going nowhere.'

After chatting to Del-Coffey, I headed downstairs. There I heaped more coal onto smouldering embers in the fire-grate, soon flames were leaping up the throat of the chimney, while kicking out plenty of glorious heat – something which felt good, I can tell you, in that cold tomb of a house.

I decided to conduct an audit of our assets (yep, that's the type of phrase that Del-Coffey would offer to us humble folk; maybe his personality was encroaching on mine, parasite-fashion?). Carefully, I checked doors and windows. Tasmin's people had brought me to the house when I was semi-conscious, due to the fever, so I hadn't seen the place properly. The house was a stout beast. It was brick-built, probably a hundred years old at least, with big square rooms and high ceilings. Long before the mind-busting epidemic had struck three years ago, there'd been a severe problem with rural crime – agricultural equipment being stolen, farmhouses broken into. Farmers have, or had, rather, a reputation for keeping large amounts of cash at home (they were famous for selling produce to locals for cash, and they preferred not to pay income tax on some of their transactions, if they could avoid that particular fiscal unpleasantness), so lots of farm owners turned their houses into forts to deter thieves. This house was no exception. Every window downstairs was protected by criss-cross patterns of steel bars, which were thicker than my thumb. All outer doors were formidable barriers, constructed from thick steel, over which a wood-effect veneer had been placed. Each door, too, boasted a heavy-duty lock and massive bolts. Yep, one hell of a fort. I even imagined Del-Coffey state in a hifalutin way, 'This house would indubitably keep out an entire army. The building is a veritable bastion.'

Food? Drink? Plenty in the larder. A couple of camping stoves occupied the huge slab of wood that formed the kitchen tabletop. Also, there were spare cannisters of gas on a shelf, in case the ones in the camping stoves ran out. Another room, leading off from the kitchen, had metal shelves fixed to its walls. On these, Tasmin's people had left us equipped with a bunch of guns – a pump-action shotgun, along with five cartons of shells. There was a submachine gun with a curving ammo clip that contained thirty rounds. And ten full ammo clips had been stacked on a shelf. There was a heck of a lot of firepower with that submachine gun alone. They'd also left my own hunting rifle that I'd collected from New Home, together with plenty of ammo. In addition to those weapons, there were five pistols of differing calibres.

If the Creosotes did manage to get out of the cage and come looking for us, the guns would easily blast those creatures into the fires of hell which so surely awaited them.

Moving briskly now, I heated spicy tomato soup, fed my two patients upstairs. That done, I looked out through the windows for the return of Gorron and the others, and to check for unwanted callers. There were only vistas of snow, outbuildings, black trees without a leaf in sight. At one point, I did see a herd of deer moving across a field out back. Fresh meat on the hoof. Perfect! However, by the time I had collected the rifle they'd vanished, timorous beasties that they are.

After returning the rifle to the armoury, I headed back to the kitchen to make coffee. Suddenly, my legs went boneless again.

'You're doing too much too quickly, Jackie boy,' I told myself.

I sat down and put my head down on the tabletop, intending to rest for a moment.

Twenty minutes later, I woke up, groggy and sluggish again. Yep, too much too soon. I had to pace myself. The bug hadn't quit my blood yet. Deliberately walking at a slower pace, I climbed the stairs where I checked on Tasmin. There she was. Sleeping soundly, her shining black hair washing over the white pillowcase in an ebony tide. Carefully, so as not to disturb her, I pulled the blankets up to her chin before going to take a squint at Del-Coffey.

The high, gleaming forehead poked out above the pale blue sheet. His own blonde hair was sticking up in a quiff. Certainly, not his usual style of having his hair neatly combed to one side. When I adjusted his bedding, so that it covered him properly, he lifted his eyelids to reveal tired eyes.

He murmured in a sleepy tone – his voice was hesitant, almost fractured, 'Jack. Why...why do they talk like that?'

'The Creosotes in the cage?'

'They each say a...a few words...the next person continues the sentence...anomalous...'

'It's weird, that's for sure.'

'And they don't refer to themselves as "us". They say "I" as in "I don't want my mind to die again." What does that mean, Jack?'

'I haven't a clue.'

'But it's like those human beings have become a single organism. I...I imagine if ants could speak, they would refer to themselves in the singular...don't you think? They are all individual ants, but they act like a single entity, and...and I think that...that the Creosote-Plus Type is the same.'

'Worry about that later, Del-Coffey. You need sleep.'

'Sorry, Jack.'

'Sorry? What for?'

Del-Coffey's blue eyes peeked over the quilt – there was that air of vulnerability again. 'I come across as pompous. A know-it-all. You see, I do care about my friends, and I do care about you. I try to be confident all the time...to make people believe that I do know what I am talking about...because that veneer of certainty, God willing, just might imbue within us...that is to say, within us survivors...the confidence to keep on surviving. And...and not give up...and not just lie down and die.'

'Oh...'At that moment, I felt guilty at judging him to be an insufferable 'get'.

'I award names to things...particularly to those 'things' that have no names and which threaten us, like the fever sickness...like those people in the cage. I named those people Creosote-Plus Types... because once you give them a pseudo-scientific name it stops them being a quantity that is unknown...and humans fear the unknown. You see...even the use of vocabulary can become a weapon, which makes us survivors stronger.'

'I see. Good work, Del-Coffey. I'm beginning to understand you.'

'No...you don't understand me...I'm scared, Jack. Absolutely scared to the bone. This new model of Creosote is much more dangerous than the older...brainless ones...they are cunning. Moreover...they are evolving. Their minds will become the weapon that has the power to destroy us...us, the younger people who stayed sane...who stayed sane...' He started to nod off.

'Okay, Del-Coffey. Take it easy, eh?'

I pulled the bedding higher, so it moulded warmly around the lower part of his face. As I did so, he grabbed my wrist – only weakly, yet he maintained his grip.

'Listen,' he whispered. 'I've been searching for a...a certain individual who is strong enough to keep us all safe.'

'Okay, but you're exhausting yourself now. Rest, okay?'

Those blue eyes changed – they blazed at me from the gloom with such a passionate hope. 'I'm searching for a man by the name of Nick Aten. He will save us. He is travelling with someone called Tug Slatter.' Del-Coffey's grip tightened around my wrist. 'Slatter is sheer bloody terror in human form. A monster. But he is on our side.' The eyelids began to close, bringing shutters down over those blue fires in his eyes. 'One more thing, Jack.'

'Yes?'

'I'd be honoured if you'd shake my hand. I want us to be friends.'

He wearily raised his right hand.

When I shook the hand, Del-Coffey smiled with relief. 'Thanks, Jack.'

He'd no sooner said that when I heard the sound. A fist pounding at the front door.

CHAPTER NINETEEN

COLD CALLER

Straightaway, I headed downstairs. The fist had struck the front door three times with a fierce power...then silence. As I reached the hallway, there came another three strikes against that formidable steel door.

BANG. BANG. BANG.

Possibilities danced across my brain. Maybe Gorron, together with the others of the search team, had returned. Or maybe fellow survivors had arrived at the farmhouse: young people that the adults had failed to wipe out? Or maybe the Creosote-Plus dudes had busted out of jail. The door had a spyhole, allowing me to safely look out, so I brought my eye close to the peephole.

A figure stood there – someone dressed in an Arctic survival suit. One of those all-in-one waterproof garments in bright orange, and probably stuffed with thermally effective goose-down. Red hair fluttered in the breeze. Red hair streaked with grey.

Immediately my tongue whipped the word 'Creosote!' out of my mouth.

The woman was perhaps forty years old. That is definitely mur-derously-psycho age. Yet the way she stood there didn't scream the horrendous news that she would attack as soon as she clapped eyes on me. Her posture was somehow refined looking. A straight back, head held high. What's more, the woman's expression appeared to be a pleasantly mild one, like a friendly neighbour popping round to have a word about when the wheelie bins would be emptied next.

The woman moved back across the yard, until she was about twenty paces from the door – that gave me the confidence to open it, leaving a gap of six inches or so, meaning I could slam the door shut and bolt it if she tried to rush at me. Yet her body language was just so completely non-threatening. Leaning forward, I put my face to the gap between the door and its frame. Instantly, I felt the icy kiss of cold air on my bare face.

'Hello?' My tone surprised me – it was quite calm, as if I did address a friendly neighbour.

The woman did not smile. Nevertheless, there wasn't even a hint of aggression in her demeanour. 'Hello, you. My name is Myra.'

'I'm Jack.'

'Hello, Jack. You took some finding.'

'Oh?' Maybe I was dreaming? Here I was speaking to one of the older adults in a normal way and, believe me, ever since The Day, when the madness erupted, there has been absolutely nothing NORMAL about anyone over the age of nineteen. Unless you are weird enough to call homicidal bloodlust on a global scale 'normal'.

'Adults did suffer a form of psychological apocalypse three years ago,' Myra said, as if answering a question I hadn't even asked. 'Children experience something similar when they hit puberty and become adults. All those newly unleashed hormones flooding their bloodstream. They cause psychological changes as well as physical ones.'

Why was Myra lecturing me? Yet the very fact a Creosote spoke to me in a way that was reassuringly normal did prevent me from slamming the door shut, before hurrying to grab the rifle for some face shooting practice.

'We need to have a serious conversation.' She eased a strap of her bag off her shoulder. 'Like I said, you took some finding, Jack.'

'You know my name?' Suddenly my blood got a few degrees warmer as I felt the first stirrings of anger. 'You've been talking to those animals in the cage.'

'Those animals, as you term them, are still in the liminal state. They are gradually transforming from the mentally disordered phase to the stage of complete mental equilibrium you now see in me.'

'Are you saying adults are becoming sane again?'

'More than sane, Jack. Minds have been melted down, as it were, before being shaped into something much finer and much more powerful than before.' She unfastened the rucksack. 'Therefore...' She pulled open the flap at the top. 'In order to prove to you that we wish to rebuild your trust in your parents, and older adults in general, I have brought you a gift. Take care of these, Jack. Make them well again.'

Myra upended the rucksack, tipping objects into the snow.

The entire world slipped out of focus for a second as I stared at what rolled toward me, before coming to a stop.

What lay at my feet were heads...human heads. The heads of three of my friends from New Home. Though the faces were mutilated, eyes gouged, and lips had been torn at the corners of the mouths to create overlarge smiles, I recognised Mary, Fatima, and Jonathan.

The shock of what I saw there ripped the strength right out of me.

Then I experienced a surge of fresh terror, which had such a painful, crushing effect on my heart, I thought it would burst like a ripe grape crushed beneath the heel of a savage boot. This new bout of terror was the result of seeing figures run around the corner of the house. They were speeding toward me, kicking up explosions of snow. Here they were – the man with no teeth, the woman dressed in red, the tall man with one eye – all the Creosotes, which had once been locked in the cage in the big shed, raced toward me, their hands outstretched, fingers insanely clawing the air. And the rage...the sheer rage that blazed from their eyes...

I fumbled with the door. I was trying to slam it shut. However, there was a security chain on the door – infuriatingly, the links swung between door and frame, preventing me from closing the door. The Creosotes were just ten paces away...and that chain...that fucking chain...had caught in the gap, meaning I'd have to open the door before closing it again.

I had no choice. I had to pull the door toward me. Immediately, five arms shot through the gap in the door, trying to claw my eyes out. Jerking my head back from those grasping hands, I tried pushing the door shut. However, the mass of bodies prevented me from closing the door again.

I howled these words at perfidious Myra. 'You opened the fucking cage, didn't you? You let the fuckers out!'

The door began to slowly open as all those men and women shoved at it. My feet slid back on the stone floor. Five seconds from now, they would be inside – mutilating, killing.

Tasmin. Del-Coffey. I'm sorry. I let you down.

Then, from nowhere – absolutely nowhere – a black shape flashed across the ground outside. It swiftly inserted itself between the attackers and the door. A pair of jaws opened wide. There was a flash of white teeth. A glint of a consummate hunter's eye. Then snarls as those white teeth crunched into a fleshy Creosote leg.

Howling with rage, the Creosotes abruptly backed away from the doorway. That projectile of hard muscle, fur and dagger-sharp teeth had actually scared them. That is something I had never seen before: a frightened Creosote. Today must be a day for miracles.

'Piper!'

The dog glanced back at me – its eyes were as bright as diamonds.

'Piper! Come here, boy! Come on!' I shouted the words as I gripped the door, ready to slam it shut.

The Creosotes had recovered from the shock of that lightning strike in canine form. They surged forward, swinging their fists at the dog, while screaming in fury. The Border Collie shot me a glance that was so abundantly full of intelligence, then he dashed away from the attackers. Half the Creosotes went after the dog, which loped away into the distance. The other half surged toward me.

This time, I held the security chain clear of the gap as I slammed the door shut, turned the key, then drove home the bolts. After that, I sprinted along the hallway to the kitchen and the back door. 'Piper's clever.' I panted the words as I ran. 'He knows how to get the better of those...those fuckers!'

The fingers of my right hand clawed at the key in the back door. Inadvertently, I began twisting the little metal shaft the wrong way – which immediately had me howling with frustration – before I finally turned the key the right way. And then with my fist, I pounded the handle downward while, with my other hand, I grabbed a D-shaped handle fixed to the door. The instant I hauled the door open, a black and white shape, sparkling with melted snow, bounded in, jumping up at me with absolute delight.

BANG. I crashed the heavyweight security door shut against its frame, turned the key, then shot the bolts across. Locked, bolted. That would keep the monsters out.

After that, I dropped to my knees and hugged the dog so hard there was a clear and present danger I'd crack his ribs. But Piper didn't mind, and he excitedly licked my face. And then I looked up to see Tasmin standing in the kitchen doorway.

Though almost passing out from exhaustion, she nodded and said, 'Maybe magic really does happen at Christmas.'

'Christmas?' I rubbed Piper's furry back. 'I don't even know what month it is.'

'I not only know the month. I can tell you that today is none other than Christmas Day.'

CHAPTER TWENTY

PIPER

This is the scene in the kitchen. A scene lit by an old-style oil lamp, complete with burning wick, and a glass chimney filled with golden light. Tasmin is standing there in the doorway. Me – I'm stroking Piper. I'm laughing and crying at the same time, but you know something? I don't care. This is a miracle.

Piper was looking up me, his mouth part-open in that toothy grin that dogs wear on their faces when they are happy. His fluffy tail was swishing hard, loudly thumping against the table leg. His eyes were so bright, and they pulled on my heart strings. I was happily ruffling his sweet-smelling black and white fur with both my hands, and he was making a puffing sound, almost canine laughter. So, Piper hadn't been killed by my father all those years ago, after all. Piper had survived and gone to live with new owners. My mother had not lied.

Tasmin was smiling – tears were making her eyes glittery bright. She was tired to the bone, but she somehow staggered over to me. I managed to catch her as she fell.

Outside, the wind was sighing around that big old fortress of a house. There was half a pan of spicy tomato soup on the camp stove. There was flatbread on a plate, left there by me earlier, ready for an early evening meal. On worktops, there were more pans, three bottles of red wine, a bottle of vodka, plus a box of nine-millimetre pistol ammo.

And in the middle of all this, there we were – Tasmin, Piper, and me – in a remote house, in a snowy landscape. Somehow, at that moment, we were all a lovely muddle: two people and a Border Collie. We were clustered and cuddled-up together. I was holding Tasmin up as she made a fuss of Piper, and then she was hugging me, then kissing me on one side of my face, and Piper jumped up and licked me on the other side. Both cheeks tingled with human and doggy kisses. And I thought: *I'm the happiest man alive.*

At last, with a huge grin, I said: 'Tasmin. This is Piper. This is my dog.'

'He does seem to know you.'

'See, he hasn't been trimmed in years. All this fur around his neck? Thick as a lion's mane.' I looked Tasmin in the eye. 'Okay. I know what you're going to say. How can I prove that this is Piper? There's no collar with a dog tag. Nothing to show he belongs to me.'

'Jack. I'm not going to disagree with you, because I really want to believe in miracles right now. Therefore, I do believe in this miracle – that Piper has found you again. And I want to believe that even more miracles will happen, and we won't die in this place. I want to believe that I will be alive this time next year.'

There we were, the three of us. Piper making that huffing sound as he excitedly wagged his tail – a breathy sounding 'Huff, huff' that was a joy to hear. And Tasmin and me stroking his furry back, ruffling the thick mane, and sometimes feeling the heart-warming benediction of his long, fluffy tail thumping against our legs. But then reality, in all its cold, harsh brutality, shoved my happiness back into the trashcan of life.

Tasmin still had one arm around me, a gesture of affection (I hoped) – that and to support her body, which was still so weak from the illness.

When I spoke, it seemed like I'd become a doctor breaking very bad news to a patient. 'Tasmin. I'm sorry to have to tell you this...the Creosotes have been let out of their cages.'

Her eyes widened in astonishment. 'Who by?'

'A woman, another Creosote, but she can speak. By that, I mean speak intelligently.'

'One of the Creosote-Plus Types?'

'Huh, maybe it's even better to describe her as a Creosote-Plus-Plus Type, because she appeared completely normal.'

'Appeared?' Tasmin had shrewdly spotted that I'd qualified my statement about normality with a disquieting 'appeared'.

'Yes, aged about forty, dressed properly for this cold weather, an intelligent expression on her face, then she goes and...' My mouth dried as I recalled what the redhaired woman had done. 'Then she goes and empties a rucksack onto the ground...dumps out the heads of my friends.'

'My God.'

'Even though their faces were...' I felt sick as I pictured the heads rolling through the snow toward me. 'Though the faces were... damaged...and that's an understatement, I recognized some of my friends from our village.'

'Jack...the doors.'

'Don't worry, all doors and windows are locked tight. And those doors are steel slabs that'll keep any fucker out.'

For a moment, we froze as we let the implications of what I had just told her about the redhead Creosote sink in. Then...

BANG!

Piper barked, while both Tasmin and I flinched in shock at the sound of that dangerous-sounding BANG. Why hadn't I put a pistol in my pocket? Too late, if they'd broken in. I spun around, ready to fight with my bare hands.

But then I saw a familiar face.

'Del-Coffey.' I sighed with relief.

Tasmin added graphically, 'Christ, man, I nearly crapped myself!'

'Ah...crapping oneself. Otherwise known as "crowded trouser syndrome". My apologies.' Del-Coffey stood there in a white T-shirt and red shorts, his high forehead glistening with fever sweat, while his bloodshot eyes fixed on Piper. 'Sorry. I fell into the door. My legs just don't bloody-well work like they should.'

'Here.' I helped him to a chair. 'Sit down.'

'Good looking canine.' Del-Coffey did not smile. His unsettling, wide-eyed stare suggested he'd just witnessed the nightmare gates of hell swing open to reveal demons swarming in an ocean of evil intentions. Even so, he murmured: 'Border Collie – originally bred in the English-Scottish borders for herding sheep. Gentle temperament. Highly intelligent. Virtually immune to adverse weather conditions.'

'He's my dog. Piper.' I gave Del-Coffey a hard stare, daring him to challenge the truth of my statement. 'After ten years he finally found me.'

'It's Christmas Day. Miracles are allowed. You know...Santa visiting every house in one night? Miracles are definitely permitted. Heck...I feel lousy.' As he sat there, he held his bare knees in both hands, gripping them hard, perhaps trying to use pain to drive back the fatigue that threatened to overwhelm him. 'Before I conk out, there's something you should know.'

Tasmin's wise gaze searched his face, she was no doubt trying to anticipate what he'd say, because I sensed what he intended to tell us would NOT be good news.

Del-Coffey shivered. I even saw the hairs on his arms bristle outward from the skin. That wasn't due to the cold. No, sir. That was fear.

He said: 'Look through the window. There are Creosotes out there.'

'I know,' was my reply. 'Someone let them out of the cage.'

'No.' His eyes widened again – that *I've-just-looked-in-through-the-gates-of-hell* stare of utter horror. 'There are more Creosotes out there. Thousands...no, not just thousands...tens of thousands. We don't stand a chance. We're in a situation best described as perilous.' Abruptly, his face turned red, and he yelled with surprising violence: 'Fuck that! We are dead, dead, dead!'

CHAPTER TWENTY-ONE

DREADFUL LEGION

Del-Coffey was right. There weren't just thousands of the monsters. There were tens of thousands. Maybe even a hundred thousand. And, let me tell you, they were an ugly stain on the landscape.

I'd taken the binox up to Del-Coffey's bedroom to get a better view, though it was fair to say that I'd have been rewarded with pretty much the same view from any upstairs window in the farmhouse. Tasmin and Martin Del-Coffey remained downstairs in the kitchen. Just moving from up here to down there, to the kitchen, had wiped the pair out. Del-Coffey had even fallen asleep, with his face resting in a mess of breadcrumbs on the kitchen table. Piper had come trotting upstairs after me, his claws tapping on bare floorboards. Piper's mood had become serious now, no doubt syncing with my own sombre demeanour. And, believe me, I had plenty to be sombre about. So, there I stood at the window. I was staring out, gripping the binox so hard I nearly crushed them. What I saw out there radiated cold waves of sheer fucking terror. My heart thumped hard, the pulse in my neck felt like a finger stabbing hard at the underside of the skin. Oh, yes...oh, yes, indeed. What I saw, roughly tore any sense of security from me. In its place settled a huge, quivering lump of fear. Because the invading army had arrived. Okay, I've seen large groups of Creosotes before, but nothing – *nothing!* – like this. This was Biblical. This was epic. This was like seeing the noose that would choke you.

Out in snow-covered fields, out in the cold, out in the gloom of that evil day, a hundred thousand or more had gathered, forming a vast ring of human flesh around the farmhouse. Those men and women weren't moving. They were simply staring in my direction. Have you ever had thousands of people staring right at you? And purely at you? It is like a lightning strike smashing into your face. You recoil with shock. Your heart lurches. You have a physical reaction, as if a bolt of lightning really has blazed through your skull.

These were regular-type Creosotes. The ones that had a good chunk of their minds ripped away on that first day of the madness epidemic. Lots were half-naked. The clothes that some did wear had actually rotted on their bodies, until shirts, dresses, jackets and so on had been reduced to something like strips of fabric, creating an Egyptian mummy effect. It really did look as if thousands of men and women had disguised themselves as mummies, with long ribbons of cloth flapping in the breeze – a cold, cold breeze which came barrelling down from the continent-sized ice tomb that is the Arctic.

Piper pressed the side of his body against the side of my leg. I remember he used to do that to comfort me when Dad's temper would go nuclear – that is, before it went really NUCLEAR, which was the night he attempted to murder his own family. I stroked Piper's head, finding some comfort in the feel of his soft fur against my fingertips.

'It doesn't look good, boy,' I murmured. 'Bad people are here. They want to hurt us. But we won't let them, eh? We'll be safe in here.' My God, I wished I could believe what I was saying. If those Creosotes decided to attack the house, their sheer weight of numbers would bust in doors and windows. 'Okay, Jack.' I murmured to myself. 'You have something that those monstrosities do not have. You have intelligence. So, observe them. Assess them. Then use your intelligence to calculate a solution that will save us all.'

Piper gave a little bark in agreement.

Despite everything, I shot the dog a smile as he looked up at me – his eyes were so trusting. 'You and me...we are a team again, aren't we? Dad couldn't kill us when he flipped. We are not going to let those things kill us, either.'

I raised the binoculars to my eyes. The creatures were worse in closeup. Straightaway, I made out individual faces. A guy with a nasty-looking burn on one side of his head. A woman with half a nose. Another woman with beautiful hair that cascaded down over her chest – she had no front teeth, and just one arm. The arm looked as if it had been gnawed off at the elbow by some beast or other. All the wounds on these Creosotes were old and had healed after a fashion. What struck me as odd, was that they had not rushed toward the house, like I'd seen happen before in the past, when packs of Creosotes had tried to break into houses where I was staying. Back then, the Creosotes would be snarling as they furiously blundered up to the door. No, these Creosotes were strangely still.

What's more, even though they were densely packed together, they did not come any closer than about a hundred paces, leaving an open patch of ground all the way around the house. Then I saw why.

Figures on snowmobiles appeared – they circled the house, sticking to the zone that was clear of Creosotes. They reminded me of sheepdogs – the way sheepdogs keep their flock in a compact group, while keeping them in a particular area of a field. The figures on the snowmobiles were dressed for winter weather: boots, survival suits, hats, snow goggles. Then I saw a flash of red hair, belonging to one of the figures – a slim individual, mounted on a machine that fired up spurts of snow from its caterpillar tracks.

'Myra,' I whispered. 'Piper, this is a twist I didn't see coming. The intelligent Creosotes are marshalling their flock.'

Yeah...the Creosotes looked something like a *flock*. But that 'flock' was, in fact, an invading legion. And we, their enemy, were just three people and one dog against a force of more than one hundred thousand. For a while, I stood there, watching the mass of Creosotes. The sight of them was hypnotic. I found I could not stop myself from staring at them.

'You're here to kill us, aren't you?'

I felt Piper nudge the side of my leg with his nose. Maybe a signal to reassure me that he was still at my side, and that he was there for me, come what may.

'Okay, Piper. I'm going to have to do some hard thinking and come up with a plan to save our bacon.'

I knew that I would have to figure out some way of saving us all soon, because something unusual was happening to the Creosotes. Also, I understood now why the Creosote-Plus Types, as Del-Coffey termed them, were using snowmobiles to keep the mob tightly packed. The Creosotes weren't immune to the cold. I saw some individuals on the edge of the group stumble a few steps before falling face down into the snow. The cold was killing them. The Creosote-Plus guys were keeping their army packed tight together, to try and mitigate the effects of the killing storm winds. The Creosotes were suffering from exposure. Winds chilled their blood to the extent that the red stuff grew sluggish in their limbs, then that ooze of cold blood through their veins would, for some of those wretched brutes, bring their hearts to a juddering stop. I saw men and women simply die on their feet. They dropped down into the snow, their eyes staring into eternity.

For one mad second, I imagined them all dropping down dead. However, there were tens of thousands of them. And, at that time, maybe only a few dozen or so had flopped down lifeless. The weather would have to get a hell of a lot colder before the entire bunch of killers was obliterated.

At last, I managed to stop myself watching that awful gathering outside. 'Come on, Piper,' I told him. 'We need to get ready for war.'

CHAPTER TWENTY-TWO

BATTLE PREP

And so, I prepared for war. My army consisted of Tasmin and Del-Coffey (both were still poorly with the fever). And there was Piper (a healthy Border Collie, but not adept with weaponry, alas). Then there was me, Jack Ranzic (recovering from the fever, but still not out of the viral woods yet). My diminutive army faced a mob who would like nothing more than to rip the faces off our heads, and then smash our bodies to a sticky red mess that they would, no doubt, smear over walls and floors – a gory work of art of sorts.

With Piper trotting loyally beside me, I walked around the house, checking that doors and windows were locked shut. I even opened a window here and there downstairs, in order to tug at steel bars covering the window openings. I was testing the steelwork's strength in case the Creosotes tried to break in.

'It's looking good,' I told Piper with some confidence. 'Those window bars are as strong as the cell bars you get in prisons. They won't be able to break through them.'

I also positioned wooden crates near doors and windows – on those crates I laid out pistols and spare clips of ammo. I left the submachine gun on the kitchen table, together with a couple of magazines that were full of bright, shiny bullets. As for my hunting rifle, I kept that with me, carrying it by the strap over my shoulder. After ensuring that our fortress was as secure as I could make it, with guns conveniently placed should the Creosotes come screaming in to attack us, I fed Piper with a big chunk of corned beef from a can. I ate the other chunk. Then I warmed chicken Balti in a casserole dish with some chopped carrots, which I then took upstairs. Del-Coffey and Tasmin were weary to the point of being semi-conscious. The fever had raised their temperatures – both had faces that glistened with perspiration.

Del-Coffey asked if we'd been attacked yet. Happily, I could say, 'No, they're just standing there.' I wondered whether to tell him that the old-style brutish Creosotes, with the limited intelligence, were now being controlled, even herded into a big group, by the intelligent Creosote-Plus Types. I decided against sharing that information with him. I didn't want to activate that powerful mind of his again. The guy deserved to sleep. Not devoting himself to solving problems.

Tasmin sat up in bed as I used a fork to feed her.

'Hmm.' She managed to smile. 'That's nice. It's got a kick.'

'Chicken Balti.'

'Ah, I remember going to restaurants. I'd love a zingy curry, plenty of golden naan bread, all gooey and hot with butter.' Her smile faded a little, and a wistful expression came to her face, remembering good times from the old life. 'We'll never visit a restaurant again, will we?'

'There's nothing to stop us opening our own restaurants.'

'What, when we've cleared away the ruins of the old world, and built a new civilization?'

I used the fork to stab a large piece of chicken in the dish, then slipped the tasty nugget into her mouth. 'Well, Tasmin. Welcome to Jack Ranzic's Glorious Good Food Café. Here we serve the tastiest gourmet cuisine.'

'Am I your first customer?' The smile grew warm enough to light me up inside.

'You are. What do you think of my dish of the day?'

'Delicious.'

'Warm enough?'

'Just right.'

'Would madam care for flatbread?'

'Please. Just a morsel, though.'

'There you go. Oops, sorry...I missed your mouth.'

I used a tissue to wipe a glossy smudge of oil from her cheek, which was left by my mis-aimed attempt to feed her.

Tasmin laughed softly. 'Don't worry. I'll still leave a nice tip.' She raised her hand, lightly touching my fingers that held the tissue. 'Thank you, Jack.'

'You are very welcome, madam.'

'It's lovely joking like this. I appreciate what you're doing.'

'I'm not doing anything out of the ordinary...in fact, I've succeeded in getting some Balti sauce in your hair. Wait a minute, let me clean that for you. There.'

She laughed again, but the laugh broke into a sob. 'That's just it. You are managing to make everything ordinary in here when there are monsters out there. You are giving me food. You are making me feel safe. That is amazing, Jack. You really are doing something amazing.'

'Listen.' I went as if to dab her chin with the tissue, to remove more sauce I'd smudged there, but my movement subtly evolved into gently holding her face with my two hands. 'What is important now, is that we do not die. We will get through this. We will live. Trust me.'

83

'I do, Jack. I do.'

My fingers tightened on her face. Hurting her. She gasped, flinching back, trying to break free of my grip.

'Ouch...ouch! Jack?'

'Uh.'

'What's wrong?'

I grunted. 'My arms. I can't move them. I can't move my fingers, either. Ah...my back's hurting. And my legs. Uh...damn it...I can't move.'

'That's a symptom of the fever. It's a good sign.' She used her own hands to gently pull my hands away that gripped her face.

'Uh, I can't move...how can that be a good sign?'

'People who get the fever go through an entire sequence of symptoms: high temperatures, lethargy, bouts of unconsciousness, but as you get better there are episodes of paralysis when the body's muscles go into spasm.'

'Damn...it fucking hurts.'

'Yes. But it won't last long. The upside is, it proves the virus is dying inside of you. Soon you will be back to normal again. Virus free. Healthy as a pig.'

Grunting with pain (yes, inadvertently grunting piglike, at that), I managed to lower my arms.

'Here, Jack. Lie down here. Right next to me...that's it. Let me cover you up. Stay warm.'

Exhaustion robbed Tasmin of pretty much all her strength. Even so, she managed to arrange the bedding over us, while I snuggled down beside her. Tenderly, she embraced me. Our heads were side-by-side on the pillow. She moved her head closer. As before, deliciously cool strands of her black hair touched my face. That felt so nice. Comforting. I loved the softness of that silky hair of hers against the bare skin of my cheek and lips.

Even talking became amazingly difficult as I mumbled, 'Uh...Taz...Tasmin. I can't just lie here. I need to check that they haven't got any closer.' Yeah, 'they' – the Creosotes that surrounded us.

'Shh, Jack. Just lie here until it passes. You've been working too hard. Rest.'

'I daren't rest. I've got to keep watch. They're going to attack. S'only a question of when...'

She held me tighter, more hair drifted over my face, a covering of silky softness that comforted...that felt as if those strands of hair formed a magical protection that would safeguard me from the tide of evil that that had crept over the countryside toward us.

My mind remained completely clear, even though the virus had effectively paralysed my body. Thoughts trundled through my head like normal. Also, that sense of danger continued to pulsate inside my skull. It was warning me that we might be savagely killed at any moment. Sternly, I told myself I must get out of bed. Time to stand guard, rifle at the ready. Prepared for war...

However, warmth, comfort, her tender embrace – that was the magic that took control of my body now.

'Okay,' I murmured as I looked into her eyes that were just five inches from mine. 'I will lie here...but just for a minute.'

I awoke an hour later. A voice that possessed absolute clarity had woken me.

'Jack. Let me in. I want to talk to you.'

With a movement that was nothing less than explosive, I sort of erupted out of the bedding that covered me. Tasmin tried to sit up.

Then it came again: 'Jack. It's me.'

I knew that voice. I rushed to the window, pulled it open, and I found myself looking down at that dreadful woman who had thrown my friends' heads at me.

'Myra.' I glared down at her as she stood in the yard, staring up at me. 'What do you want from us?'

Her red hair fluttered in the breeze. 'Jack.' She smiled. A warm smile that oozed with the purest of goodwill. 'Jack. Open the door. Let me in.'

'Not a chance.'

'Let me in, Jack.' Myra stood just a hundred paces away from her legion of death that was a hundred thousand strong. 'We must talk, Jack. I have something important to tell you.'

Tasmin grabbed my arm. Somehow, she had found the strength to totter from the bed to where I stood at the window. Tasmin stared down at the redhaired woman.

Tasmin clearly understood what must be done. 'Jack,' she said in clear tones. 'Shoot her. Shoot her now.'

I grabbed the rifle from where I had left it leaning against the wall, pulled back the bolt, then hurried back to the window – flakes of white were blowing into the room on blood-freezing winds.

After putting the rifle to my shoulder, I leaned out.

Myra had gone. Just her footprints remained in the snow.

Then the sound came. The hundred thousand had begun to chant.

'LET...ME...IN...LET...ME...IN...'

CHAPTER TWENTY-THREE

'LET ME IN'

When a hundred people chant close by, it is loud. When tens of thousands chant...well, that muscular punch of sound knocks the air from your lungs. You don't even hear the sound as such, you feel that chant shake your belly. You feel its savage beat inside your skull.

After that bout of paralysis, the muscles in my back, my shoulders, and arms and legs felt tight, even painfully so. But my mind was perfectly clear. Even though I moved scarecrow-stiff on aching legs, at least I could walk quickly. With Piper following me, ready at my side if anything should kick-off, I headed downstairs, rifle in hand, my heart beating fast, and ready to fight for our lives if those creatures tried to break down the door.

I took up a position in the living-room, close to one of the windows. Like all the downstairs windows, this had steel bars over the opening. Clearly, even back before the collapse of civilization, the homeowner had taken security seriously enough to spend a lot of money on formidable steel doors, and bolting fuck-off metalwork over the window openings to keep intruders at bay. Outside, the cloud had begun to break, revealing areas of blue sky. Tree branches were still black claw shapes against all that frozen whiteness. And the Creosotes, all one hundred thousand of them, still chanted.

'LET ME IN...LET ME IN!'

The rhythm of their words had quickened. It was more urgent sounding – heck, more *dangerous* sounding. I saw thousands of figures out there, surrounding the house in a mob. The breath of all those people was creating a layer of white mist just above their heads. They did not come closer to the house. The only thing moving was their mouths. This was shocking because the old type of Creosote never even uttered so much as a single word. Something had changed inside their heads, giving them the ability to chant those three words. Three utterly dreadful words, because if those creatures ever did get into the house...images of our bloody murder spat through my brain.

The nearest Creosotes were perhaps a hundred paces from me. They were dishevelled-looking creatures. I saw faces ruined with scars and part-healed wounds. Men had beards that came halfway down their chests. And all those mouths were opening and shutting to the rhythm of their chant. Many of those mouths were missing front teeth. Come to that, some mouths even lacked a lip or part of a jaw.

And the cold was slowly killing them. Every so often, a man or a woman would totter away from the mob before they flopped down. They would slowly writhe on the ground, unable to get to their feet again as bitterly cold air stole away what remained of their body heat. Already lying out there, in a sort of border zone between the mob and the fresh snowfall in the yard, were frozen corpses with stiff arms and snow-speckled faces. They had staring eyes – their lips were curled back to expose teeth that were either black or broken.

Piper stood beside me. His dark eyes were fixed on my face. I knew he understood that the expression I wore was one of profound worry.

'Why have they come here, boy?' I murmured. 'What do they want?'

Piper tilted his head to one side as I spoke, listening closely to every word. I reached down to rub the soft fur on his head, one half of which had perfectly white fur, the other half was perfectly black.

'They're dying out there. The cold is killing them. So, what are they hoping to achieve before they all die?'

Of course, Piper wasn't going to answer that one. *So, why are they here? To kill us?* Yeah, that is a distinct possibility. But why did a hundred thousand or more home in on this particular farmhouse, in the middle of nowhere? Usually, when Creosotes attack it's in packs of a few dozen, or maybe up to a couple of hundred on rare occasions. But there were thousands besieging the house. Those kinds of numbers were unheard of – at least they were in my experience.

As the multitude did their blood-freezing chant, I flexed my fingers, then rotated my shoulders and raised my knees a little, testing my body, checking that muscle and sinew were supple again after that frightening bout of paralysis. Okay, Tasmin had reassured me that the seizure was the final bit of fun stuff that the Yipno-Fever had flung at me, and that I'd soon be fully recovered. Even so, not being able to move my arms and legs, which left me so helpless again, albeit briefly, was no laughing matter. In fact, not being able to walk or even raise my arms had been bloody terrifying.

'LET ME IN!'

In response to the demand, I fired back a full-blooded yell of, 'Oh, why don't you just fuck off!'

My shout dismayed Piper. His ears went flat to his head as his worried eyes looked up at me. He even raised a front paw, a gesture I recognized from ten years ago when he needed reassurance. I gently shook his paw.

'It's alright, Piper. I'm not shouting at you. You're a good boy, not like those things out there.'

Happy once more, he wagged his tail.

Just then – *crack, crack, crack!* That was the sound of gunshots. I knew straight away they'd come from upstairs, whereupon I bounded up the staircase to discover Del-Coffey leaning against the landing wall, his arm out of the window. The guy could hardly stand. Even so, he'd found the strength to somehow fire a snub-nosed .38 at the Creosotes.

'Del-Coffey.' I ran toward him. 'Don't do that. You'll only make them mad.'

'That noise...that chanting...I can't stand them shouting.'

He fired off another couple of rounds. Though what he hoped to achieve by shooting that titchy pistol into a mob of thousands, maybe only God alone knew. The low-velocity rounds would barely reach that mass of lunatic humanity, never mind killing any of them.

He fired another bullet. Then in a groggy whisper he managed to utter, 'I think I...hit one of them...big guy...bald head. I see... bleeding.'

'Okay, Del-Coffey. Good shooting, now give me the pistol...there, I've got it. C'mon, let's get you back to bed.'

Del-Coffey allowed me to haul him back to his bedroom.

'Did I kill many, Jack?'

'Five or six,' I told him, though I doubt if he'd even lethally plugged one of the monsters. 'Get into bed. I'll bring you a cup of coffee.'

'Thanks, Jack. You're one of the good guys. Wait.' He stood there with an expression of surprise on his face. 'Listen...do you hear?'

'What?'

'They've stopped chanting.'

Del-Coffey was right. His face was flushed from fever, his eyes were bright and sort of staring, as if he'd seen something wonderful through the bedroom wall.

I, on the other hand, did not see something wonderful through the bedroom window. Far from it. Yes, okay, the Creosote death legion had stopped chanting. They were silent now. But, get this, they were on the move. Putting one bare, frostbitten foot in front of the other. They were coming this way. They had finally launched their attack on the farmhouse.

'Damn!'

I let go of Del-Coffey, leaving the man to flop back onto the bed. My heart was going WHUMP-WHUMP! WHUMP-WHUMP! That's the sound of one hell of a scared heartbeat. Taking a deep breath, I headed along the landing, then down the stairs.

This is it. Time to fight.

CHAPTER TWENTY-FOUR

THIS IS IT...THE ONSLAUGHT

Piper rushed down the stairs in front of me. He headed for the lounge, where he started barking – a harsh, furious bark that hurt my ears. Keeping a firm grip on the rifle, I headed to one of the lounge windows. They were large ones that opened in the middle and swung open like a pair of patio doors. This window opening, too, had its covering of robust metal bars.

The moment I tugged open the pair of windows, cold air flooded into the room.

Instantly, my eyes gulped in that terrible view. At the far side of the yard, covered with its pristine covering of softly undulating snow, was a field. And in that field a mass of Creosotes were clustered. A quick glance left and right confirmed, yet again, that in all likelihood they surrounded the house. An icy wind blew, raising twisting ghost shapes of snow particles from the drifts – they went spiralling and dancing across the yard.

Piper stood beside me, his front paws were up on the windowsill, and he was barking at the death legion, which now moved toward the house. A moment ago, they'd simply been this anonymous group of people. Now, I focussed on individuals – a guy with straggling side curtains of white hair that descended from his head, leaving a bald dome at the top. A woman with black hair, and with lips that were blue with cold. One of her eyes was missing, exposing a diseased socket of red flesh that stretched back toward her brain – a cave, of sorts, which was utterly revolting to see. The mob came toward the house.

The breeze surged, filling the room with a hissing sound. No... not a breeze...that was the enraged panting of a hundred thousand creatures.

My heart pounded. Terror burned itself deep into my brain. Nothing else for it...I raised the rifle. I aimed the weapon at the Creosote with the straggling side curtains of hair. I squeezed the trigger...**BANG**. I parted the skull down the middle, the bullet cutting a crimson groove through the top of the bald bulge. He fell into the snow. Behind him, the same bullet punched through more heads, faces, throats. Perhaps five men and women slumped downward. Others fell into the snow, too – these were so debilitated by hypothermia they could no longer remain upright on their feet. That was a small miracle. As was the fact that my single bullet had knocked half a dozen of the murderers off their feet.

But just think about it...my rifle carried a maximum capacity of five bullets. If each bullet killed five people...that's a total of...yeah, not bad, not bad at all...but one hundred thousand homicidal people were marching toward the house.

Soon, they'd break down doors, even though they were made of steel.

I fired again and again into the tightly packed mass of humanity. Some of those individuals clutched at their chests or bellies, where bullets had smashed through skin, blood vessels, muscle, bone. I watched figures topple as I fired the gun. But I needed machine guns. I needed grenades. I needed fucking napalm. That might be enough to stop them. Not me with a rifle that was now down to the last miserable bullet.

The mob was halfway across the yard. Another fifty paces and they would be here at the window.

Piper barked. His gleaming white teeth were exposed. His instinct told him that to show his teeth could be enough to discourage an aggressor. Not, however, this bunch of slaughter-hungry maniacs. They hardly ever ran away when attacked. Shit, they never even seemed to feel pain the way you and I do. I've even seen a Creosote with an arm hacked off by a chainsaw, and most of their face blown away by a shotgun blast, and they still come at you, raging in all-out fury. Only an instantly fatal wound stops them for sure. Once, Gorron shot a Creosote in the backbone. It was a guy of around eighty with stumps for fingers (maybe bitten off by a dog, Gorron had later speculated). Anyway, Gorron shot this Creosote in the bottom of the back with a pistol (as the guy lunged at me), which severed the spinal column – and still the guy tried to attack us. Even though his legs were limp, he dragged himself along pretty much the way a seal moves across the beach – belly-down, front flippers hacking down into the sand, pulling itself along. The guy undulated toward us on his stomach. His mouth was open, his finger stumps were digging into the dirt, dragging himself forward. My pistol-shot to the old guy's face finished the job.

Now...a strange calmness floated over me. Maybe this is how it feels when you know you are about to die? I didn't even fire the last bullet in my rifle. What's the point?

Thousands moved toward the house, their feet crunching loudly into that crisp whiteness. Then, to my surprise, came the howl of engines. As I watched, feeling so helpless, the snowmobiles returned. These were ridden by the Creosote Plus Types.

Like sheepdogs, the snowmobiles moved swiftly backwards and

forwards along the front edge of the mob, slowing it down, then the machines altered course, to nudge people back, bit by bit. The new version of Creosote – the ones that could speak lucidly and had minds that appeared to be sane – worked hard, and with absolute determination, to push the Creosote hoard back to its original position in the field. The old Creosotes, which only possessed a stunted vestige of intelligence were, I believed, in the service of the new Creosotes – the old version was seemingly incapable of responding to verbal commands and, therefore, had to be herded like sheep. And gradually, the efficient toing-and-froing of A-Types on their snowmobiles succeeded in shifting the mob back.

Even Piper sensed that our enemy was retreating from the house – order was restored, the attack was over. For now.

Just as relief came surging through me, I felt that sensation again in my arms and legs. Muscles tensing – going into spasm. A fiery pain was burning through my body as the muscles that encased my skeleton went rigid. I moved backward from the open window, intending to go upstairs to check on Tasmin and Del-Coffey. As it was, I only made it to an armchair, just three paces behind me, before flumping down, dropping the rifle as I did so. My legs painfully stiffened until I could not move them. There I sat, feeling cold air flowing through the window to run its icy touch over my face. Piper couldn't understand what had happened to me and, after staring up at me with undeniable concern in his dark eyes, he began to nudge my hand that now hung down over the side of the chair. Damn it, I could not even lift my hand to reassure him with a pat on the head.

I did manage to speak, only with difficulty, though. 'S' okay, boy. I'll be alright. It'll pass in a minute.'

Then something awful happened...

Faces began to appear at the window. They were looming right up to the other side of the criss-cross pattern of steel bars that covered the opening. These were the clean faces of the A-Types. Their eyes were bright with intelligence. Worryingly, they possessed the knowing expressions of people who had already passed judgement on someone that was the object of their scrutiny. I recognized individuals from the cage – they were part of the group that Tasmin's squad had captured – and which Del-Coffey had planned to study. He grandly claimed that he'd dissect their psychology and thereby understand their behaviour. Now it felt as if the situation had been reversed. They stared in at me. They studied the expression of pain on my face. They understood perfectly that I was paralysed. And there I sat, waiting – waiting, perhaps, for a more bodily dissection.

Piper watched those intruders...he was silent now...tense...ready to attack if they attempted to break in.

The group was prepared for cold weather, unlike the old type of Creosotes, which were a mixture of the half-naked and entirely naked. These A-Types either wore multiple layers of clothes, or the all-in-one cold-weather survival suits. Once again, they spoke in that strange way. A guy in a yellow beanie hat starting speaking, then another individual supplied a few words, before another made their own contribution.

'Jack, you...'

'...know you cannot...'

'...possibly hope to survive like...'

'...this. Let me in, so...'

'...that we can discuss what...'

'...must be done to help you and your friends.'

That unholy chorus of men and women detonated such terror inside of me. Those knowing expressions. The alien way in which they had spoken. Taking a deep breath, I tried to override the paralysis that left me so helpless in the chair – sitting before my audience of six vile creatures that had once been ordinary men and women, no doubt with careers, and families, and who had once enjoyed innocent pastimes of watching television, reading, cooking, listening to music, maybe with a glass of wine or two. Not anymore. Their mutant brains had turned them ugly in mind and spirit...and intent. If those steel bars hadn't prevented them from climbing into the room, they'd have wasted no time in ripping my face off the front of my skull.

With a huge effort, I tried to reach the rifle that lay on the carpet. If I could grab the gun...just shoot one of the fuckers...that would feel so good. That would feel like I'd performed a sacred duty.

My fingers moved closer to the gun. My hand trembled. My shoulder ached. Closer, closer...almost touching the barrel.

At that moment, Piper's sharp snout pointed in the other direction as he looked at something behind me. He began to move backwards. Fur was rising on his neck and bristling along the line of his backbone. His white teeth glistened as he drew his lips back.

Then two things happened simultaneously. The six standing at the window suddenly reached in through the bars. They succeeded in grabbing hold of Piper by his bushy fur.

Then another hand swum into view. That hand picked up the rifle I had struggled to reach. With another huge effort, to overcome the cramp stiffening my neck, I turned my head a little – to see the new arrival in the room.

Myra stared at me. Her bright green eyes seemed to be devouring the image of me, as I sat there in the chair. She still wore the orange cold-weather suit, while her hair looked as if it had been washed recently – it hung down over her right shoulder in waves of shining copper.

Myra curled a finger around the rifle's trigger. 'No bars on the skylight. Quite an error of security planning, don't you think?' She pressed the muzzle of the rifle against the centre of my chest. She pressed hard until it hurt. 'I'm here with an offer. It's time we finally made a deal.' She smiled. 'That's right, Jack. I came here to save your life.'

CHAPTER TWENTY-FIVE

BETWEEN THE DEVIL AND THE DEEP BLUE SEA

Myra. The woman with all that curly red hair, which flowed down over her right shoulder, smiled at me as she pressed the rifle's muzzle into my ribs. Meanwhile, the dozen hands that had reached through the window bars to grab Piper by the fur still held on tight, even though he twisted his head, his jaws opening wide before snapping at fingers and wrists, drawing bright beads of ruby-red from bite marks. The Creosotes holding him did not react when the dog bit them with sharp, wolfish teeth. They did not seem to feel pain. Their faces were pressed to the bars – all of them were staring at me with such an expression of gloating.

I tried to stand, but the paralysis had me in its grip. I could not even raise my hand to bat the rifle away. What now? Would the woman pull the trigger? There was a final bullet in the magazine. Just one twitch of her finger would send the bullet crashing through my ribs to rupture my heart, before punching out through the back of my torso.

Myra smiled again, then her face became grave. Her eyes were suddenly distant, like she remembered terrible events.

When she spoke, her voice was coldly distant, too, as if grim memories had taken her back to a dreadful place. 'Everyone over the age of nineteen lost their minds. Me included. It felt like the death of the soul. Adults ran amok, killing the young – even killing their own children.' Her eyes abruptly focused on me with a burning intensity. 'Jack. We did not enjoy killing our own. Adults weren't angry with young people. We did not hate you. No...' Tears glistened in those big green eyes of hers. She moved the rifle muzzle from my chest and put the weapon down on a table. 'No... adults were terrified of you. We feared our own young. You see, for some reason, which had its root in mindless paranoia, we believed you would kill us. Our own children struck terror into our hearts.'

The hands grasping Piper tugged him so brutally toward the bars that he let out a squeal of pain.

Again, I tried to rise to my feet, but my leg muscles had locked tight into painful cramps that made my body blaze with nothing less than waves of agony. Though I could not move my limbs, I could move my lips.

In a gasping voice, I begged, 'Myra. If you have human feelings, tell those people to let go of my dog...they're hurting him. Make them let go...'

The Creosotes at the window instantly replied with the following mendacious statement, each one speaking a word, or a few words, before passing the verbal poison baton to their companion.

This is what they said, the vile fuckers:

'Jack. This is...'

'...not your...'

'...dog.'

'The dog...'

'...you loved, Jack, died...'

'...died a long time ago.'

'The dog you loved is just...'

'...rot...'

'...and bone...'

'...and death...'

I erupted. 'You liars...fucking liars. That is my dog. And just you let go of him or I'll fucking blow your heads off!'

I struggled to my feet. Then I was reaching out to where Myra had left the rifle on the table. However, that cramping paralysis simply would not let me do what I oh-so badly wanted to do. To kill those monsters that held onto Piper by his fur, hurting him, making him writhe, and yelp, and whine. No. My legs didn't work like they should – when I tried to take a step toward the table, I lost my balance and crashed back down into the armchair.

Piper yelped again. Cruel hands were pulling his fur, holding him there – his dark eyes fixed on me, pleading for help.

'Myra!' I shouted. 'Prove to me that you're human! Tell those fuckers to let him go!'

Softly, Myra uttered one word: 'Release.'

Twelve hands instantly let go. Piper flew across the room toward me, ears flat to his head, his body held low, his belly almost sliding across the floor. He pushed himself against my shins as he sat down.

'Thank you, Myra,' I said, and I genuinely meant it.

She appeared bemused by my relief that the dog was free. It was like she didn't understand that while my dog was hurting, I was suffering, too, as I watched that appalling ill treatment.

I managed to lean forward a little, then I stroked Piper's head while murmuring, 'There, boy. Good boy. It's okay. They won't hurt you now. Shush...take it easy, stay there, that's a good boy.'

The tone of my voice and stroking his head did soothe him. He slithered down until he lay on his stomach – though his head remained high, and his gaze was on high alert as he stared at the people who'd hurt him on the far side of the steel bars.

'Okay, Myra,' I said at last. 'You said you wanted to make me an offer.'

'Thank you for being prepared to listen to me, Jack.'

'But first, where are my two friends? If you've hurt them...'

'They're safe.' She spoke quite gently as if wanting to be my friend, too. 'They locked themselves into one of the bedrooms upstairs. They told me they have a gun and will kill me if I try and break down the door.'

'And will you?'

'No. There should be no more violence, Jack. It's time the older generation and the young people made peace.'

'You have a weird way of showing it.' Piper raised his head – his cold nose softly prodded against the bare palm of my hand, encouraging me to keep stroking him. 'Why did you throw the heads at me...the heads of those young people you killed.'

'I'm sorry.' And she did look repentant. 'I apologise for my lack of sympathy. Believe me, I had nothing to do with that attack on your village. I brought the heads to you because I could not carry entire bodies. I believed you would want to give them the decent burial they deserved.'

'But you cut their heads off first. You did, didn't you? That's hardly the decent thing to do to the bodies of human beings. Butchering them like dead pigs.'

'Jack.' She crouched down and placed a hand on my knee. Piper gave a warning growl – he was ready to bite her if she attacked me. 'Jack. Three years ago, my mind just...just exploded into nothing less than madness. All over the world, an epidemic of psychosis infected adults overnight. I don't know why it happened. And I can't begin to describe how terrified I was. How it felt to be trapped inside a nightmare. I was running through streets, attacking young people with my bare hands, because I truly believed they would kill me. I existed in a state of absolute terror. Every so often, just for a few minutes, I became sane again. I'd look at the blood, all disgust-ingly smeared on my hands and on my clothes...blood that wasn't my own, and I was just so scared, because I simply did not know what terrible things I must have done. Back then, during the madness, it was, for most of the time, a mixture of nightmare images that seemed to be an awful dream, not reality...but then I'd be me again. I'd know I was sitting on a bench in Burger King with my niece's head in my lap and one of her eyes lying there in the palm of my hand. I'd look at Tanya and I'd wonder what had hap-pened to her body...had I cut off her head? Yes, you can look at me strangely, because I'm so calmly describing what happened...me, sitting there with my sixteen-year-old niece's head resting on my legs and her eye...her gouged-out eye in my hand. At the time, I was screaming with horror. My niece, my poor niece, and I'm wondering if I was the one who'd killed her. But, seconds later, my sanity fractured again. I have bizarre memories of me running through Doncaster, swinging Tanya's head by the hair. After that, I don't remember anything until a few weeks ago, when I found myself coming out of a mental fog. My mind was clear again. I realized I was half naked. I was wearing a few ragged clothes. I didn't have shoes. My hair was all messed up. My fingernails were as long as claws. So, I found a house, got myself cleaned up, found these clothes. No, Jack, please don't ask any questions yet because I still have something important to say.' Those green eyes of hers were beginning to glisten with tears again – the memory of what happened had brought fresh torture to her. 'Yes, I threw the heads at you. It was weird, insensitive, grotesque – that is because though my mind is healing it is not completely back to normal again. Then again, I doubt if I ever will be the same person I was before that day when madness engulfed me. Yes, Jack, I have spoken to other young people. I know something about what you all suffered and how you had to fight for survival.' She abruptly leaned forward, taking my hands in hers, as she brought her face close to mine. I could feel her breath on my face when she spoke. I could smell the fragrant aroma of shampoo she'd used to clean her hair. 'Please, Jack, be patient with me...because I will continue to say strange things. I will still behave in bizarre ways every now and again because my mind isn't yet fully restored.' Her voice then sounded strangely flat, as if I heard her speaking from the wrong side of a tomb door – that is, from the other side, where the dead sleep for all eternity. 'Jack, three years ago, my mind died. Slowly, it is returning to life...but is it a Frankenstein mind? Could you love someone like me? If we went to bed together, could you bring yourself to touch my body when it was naked? Dare you fuck me? Or would you be frightened that, during the fucking, I would reach up and tear out your lovely eyes?'

The woman's breath came in gusts from her lips, blowing forcefully into my face. That air from her lungs...Dear God, I had to suck it into my lungs because my neck muscles had cramped up tight and I couldn't turn my face away from her. Myra was panting now. Was that lustful panting? Was it a sign of sexual arousal? Or was it murderous excitement?

Piper gave a yelp of protest. He didn't like the woman being so close to me. He jumped up, almost as if trying to lie on my chest, and he put his paws on my shoulders. He began pushing his own furry body between mine and hers – clearly an attempt to protect me. A warning growl rumbled in his throat.

Myra abruptly drew back – a spell had been broken. 'You see,

Jack. I'm not free of strange thoughts yet. Bizarre impulses some-times take control, just like when I threw your friends' heads at you. Please trust me, though. I do want us to be friends...allies... mutually advantageous comrades. Ha!' She seemed embarrassed by the sudden burst of irrational laughter that left her lips. 'Sorry, Jack. I am getting better. Trust me.' She pointed at the figures clus-tered on the far side of the steel bars, which covered the window opening. 'These ladies and gentlemen are somewhat behind me in regaining their sanity, but they are much closer to being sane again than those thousands of sorry wretches out there in the fields.'

'Will those sorry wretches – as you term them – ever become sane?'

'I don't know. However, please do not permit your companions to fire guns at them again. That kind of action will trigger the swarm to attack you. We only just managed to bring them back un-der control. Next time, we might not be so lucky. Next time, they might be carrying your eyes in their hands – your blood will be their sacrament. They will be...' She closed her eyes as she strug-gled to regain control of runaway thoughts that were as dangerous as they were strange. 'Just don't antagonize the Creosotes, Jack. They are more frightened of you than you are of them. That's what makes them so dangerous.'

Piper relaxed a little and backed off a pace or two from the armchair where I sat. Nevertheless, he kept a beadily alert eye on Myra, just in case she got too close to me again. My dog hadn't liked her doing that, no he had not.

'Myra.' I flexed my fingers. The cramps were easing. 'Myra. You said you wanted to make me an offer?'

'Yes. And there isn't much time, so you need to think carefully about what I'm going to say next, then I urge you to accept.'

'And that offer is?'

'Give me Del-Coffey.'

'What?'

'Give me Del-Coffey and Tasmin. Yes, we know their names.'

'You are mad...absolutely crazy. I can't just hand over two people to you and your fucking mob.'

'You have until midday tomorrow – that is twelve noon, prompt, to hand them over.'

'Why?'

'We know about Del-Coffey. He understands our condition. He has the power to help us become sane again.'

'No.'

'You must, because noon tomorrow is the longest I can hold all those thousands out there in check. If you don't agree, and if Tasmin and Del-Coffey don't walk out of that front door tomorrow and give themselves to us, then the Creosotes will attack...and they will break down these walls with their bare hands, and they will tear out your hearts and your lungs and your throats.' She panted with what might have been sexual hunger. 'Sorry...you see, we need Del-Coffey's help. The man is a genius. He understands what is wrong with us. He can heal our kind.' Myra appeared to be trying to hold back some powerful urge. She failed...because, at that moment, she thrust her face toward mine and then kissed me on the mouth – a hard kiss. One that blazed with such craving. 'Sorry, Jack,' she muttered. 'I shouldn't have done that.' Her face began to glisten with perspiration. 'At twelve, tomorrow. You must open the door and make sure Del-Coffey and Tasmin walk out across the yard. We will look after them. They will become a breeding pair. Yes? A dynasty of genius.'

'Myra. Listen to yourself. You are saying crazy things.'

'Give them to us, Jack.' She backed away across the room, toying with her long red hair as she did so. 'And I will give myself to you.'

'Fuck off. Just fuck off.'

My body began to respond to my brain now. I managed to stand.

'Even if you don't want to love me, Jack, I will promise you your safety. Give me your two friends. I guarantee that you will not be hurt. You can leave here, start a new life.'

Myra turned and walked away. A moment later, I could hear her running upstairs to where she'd no doubt exit the farmhouse through the skylight in its roof.

'I'm not giving you Tasmin,' I shouted after her. 'You're not having her. And you're not taking Del-Coffey. Do you hear me? You are not taking them from me!'

CHAPTER TWENTY-SIX

TIME TO START THE COUNTDOWN TO DOOM

Martin Del-Coffey was amazed.

'They want me? You've got to be kidding!' Despite the fever draining the guy of his strength, he'd still managed to shout the words in disbelief.

'I'm not joking, Del-Coffey. They want me to send you out there. Myra believes you have the knowledge to heal their minds.'

'Am I expected to feel flattered by what that lunatic said? For the love of God, they'll rip me apart.' Drops of spit flew from those pale lips of his as terror exploded inside of him. Yup. The boy was scared. 'Do not make me go out there. I can't help them. Before you know it, there'll be some Creosote dancing around wearing my ripped-off face on his head like a bloody hat!'

By this time, the Creosote A-Types that had gathered at the window earlier had gone, and I'd closed and locked the window. No way, did I want to be stared at by that menacing bunch again.

Tasmin stood in the doorway to the lounge, swaying with exhaustion. Nevertheless, her eyes were clear, and her was voice firm. 'Jack, I won't let you push Del-Coffey out of the house.'

Del-Coffey's wide-eyed stare grew even more boggle-eyed as the truth sank in. 'Those Creosotes actually believe that I'm like some psychology expert who can fix their minds?'

'Yes.'

Tasmin scowled. 'I will not let you hand Del-Coffey over to them.'

I looked at her standing there. And at that moment, I found myself reliving the shocking moment when the Creosote, Myra, had kissed me. I scraped the back of my hand across my lips, hoping I could wipe away any residue of Myra's saliva. *Vodka...get vodka...rub the spirit on your mouth. The spirit will kill any bugs worming into your skin.* That's what I wanted to do right then, but clearly Tasmin and Del-Coffey were hellbent on ridding me of any temptation to turf Del-Coffey outdoors into the welcoming arms of you know who.

'Jack.' Tasmin glared at me. 'Did you hear what I just said? Del-Coffey is not going out there.'

'They'll kill me.' Del-Coffey clearly wished to drive the point home that his life would very swiftly desert him if he walked out amid those thousands of homicidal maniacs. 'They'll break my bones – they'll rip out my belly.'

Tasmin insisted: 'Del-Coffey stays. We don't do deals with Creosotes.'

'Tasmin,' I said, 'they want you as well. Myra told me that you and Del-Coffey will become a breeding pair. They want to see you mate with one another.'

'What?' Just when I thought that Del-Coffey's eyes couldn't get any more gigantically humongous with amazement, they did just that. They enlarged into two huge, shining pools of astonished blue.

'No fucking way!' Tasmin clenched her fists, getting ready to punch any plans I might have for treachery right out of my skull.

In fact, both kicked-off in an absolute swear-storm of yelling. This went on for a full three minutes before I finally managed to calm them.

'No,' I told them when they'd finally stopped shouting so loudly that my ears hurt. 'No. You aren't being given to the Creosotes, Del-Coffey. And neither are you, Tasmin.'

Tasmin's voice was nothing less than fiery. 'I'm glad to hear it.'

Del-Coffey shook his head in astonishment. 'Those creatures believe that I have the intelligence to not only diagnose their condition, but reverse their insanity and render them normal again. What an extraordinary assertion on their part.'

Yup, the man was pleased with the Creosotes' 'assertion', though I preferred the word 'delusion'. Their madness made them believe that nineteen-year-old Martin Del-Coffey had the wisdom to heal fucked-up crazies. He even ran his fingers through his blonde hair. *You actually doing that, smarty-pants? You actually preening yourself? Is your ego being oh-so pleasantly stroked by the mob outside?*

'Okay,' I said, getting serious, and ready to reveal just how worrying and dangerous things really were. 'Myra gave me an ultimatum. You, Tasmin, and you, Del-Coffey, must walk out through the front door tomorrow, then hand yourself over to the Creosotes, otherwise they will attack this place and kill us all.'

Tasmin's shrewd eyes burned craters into my soul. 'What about you? What do you get, if you throw us out to the mob?'

'Myra promised me the freedom to leave here without being harmed.' Yeah, she'd also appeared to promise me sex as well, but I thought that would only complicate the situation if I told them that she'd hinted at red-hot erotic playtimes.

Del-Coffey tottered toward me. 'Tasmin, despite what Jack has just said about not handing us over, he's going to trick us into going

101

out there. The treacherous rat's going to sacrifice us so he can save his own stinking neck!'

Del-Coffey appeared to have set out with the intention of beating me senseless. The fever still gripped him, though, draining him of energy. After a few steps, he wearily flumped down onto the sofa, where Piper lay curled up at one end, recuperating from his own violent encounter with the Creosotes.

For a moment, Tasmin and Del-Coffey were silent. Both were drained by what had been, for them, an exhausting journey from their bedrooms upstairs, down to the lounge. Now Tasmin did the tottering forward. I caught her before she fell and sat her down in the armchair. Of course, I reassured them that I would not be using their bodies as payment to the Creosotes so I could leave here in one piece. After all, what would the new, sort-of-sane Creosote A-Types do to Del-Coffey when they eventually realized that he did not know how to heal their minds? My guess is, they would ease their disappointment by taking a bath in Del-Coffey's lukewarm blood, while sponging themselves down with his lungs and ball-sac.

We sat there in the room, a blizzard dumping so much snow out of the sky that flakes created a thick, grey fog that hid the Creosote legion from our anxious gaze. I told Tasmin and Del-Coffey about what had happened earlier. How the Creosotes had appeared at the open window to tell me that Piper wasn't my dog. 'He is my dog,' I told the pair. 'You can tell he is, can't you? The way he definitely knows me.'

'Does the dog answer to his name?' asked a weary Del-Coffey.

I looked at the black and white Border Collie, curled up on one end of the sofa. 'Piper. Hey, Piper.'

The dog raised his head, looking directly at me – those bright eyes, no doubt accurately reading the expression on my face. An expression that suggested I desperately needed reassurance that he really was mine, and that he'd shared my childhood home before Dad tried to murder my mother, my sisters, and me.

Tasmin smiled. 'Of course, he is your dog, Jack. That's Piper, alright. He knows you, there's a bond between the pair of you.' Then her face turned serious. 'Okay...it's two o'clock in the afternoon now, so that gives us twenty-two hours until Del-Coffey and I walk out the door to join the Creosote gang. Because if we don't...' She shrugged and left the horror of what would inevitably follow unsaid.

'We have intelligence,' Del-Coffey told us. 'That means we can intelligently work out a solution to our problem.'

'But, to put that horrendous problem into words,' I said, 'there are three of us. You two are sick with fever. Every thirty minutes I get hit with a bout of paralysis. Okay, it doesn't last any longer

102

than a few moments, but during that time I'm as helpless as a baby. We have guns, yes. The downside is, we are surrounded by thousands—'

'Tens of thousands,' corrected Del-Coffey.

'Okay, tens of thousands of men and women who want to destroy us. They are only just kept under control by a few Creosote A-Types on snowmobiles.'

Tasmin nodded as she digested what I'd said. 'Therefore, how do we come up with a plan to escape an impossible predicament? Yes, we have those guns, but no transport, and no way of communicating with the outside world.'

'Flying out would be good.' Del-Coffey wore a thoughtful expression as he stroked Piper's head. 'But seeing as not a single aircraft has flown since civilization rolled over and died, flying away from here isn't likely, is it?'

I sighed. 'No, Del-Coffey, it isn't likely. So, if we get rid of any notion of flying through the air, or escaping by secret underground tunnels, because I'm pretty sure there aren't any, it means that we have to somehow walk through loads of Creosotes that are tightly crammed together, shoulder-to-shoulder.'

'And,' said Tasmin, with a bleak expression on her face, 'considering that Del-Coffey and I are still so poorly with the fever, I doubt if we could walk even a hundred yards without needing to sit down and rest for a long, long while.'

Del-Coffey rubbed his belly, perhaps the raw deluge of anxiety made it ache with a merciless intensity. 'To sum up: we can't fly away into the great blue yonder, we can't tunnel out, we can't even walk away from here, and we can't call on people to save us, so...'

'So...what?' Tasmin's head lolled back. Fatigue had got into her bones again. 'So, how do we save our lives?'

Del-Coffey yawned. That high forehead of his had turned crimson, suggesting the fever had raised his temperature again. 'How do we save our lives? Sorry, I haven't a clue. I can't think of a single method to get us out of this...this...shitstorm.'

At the best of times, I don't like sitting still for long. And this was the first time, since being struck down by the fever, that the old edgy, can't-sit-still-for-a-minute habit had got me back onto my feet again. I began pacing around the room.

I took a deep breath. 'Okay. Del-Coffey reminded us that we have intelligence. Which means we can work out a plan to get away from those fuckers outside.'

Tasmin was becoming sleepy as she murmured, 'How?'

I mooched back and forth across the carpet as I talked 'We have intelligence. We have guns. What else do we have here?'

'A house,' offered Tasmin.

'Some old farm equipment,' added Del-Coffey.

'I went to the window. I saw that as quickly as the blizzard had begun it had ended. Outside, not so much as a flake of snow fell. Fresh snow on the ground was so bright I had to shield my eyes. The Creosotes were still there, of course. Hunched figures, shaggy hair, hating eyes. The building's security measures would prevent them getting in for a while, until they decided to attack after the deadline expired tomorrow and we could kill a few with our guns. Eventually, they would break through the barred windows, and even through those substantial doors. Maybe Myra would show them how to enter through the skylight on the roof. Ultimately, they would get inside the house.

I stared out at the Creosotes – many had a covering of snow on their shoulders and tops of their heads. They pressed tight against each other, a pack of men and women forcing their bodies against those of their neighbours, using close proximity of flesh to keep cold air at bay. On the whole, it worked, though those at the edge of the mob were more vulnerable to low temperatures. Every so often, one of them would sink to their knees, where they'd stare blankly into space for five minutes or so before they simply flopped down onto the ground – and there they lay, their death unnoticed and definitely un-mourned by their fellow Creosotes.

Once again, the snow returned – all those billions of snowflakes creating a fog so dense that it reduced visibility to almost zero. I could barely see the ground just beyond the window, let alone the Creosotes a few dozen paces away.

'We have intelligence, guns, and...' I pointed out of the window, '...a cloak of invisibility.'

'What?' murmured Del-Coffey, so tired he could barely raise his eyelids.

Tasmin, however, seemed to wake up, her eyes becoming sharper. 'Cloak of invisibility. You mean they can't see us?'

'It doesn't last long. Those heavy snow showers blast down for maybe five minutes at a time. When they do, you could stand an arm's length from a Creosote, and they couldn't see you.'

Del-Coffey gave a groggy shake of the head. How does that help us? We can't just amble through the mob, hoping they don't notice we're there.'

'Besides,' pointed out Tasmin, 'Del-Coffey and me can hardly get upstairs, never mind start running away.'

My body began to tingle, a slow burn of excitement. 'Don't you see? This is the start of a plan. When the blizzard comes, that allows me to walk through that lot without being noticed. I become invisible to them.'

'For five minutes, maybe, until the snow stops, then...' Tasmin shrugged – a fatalist shrug at that.

Yeah, she had a point. Okay, I could cover a little bit of ground beneath that heaven-sent cloak of invisibility. That's all. How would that help Tasmin and Del-Coffey? And what happened if another bout of paralysis hit me? I'd have to sit down there and then, waiting for it to pass. With me incapable of firing a gun, that would make me a nice easy victim. Nevertheless, I had found something that might help us. If the Creosotes couldn't see me, even for as little as five minutes, then that should be useful. Incredibly useful. Now, I needed more useful elements to build a cogent plan that would get us to safety.

Outside, the blizzard began to ease, visibility improved; within seconds I could make out the silhouettes of our enemy. The silhouette images made those figures appear even more monstrous – they were menacing creatures without heads – or so it looked to me. I shivered.

The blizzard then ended as suddenly as if someone had clicked 'Stop' up there in the snow-yielding clouds. I could see the huge shed, which contained cages that had once housed the Creosote A-Types. Next to that shed, there was another one of a similar size. A huge warehouse-sized building. At one end of the structure was a tall pylon, topped with a windmill arrangement of blades that spun round and around. They were making a faint *click-click-clack* sound.

I stared at the second shed for a moment. 'What,' I began, 'is in the other shed? The one next to the building with the cages?'

'I checked all the buildings,' said Tasmin. 'There's farm equipment in there...ploughs, threshing machines, a hopper that pumps out fertilizer and...' She paused, then shivered as if someone had doused her back in cold water. 'And...there...is...' Her eyes suddenly flashed all bright and beautiful – they were full of nothing less than hope. 'A truck. A big truck. A huge one.'

'See?' Del-Coffey looked pleased with himself. 'Engage intelligence with your observation of what assets lie within your reach, and you will develop a coherent plan.'

I grinned. 'Does that mean we all now agree on how we get ourselves out of here?'

Tasmin grinned, too. 'With a truck that size, we can simply bust out through the doors and drive over that bunch of psychos out there, then we vanish into the hills.'

'However...' Del-Coffey appeared to have identified a problem. 'However, the truck will have stood there for years. Its tyres will be flat, the battery fucked.'

The elation I felt wasn't going to be beaten down to a sad death by that guy's doom-laden 'However'.

'Look,' I said, 'when the blizzard comes back, I can reach the truck shed without being seen. When I'm there, I lock the door behind me, keeping those devils out. After that, I work on the truck. Get the engine started.'

'Tasmin shot me a searching look. 'How are your mechanic skills?'

'Well...you know...how hard can it be?'

'Very hard...especially if you don't know what you're doing.'

'I'll manage.'

'Will you hell, Jack. I'm coming with you.'

'No way.'

'I'm coming.'

'You can't even walk that far.'

'Carry me.'

'If the blizzard stops, they will see us, then we become nothing more than a big red smear on the ground.'

Del-Coffey's laugh was a bitter one. 'Vividly expressed, old man.'

'Tasmin. You are not coming with me.'

'Jack, listen. No, properly listen...look at me while I tell you this. Back there on Sugar Island, who do you think got those security vehicles working? Their motors hadn't run once in the last three years. I, Tasmin, got them started. I put air in the tyres. Then we drove here in those 4x4s.'

I didn't reply. No doubt I'd got my brooding face on, which was all neatly matched up with my sullen stare. 'I can get the truck's motor running.'

'Have you ever done that before? To a machine that hasn't run in years?'

With grudging reluctance, I shook my head.

Del-Coffey came up with Plan B. 'We could always just wait here and hope that Gorron and the others come back. They could shoot their way in.'

I sighed. 'Gorron and the others should have been back here a couple of days ago. We have twenty hours until the deadline. We can't risk waiting. Heck, come to that, even if they do come back, how can two cars cut through all those thousands of people out there?'

Tasmin's eyes were bright; she wanted me to say the right thing. 'Well, Jack?'

'Okay. We go across there together. And we need to do it when the next whiteout blows in.'

Tasmin held up her hand for me to help her to her feet. 'Then there's no time like the present. Help me get my boots on.'

Del-Coffey managed to combine an expression of hope and pure terror at the prospect of us going out there into...well...let's call it the Death Zone.

Slowly, he rose to his feet – then he uttered: 'Just don't forget to take the truck's keys with you.'

Outside, the snow began to fall once more.

CHAPTER TWENTY-SEVEN

'WHAT ABOUT POOCH?'

That's when things started moving quickly. Well, for me, they moved fast. Del-Coffey had fallen asleep on the sofa. The illness stripped him of his ability to even remain awake. As that quaint phrase describes oh-so vividly: *the man was knackered.*

Tasmin was in better shape. She sat on a straight-backed chair, hunched over forwards, long hair reaching down until the tips swished on the carpet as she slowly tied her bootlaces.

I crouched down in front of her. 'Here, let me.' Quickly, I tied the laces for her.

'Thanks, Jack.' She smiled; her face was so close to mine our noses almost brushed against one another. If that had happened, I know it would have been a nice sensation.

After tying the laces, I said, 'I'll help you with your jacket. Right arm first...there...now left. Can you stand? No, it's okay. I'll help you up.'

Tasmin did try very hard to get herself kitted up for our trip to the shed where the truck was parked. Though, like Del-Coffey, the fever made her groggy. Her movements were slow, her eyelids drooped. When she was standing upright, I zipped up her water-proof jacket. The jacket was bright red, and I hoped it wasn't so vividly red that it would instantly attract the attention of the Creosotes when we made what would be a hideously dangerous journey across the farmyard. That would be a hazardous three-minute walk, believe me.

'Okay, Tasmin,' I said. 'Sit down here until we're ready to go.'

'I want to help.'

'I know you do.' My voice was gentle. 'You need to rest, though. Try to hang on to your strength.'

'You, too. You might conk out again, yeah?'

'Yeah. That's a risk we must take. Alright, when I've got the guns from the store, I'll sit down for a while.'

She regarded me with those big dark eyes that were so wise and so solemn. She knew I'd fibbed. I would not rest. Because that great pulsating light of **URGENCY** was flashing inside my skull. Damn it, I had to get everything ready, then we just had to go for it.

I rushed into the kitchen, Piper following me, his eyes on my face all the time. He knew that I was pumping myself up to leaving the house in a hurry. If that dog could speak, he'd have been saying 'I'm coming, too. Don't leave me here. I'm coming with you.'

'Piper. You stay here with Del-Coffey. I'll come back for you, boy. Promise. Cross my heart and hope to die.'

Those gentle eyes were fixed tight on me, they melted my heart. I just wanted to cry.

So, I began moving even faster. My heart pounded, my blood thrusting along arteries, lungs whooshing the air through my throat, I grabbed all the ammo I could feasibly carry before stuffing it into a rucksack. Into that bag went food and a camping stove. Thankfully, I didn't need to carry water, which is so heavy to lug about if you need to take a lot with you. We could melt snow for drinks and cooking. All the time, my mind spun out images of my plan. Get to the shed, get the truck started. Collect Del-Coffey. After we drove away from here, we would have enough food in my rucksack to last for a couple of days. That gave us ample time to find supplies.

I kitted myself up. Boots, waterproof jacket, hat, gloves. Added a knife in its sheath to my belt. Grabbed the submachine gun, checking the mag was full of those bright, golden bullets, then I reloaded my rifle and leant it against the sofa, within easy reach of Del-Coffey. I put a loaded pistol on a coffee table.

That done, I tugged the straps of the rucksack over my shoulders. Dear God, that was one heavy bag. Also, I was mindful that I'd probably end up carrying Tasmin. I could only hope that paralysis didn't sneak up on me again. The notion of lying there helpless in the yard filled me with just one big purple bonfire of dread and terror. I tried shutting those malignant images out of my head – of me lying there, my legs and arms all cramped and useless, and Tasmin so helpless with fever fatigue that all she could do was crawl through the snow as the Creosotes lunged toward us, hands stretching out, eyes wild with fury, and lusting for...*NO. STOP IT. STOP IMAGINING WHAT MIGHT HAPPEN. DO NO DIE OUT THERE. YOUR MISSION IS TO SURVIVE.*

First, I spoke to the dog as he stood by my side. 'Okay, Piper. Look after Del-Coffey. Keep him safe, eh?' I then turned to Tasmin, who sat there so limply I wondered if I was doing the right thing, taking her away from the house. 'Tasmin? Are you ready?'

'As I ever will be.'

I shook Del-Coffey until he woke up. 'Del-Coffey? Can you hear me?'

He grunted some words I couldn't make out. I shook him again with plenty of force, causing his head to flip-flop from side-to-side.

'Del-Coffey. Wake up. Tasmin and me are heading out to get the truck.'

'Uh...' Del-Coffey rubbed his eyes. 'Take me with you.'

'No, I can't carry both of you if you pass out on me.'

'You're in the paralysis phase of the illness,' he muttered. 'You might be incapacitated yourself.'

'Trust me. I will get the truck. After that, we find Gorron and the others.'

Tasmin leaned against the doorframe for support. 'Del-Coffey, just be ready to leave when we come back.'

'I'll get my boots on. What about pooch?'

'Piper's staying here.' I patted the sofa cushion beside Del-Coffey, encouraging Piper to jump up. 'The pair of you will look after each other while we're gone.' I glanced out of the window. 'When the next blizzard comes, we'll make a run for it.' I turned back to Del-Coffey. 'We'll leave through the front door. You lock it behind us. Okay? Do you think you can manage that?'

'I'll manage. Wait...don't forget the keys to the truck.' He gave a sardonic chuckle. 'I forgot some keys once and everyone got mad at me.'

'Don't worry.' I patted my bulging pockets. 'I've got every key I could find.'

Tasmin looked stronger – at least, that's what I told myself. Maybe, however, that was optimism naively attempting to defeat reality. Though maybe, sometimes, if we believe in something hard enough, what we long for will come true.

'Ready, Tasmin?'

She nodded.

'Okay.' I tightened my grip on the submachine gun. 'Now we wait for the snow to start falling again. It needs to come down so thick and so fast that mob outside won't see us.'

And after all that rushing around, grabbing guns, ammo, food, keys, this was it.

CHAPTER TWENTY-EIGHT

OUT INTO THE DEATH ZONE

We stood behind the steel door with its wood effect panels. A formidable barrier, indeed. Beside the door, a window protected by bars granted a view of the outside world. Just a hundred paces away stood the Creosotes. There was no sign of Myra, however, or the other A-Types. They were more vulnerable to cold than the old-version Creosotes, with their no doubt atrophied sense of cold and heat.

Littering the ground in front of that densely packed barrier of human flesh were dozens of dead men and women. Their fellow Creosotes showed no interest in the corpses, nor any inclination to remove the bodies. There they would stay and rot.

I said: 'Crows are going to get fat.'

'Uh...pardon?' Tasmin sat on the bottom step of the staircase, trying to preserve what little energy she had. 'Crows?'

'No, it's nothing, Tasmin. Just me thinking aloud.'

'Any sign of it starting to snow again?'

'Nope.'

'I hope it does, or we're stuck here.'

'Yep.'

'If we're stuck here, when the deadline comes...'

'Don't think about it,' I told her. 'We're getting out of here. And we are going to live. We're going to live until I've got white hair and wrinkly skin.'

'Me, too.'

'No, Tasmin. You'll always be beautiful.'

'Thank you.' She smiled, though her head drooped as she became drowsy again.

Piper appeared in the lounge doorway. His brown eyes locked onto my face. That stare tugged my heartstrings.

'You're staying here, boy,' I murmured. 'I'm sorry.'

'Tasmin lifted her head. When she spoke, it was in a puzzled tone: 'Why are you apologising to your dog? What are you planning to do?'

At that moment, something else grabbed my attention. 'Uh-oh...starting to snow again. Get ready.' I called through into the lounge. 'Del-Coffey. You need to be through here to lock the door after we're gone. Hey, Del-Coffey?'

'Coming,' said a tired voice.

'It's okay. I'll give you a hand.'

Quickly, I went into the lounge. Del-Coffey was using the rifle like it was a crutch, trying to hobble across the room. Taking him by the arm, I helped him into the hallway. There was a straight-backed chair against a wall. I hooked one of its legs with my foot, dragging it close to the door. I helped Del-Coffey sit. That done, I propped the rifle against the wall where he could easily grab it if the house came under attack.

'Del-Coffey. Sit here, try and rest. All you need do is get yourself out of the house when I come back with the truck. Don't bring anything else. Just *you*. Got that? Be sure to move as fast as you can from this doorway to the truck. Because the Creosotes will go absolutely berserk when they see us outside.'

'What about Piper?'

'Trust me, he will zip across to us, fast as a rocket.'

Tasmin got to her feet. 'The snow's coming down faster. It's time we went.'

Holding the submachine gun in one hand, I pulled the door bolts back with the other. Tasmin moved as best she could toward me.

Del-Coffey suddenly reached out to grab my wrist. 'Wait. It's not snowing hard enough. I still see Creosotes, that means they'll see you.'

'Okay, we'll give it a minute.'

Del-Coffey clearly intended that we appreciate the danger. 'Remember, if they see you, your life expectancy can be measured in seconds.'

Tasmin put her hand on his shoulder, then uttered in a very dry tone, 'Yes, Del-Coffey. We do understand that might be the case.'

'Sorry. But I care about you.' Del-Coffey swallowed hard. There were tears in his eyes. 'Jack's right. What is important, is that we stay alive. We owe it to ourselves to—'

'Del-Coffey.' I spoke quickly as a sense of urgency gripped me. 'Sorry to interrupt. We've got full-on blizzard.'

I turned the key in the lock. Piper tilted his head, those beseeching eyes of his sang out so loud and so clear: *Take me with you*. Just the way Piper looked at me made me want to sob my heart out. After being parted from my dog for ten years, being reunited with him was nothing less than a miracle. Now, I was leaving him here.

I took a deep breath, focussing on what I must do. 'Remember, Del-Coffey. Keep the rifle close. Lock this door. When you see us coming, just get out of the house and run to the passenger door.'

When I spoke the next words, I couldn't help but glance in Piper's direction. 'It's human life that matters.'

The moment I pulled open the door, ice-cold air rushed at my face, stinging my cheeks and nose. A mass of white flakes blasted in, landing on the hallway mat, the stairs, and on Piper, speckling the black parts of his fur.

Tasmin did her best to reassure Del-Coffey. She patted him on the forearm as she said, 'We'll be back soon. Take care.'

With the rucksack weighing heavy on my back, and the memory of Piper looking up at my face weighing even heavier, I headed outside. Tasmin followed.

This is it. And I had fiercest of premonitions that the short distance we needed to cover would be the longest journey of my life.

CHAPTER TWENTY-NINE

ONWWARD...ONWARD...

Out into that world of grey. Snow crunching beneath my feet.
Tasmin holding onto a strap of my rucksack. Connecting us
together in this life-or-death march across the yard in the direction
of the big shed, which was now invisible in the blizzard. A thick
grey fog – that's what the falling snow resembled. Our precious
cloak of invisibility. And that landscape-vanishing fug was created
by billions of snowflakes, which blasted out of the gloom at us, on
an as-cold-as-your-tomb wind.

I thought: *Keep moving forward. Don't stop. Get to the big shed.
Make the truck work. We're getting out of here.*

Hard snowflakes stung my eyes until they watered, while the
intensity of the snowfall rendered the Creosotes that surrounded
the house invisible, too. When I extended my arm into the chaos of
snowflakes, my hand vanished into murk. Dear God, visibility had
dropped until it was less than the length of my arm. Tasmin stayed
close beside me. Snow glued tight to her clothes, her hair, her face.
She had become an ice nymph. A beautiful woman sheathed in
white.

Tasmin had already begun to slow down. Hardly surprising, she
was so dreadfully ill with fever.

'Jack.' She gave a gasp. 'Sorry.'

Her legs folded at the knees. Fortunately, I caught her before she
fell. With absolute determination, I pulled her left arm, so it went
around the back of my neck and over my left shoulder. Supporting
her like this, and with the submachine gun gripped hard in my
other hand, I ploughed on through snow that now lay knee-deep.

This became my tiny world. A man-sized sphere with nothing
beyond its outer edges I could see. Grey beneath me, grey above,
grey to the left, grey to the right – and, yes, ahead and behind.
Nevertheless, some white-hot core of energy (created by a huge
injection of adrenalin, no doubt) powered me forward. I kept my
hand, which clutched the machine gun at its midpoint, way out in
front of me. The gloved knuckles of that hand had become a vital
sensory organ in the gloomy murk.

It had to happen. But when it did, the shock nearly ruptured my heart. The outstretched hand, which clutched the gun, struck an object.

Creosote?

Must be.

Damn it.

Can't be anything else.

Stop here?

No way.

Onward, onward...

As I approached the thing, which my knuckles had softly touched (but what my eyes could not see), my heart pounded so hard it felt like panicky, scrambling feet inside my chest. A weird description, I know, but at that moment it seemed like my heart would erupt out through my mouth.

Holding onto Tasmin's arm, I moved forward, while slowly, just ever so slowly, a gaunt apparition formed in front of me, growing clearer as I got nearer. It was a woman of around sixty. Hair as long as my arms streamed out, fluttering in the cold blast. Storm winds caused the snow to cake on her naked torso. I saw the scars of old battles on her face. Her bare belly was shrunken, and it was pinched inward with hunger. I had to push by her, while hoping that beneath the concealing veil of the blizzard the damaged remnant of her mind would harmlessly identify me as one of her own kind, not fresh prey. Hanging onto Tasmin, I squeezed past the woman. I saw that I was hemmed in at the other side by a man with a bushy white beard, and with lips that were a death-beckoning blue.

As I squeezed by the woman, her breasts scraped against my own body. One of her nipples was missing, perhaps ripped away from that battle-scarred body of hers, during some fight in the past few months.

No...don't let your mind prey on things like that, I told myself, as I pushed onward into a deadly forest, created by men and women standing tightly packed together. *Keep moving forwards.*

This really was like moving through a forest of densely packed trees. There was virtually no space to pass between those people. Some were partly clothed in ragged jackets and sweaters and trousers and skirts – some were entirely naked: no doubt their clothes had simply rotted away, and their broken minds hadn't told them to find replacement clothing, or even shoes, because most stood barefoot in the snow, frostbite causing feet to shed toes. Or even legs to shed feet. Yet, somehow, the instinct to kill young people drove them on, gifting them the ability to balance and move on legs without feet, or to even walk on knee stumps. Necrosis – decaying flesh. There was plenty of that. Though they did possess beating hearts, these people were a mass of barely-alive rot. If this had been summer, the stink of decomposing skin and muscle would have been unbearable.

'Keep snowing,' I muttered to heaven as I threaded myself through all those people.

At times, I had to gently push my way through, with bodies pressing against me at both sides. Gaunt faces possessed dull eyes that stared but did not see. Or so I decided. Because even when I was close, they did not move their heads to look into my face. Just gaunt totems. Unmoving pillars of flesh.

Dare I believe they cannot harm me? Just asking myself that question gave me a rising sense of excitement. They had frozen into something resembling statues. Harmless statues. Immobile. Inert. Incapable of hurting us.

Oh, how wrong I was.

As I pushed by a short guy, with burn scars down one side of his face, leaving him with half a beard, those dull eyeballs of his suddenly swivelled in their sockets. When they fixed on my face that's when life blazed into him. Life, and absolute homicidal fury.

With a howl, he pushed his comrades aside so could launch himself at me, his hands flashing through tumbling snowflakes to grab me by the throat.

Another hand appeared, grasping a knife. The blade crunched through the man's right eye, the knifepoint no doubt penetrating the front of his brain.

I turned my head to see that Tasmin had delivered the killing blow. As the man fell dead, dragging the knife from her hand as he did so, she whispered forcefully into my ear: 'Move faster, Jack. Get us to the shed.'

When a problem comes storming into your life, to upset your plans and inflict misery on you, isn't it always the case that the first problem brings its brothers and sisters with it? In no time at all, you don't have just one problem – no, you have lots of problems to deal with. Like you accidentally burn your hand on the pan when cooking. That then makes you flinch, so you knock the other pan with boiling water all over the kitchen floor, then you slip on the wet mat, you go down with a painful thump, and bruise your backside – and by the time you've wiped up the spilt water, the pan on which you first scorched your hand is now making a loud sizzling sound and pumps out black smoke, because in all the chaos you forgot to turn the gas off, and the steak you were frying has turned into something resembling a slab of burnt wood.

So, it was here...during what should have been a three-minute walk from the house to the shed that garaged the truck. First problem: the guy with the burnt face had identified us as young people, that meant we were non-Creosotes, that meant we were THE ENEMY. And that is the enemy that his warped instincts urged him to destroy. He'd attacked us. Fortunately, Tasmin is good with a knife. Problem solved. Only his attack on us had alerted another swathe of Creosotes that their enemy was amongst them, so they vented howls of fury as they lunged at us. And Tasmin was so exhausted by illness that she could not run, so I carried her.

OH, YES...THEN THERE HAS TO BE YET **ANOTHER** PROBLEM – THE INEVITABLE INVOCATION OF THAT ROTTEN FUCK-AWFUL TRUISM KNOWN AS **'SOD'S LAW'**, MEANING THAT LOTS OF OTHER PROBLEMS BLOW AN ENTIRE SHITSTORM INTO YOUR FACE.

I managed to weave through the furious men and women that lunged at us. I felt hands claw at my arms, shoulders, head (my hat vanished as hooky fingers snatched it away), another hand yanked out a chunk of my hair. *Ouch!* Still, I clung onto Tasmin as we ducked and swerved our way through the huddle-muddle of monsters that lunged at us from all sides. Thankfully, visibility was so poor due to the blizzard that I only needed to take four or five steps before we vanished into grey fog again, and we became invisible to our attackers. Of course, there were hundreds of those crazies. Thousands. Tens of thousands! The moment I got Tasmin clear of one group, we found ourselves in another mass of tightly packed mad, mad flesh. Luckily for us, it took those folk with their smashed-up minds a moment or two to recognize that we were their enemy, then they had to get their frozen limbs to work in order to attack us. All of which meant that we were granted a few valuable seconds to move forward, unmolested, before they lunged at us again.

Thereafter, we launched ourselves into a sequence of: be attacked, evade our attackers, duck back into the invisibility cloak of the blizzard, then a moment of safety, then the next tranche of Creosotes would ID us as prey, and so on, and so on...

Because I was carrying Tasmin, I didn't have a free hand to cock the submachine gun and start shooting...not that it would have helped, if truth be told. The magazine held thirty rounds. We were virtually drowning in an ocean of Creosotes. I couldn't blast them all.

No. Somehow, I had to get through this legion of killers, then scramble into the shed, grab the truck and...well...you know the plan.

Ducking, dodging, weaving, feeling cold fingers (often lacking fingernails) swiping at my bare face, and hands clutching at my rucksack and clothes, we pushed on. Constantly vanishing into the murk that concealed us so perfectly. And then...shit!

'Tasmin.' By this time, yours truly was panting hard. 'The snow's stopping...it's thinning. I can see further...'

'And they can see us! Jack...drop me here. You can't carry me through that lot.'

'No fucking way.'

My arm tightened around her as I tried to shove my way through. I saw more Creosotes as the blizzard eased. Previously, I only saw two or three at a time. Now I saw fifty raging faces. Eyes blazed at us. They tried to push each other aside so they'd be the first to gouge our eyes and dance on our bloody guts.

I swiped the gun at those murderous creatures when they got close enough. The gun's solid metalwork opened gashes in faces – it was breaking noses, splitting lips, releasing blood and roars of fury, but those fuckers do not let pain stop them. Even breaking a jaw here or splitting an eyeball there doesn't even slow them down.

A woman, with a leg missing below the knee, toppled forward, her hands stretching out. The creature, which was all shrieking mouth and wild, staring eyes, grabbed Tasmin by her hair, then hung on. Tasmin howled with pain. I swung my boot, kicking the woman's remaining leg so hard the blow snapped her shin. It became sort of hinged halfway between her knee and her bare foot. With the ability to stand destroyed, she fell – though she still hung on tight to Tasmin.

By this time, Tasmin had pulled a revolver from her pocket. She fired a single brain-destroying bullet through the centre of the woman's forehead.

Then we were moving forward again. By now, I could see the big shed fifty paces away. But, damn it, so close, yet so far. There was still a blockade of maybe five thousand Creosotes between us and the shed door.

Tasmin gave a moan of despair. 'It's almost stopped snowing. They can see us.'

'We'll never get through while we're visible to them.'

My eyes scanned the ground between groups of milling Creosotes. Because there was so many, they got in the way of each other, otherwise they'd have slaughtered us in a heartbeat. Lots lay on the ground, either part-covered by snow or simply turning into soft mounds of white where they'd been covered entirely. Plenty were dead. Some were still alive, squirming weakly.

And the blizzard was almost over, the air getting clearer by the second. Visibility becoming perfect.

'There's only one thing for it.' My heart was pounding with dread. 'We have to get where the Creosotes are thickest. Into the densest part of the mob.'

'You've got to be joking?'

'No...we're going to exploit those monsters...we hide amongst them until the snow starts to fall again.'

By this time, I was fully carrying Tasmin. Fatigue had ripped the strength right out of her, the hand that held the pistol was limply swinging backwards and forwards. When the Creosotes realized we were from the cohort of young people that they wanted dead, they scrambled to attack us. However, they were so densely packed together their movements were restricted, many having their arms pressed to their torsos by the huddle of Creosote flesh against which they were rammed. Some of those Creosotes tried to bite me as I forced my way through the crowd. One succeeded in raking my right cheek with tatty remnants of fingernails. That stung like fury. I let out a yowl of pain.

Tasmin shouted, 'No, Jack! Don't go deeper into them! Get us away from here!'

'They're crammed together so tightly they can hardly move.'

'Neither can we!'

'Look at them, they can't attack us properly. Most can't even get their arms free – they've got themselves tangled into one big fucking knot!'

As if fate had decided to nimbly contradict the statement I'd just made, an elbow viciously swung up and smacked me in the mouth.

Swearing loudly with frustration, and pain, I stared up into the grey sky. I was craving the arrival of more snow. Nope. Hardly a flake.

'Jack,' Tasmin yelled. 'They're going to overwhelm us. Your plan isn't working.'

I made a decision. 'Down!'

I folded my knees, drawing my feet up toward my backside. For a moment, the press of bodies all around us was so formidable that I hung there, held in place by men and women's bellies, buttocks, torsos. Snowmelt on my clothes helped me. Moisture was creating a degree of lubrication. Gradually, I slipped downward to the ground, taking Tasmin with me. Now we lay there in the trampled slush with all those feet shuffling around us, sometimes buffeting our heads and bodies – not deliberate kicks, however. And although the Creosotes attempted to find enough space in order to attack us, the others, pressing forward to take part in the slaughter, shoved the others, so there was a kind of pushing battle going on. They were like a crowd of drunks in a street, milling around. A big man forced a silver-maned woman out of the way, to give himself enough space to reach down to us, maybe intending to gouge our faces with his big thumbs, but then an even bigger man roughly smacked him out of the way so he could launch his own attack on us.

Tasmin jammed the pistol up between the bigger guy's legs and shot him in the nuts. From that angle, the bullet would have ripped a corridor through at least one of his testicles, then the bullet would have carried on, up through his stomach, maybe even rising high enough to pop his heart. Instantly, he clutched his bollocks, which squirted blood – after that, he dropped down with a bull-like grunting, his eyes bulging as the life drained out of him.

I grabbed a fistful of Tasmin's jacket. 'Crawl...Crawl.'

She did manage to crawl after me, through the dense forest of legs. Legs that constantly moved, if only by a few inches at a time. My plan, crazy though it was, had worked. We were in such a dense crush of people that they couldn't even bend down to grab us. Feet with boots, feet with sandals, feet with nothing but bare, frost-bitten skin, they tramped around us, almost like those vineyard workers who used to stand in huge tubs full of grapes, walking on the spot, as they crushed juice from the fruit. However, these people weren't trying to crush us – they merely jostled haphazardly, maybe sensing that their enemy was nearby.

There were corpses on the ground. I dragged the body of a woman toward Tasmin, then hauled a lanky dead guy, with an emaciated face resembling a skull, toward me.

I urged Tasmin to lie still and partially rolled the woman's corpse over onto her. This became protection to a certain degree from all those shuffling feet. That done, I pulled the cadaver of Skull-face over onto me. I reasoned that when the Creosotes realized they had lost sight of Tasmin and me, they might decide that we'd crawled further away, resulting in them searching elsewhere.

Skull-face was naked from the waist up. His ribs formed corrugated ridges the full length of his chest, from a pinched-in-tight belly to a scraggy throat. On one arm was a tattoo of a blue heart. On the other arm, in green tattooist ink, the words *Luv U Mamma*.

Glancing up, I only had a partial view of the crush of bodies. White vapour vented from mouths. Creosotes grunted and made panting sounds like aroused beasts. They pushed each other, sometimes grabbing the heads of their neighbours, and turning faces toward them to check that they weren't the enemy.

Though terror flashed through my body like the devil's own lightning, I remained calm. As did Tasmin. We both knew that stillness would save us. We had to play at being dead amid Creosote corpses.

Then an absolute shock made me yell out loud because I felt movement right up against the side of my body. A cold hand glided out of the gloom, like a pale fish swimming through dark water. Skull-face was not dead after all. His eyes bulged from that gaunt face as he reached up to grab me by the throat. I punched the hand away.

Skull-face lay there, opening and closing his lips like he imitated a goldfish. The guy was on his way out...death was only a few heart-beats away, but he'd found the strength to make one last attack.

Tasmin lay beside me. She reached over my chest to push at Skull-face, trying to shove him away from me, though she was too weak to do that successfully. Skull-face, however, could barely raise own head, let-alone mount a savage assault on us. Even so, he began to speak.

Or, more accurately, he uttered a strange sound that resembled a clicking mechanism: 'Tee-kuk...tee-kuk.'

Tasmin whispered into my ear, 'Is he trying to tell us something?'

'I don't know.'

Maybe the sound was merely a symptom of respiratory failure. Or maybe he did try to communicate with us...or, more alarmingly, attempt to warn his 'friends' that we were lying down here on the ground.

The dying man's eyes were as dull as meat paste. 'Tee-kuk...tee-kuk.'

Tasmin gripped my arm as we lay there, side-by-side. 'Jack. You've got to shut the guy up – the others will hear him.'

'Tee-kuk.'

Then, when I finally understood, I almost leapt up in surprise. 'Listen.'

'Tee-kuk...Tee-kuk.'

'Tasmin. Do you know what that is? The sound he's making?'

'Jack, shut him up. Please. He'll bring the others down on top of us.'

I rolled my head until the tip of my nose was almost touching hers. 'Listen to him. *Tee-kuk*. He's imitating the sound of the window turbine. *Tee-kuk*. That's the sound it makes. A metallic squeal followed by a klunk.'

'Okay, so he's a mimic.'

Skull-face opened his mouth. 'Tee-kuk!'

'And he's getting louder,' she warned. 'Soon his pals are going to hear, then they'll be on us.'

'*Tee-kuk!*'

That was the guy's last sound because Tasmin scooped up a big handful of snow, reached over me, then rammed the snow into his mouth. Now he couldn't utter so much as a single, solitary squeak. Okay, she could have killed him with the pistol. The loudness of the shot, however, would have told the Creosotes **EXACTLY** where we were.

I helped out by pinching Skull-face's crusty nostrils shut between my finger and thumb. Skull-face feebly waved his arms, but he was too far gone to offer any effective resistance. He raised one knee, his heel scraping a grove in the snow. Then I felt

120

convulsions running through his body, an effect like a series of electric shocks. After that, his limbs sagged limp. His eyes stared upward, although he wasn't seeing the white flakes drifting down from the sky.

I hissed a single word: 'Snow.'

Tasmin, despite the fact our lives hung in the balance as we lay there on the ground, actually smiled at me. 'You're right, it's starting to fall again.'

A moment later, the blizzard returned. White out. Cloak of invisibility. The Creosotes, even at the shortest of distances away, couldn't see us again.

'We've got to get moving,' I whispered. 'It might only last a few minutes.'

I moved my hand to pick up the machine gun. Damn. I tried to make my fingers work, but that only made the cramp in my hand hurt like hell. When I moved my legs, waves of fire shot up my calf muscles into my thighs.

'Tasmin.'

'What's wrong?' Her eyes became massive with fear.

'The cramps have come back. I'm going back into paralysis again. Damn.'

'Force yourself through it, Jack.' She pressed her gloved hand against my cheek. She was willing the power of movement into me. 'You can walk. You've only got to try hard enough.'

Easier said than done. Even scooping up the gun into the stiff claw that was my hand not only hurt but was amazingly difficult to accomplish. That fever bug had returned to deliver another attack on me. And it had chosen to do so here...me, lying on the ground, in the centre of a rug of Creosote dead. However, and more importantly, a lot of living and decidedly violent Creosotes were milling around us.

'Okay,' I whispered. 'We'll have to crawl. Then, when we can, we run. Can you manage that?'

Tasmin gave the gravest of nods. 'We'll get there, even if we have to drag each other to the shed by the bloody hair.'

I don't know if that was gallows humour of sorts. Even so, I manged a grim smile. 'Okay. Come on.'

We crawled forward, sometimes getting our hands accidentally stomped on. Every now and again, legs would thump into us as the Creosotes blundered around, searching for their enemy. Thank goodness for the blizzard – all those hard flakes smacking into their eyes, blurring their vision, spoiling their search for us.

And so, we crawled through that grim multitude. The slow journey took us over more corpses. Already rats had taken a bite out of cold flesh here and there. A tip of a nose gone, revealing grey bone. Eyelids gnawed away to reveal a massive pair of blue eyes;

the woman's mouth yawned open, a silent scream frozen there on her dead face.

Then...suddenly...there were no feet anymore. Tramping-on-the-spot legs had vanished. I couldn't see much, but there was an open space now...a smooth area of fresh white without footprints. Visibility had dwindled to no more than a couple of paces. We were veiled again by the downfall.

Tasmin had noticed as well. 'We're clear of them,' she panted. 'Can you stand?'

I nodded, though I didn't know if I could. 'Just give me a minute to get to my feet, then I'll help you.'

Using the machine gun as support, I pushed myself upright. Torrents of fire shot through my arms, legs, and back as the cramping tried to overwhelm me. But this was our last chance. I had to ram the pain back into some recess of my skull where it wouldn't prevent me from doing what I needed to do next. Tasmin, meanwhile, managed to get to her knees. She'd become the snow nymph again, a figure enclosed in white. Snowflakes stuck to her, from the top of her head to her feet. Clumsy with exhaustion, she nevertheless succeeded in pushing the revolver into her pocket, then like a child wanting to be picked up, she held up her arms – a gesture of such trust that it put a hook into my heart. I realized, with a stab of utter surprise, that this was a woman I could love for all my life.

'What are you waiting for, Jack?' She gave a tired smile. 'We must do this. Get that truck. Then leave shitstorm mansion, uh?'

'Yep, time to leave shitstorm mansion.'

With desperation pushing me ruthlessly now, I picked her up. She seemed so light. My body had released torrents of adrenalin and endorphins to get me through this.

'We're not going to die,' I promised her. 'We aren't.'

'Damn right we aren't. Okay. I know you can do this.'

Through the blizzard we went. I carried her into a silent fog of grey. Once again, I could see no more than an arm's length in front of me, and no more than a yard to my left, right and rear, come to that.

Tee-kuk...Tee-kuk...Tee-kuk.

As I carried her, I gave her a reassuring squeeze. 'That really is the wind turbine this time.'

'Tee-kuk indeed.' She sounded drowsy.

My legs stiffened. Soon I had to force myself to move forward on legs that would not bend at the knees. I felt dizzy – the body's natural painkillers were working. But I was so light-headed I was in danger of falling over. Snow crunched under my boots. Flakes stung my eyes. When I opened my mouth, to suck in enough air to keep me going, those feathers of white rushed inward over my lips to melt in that distinctive tingling way on my tongue.

Then something lunged from the murk and hit me. For a second, I stood there, utterly breathless with shock. Who had just attacked me?

I couldn't see a figure. I pushed my hand through the dense murk of falling snow. Though I couldn't see my attacker I could feel a hardness.

The thing that had struck me was not human. In fact, its body consisted of a hard surface that was perfectly vertical.

'Tasmin.'

'Uh?' The woman was falling asleep.

'Tasmin. We made it.'

I set her down on the ground as gently as I could. That done, I propped the machine gun against the wall. Then came a desperate and infuriating fumble as I struggled to get the keys out of the side pocket of my jacket. I glanced back. The snow was easing again. I could see figures. Bright eyes blazed at me from the bone-white mist as full daylight returned.

'Come on, Jack, come on.' I muttered this as I sorted through key after key. They all had little plastic squares attached to them that bore a label. I read the writing there with difficulty. My sight was blurry due to exhaustion and pain from the cramps.

There were keys for 'Back yard pavilion', 'Motor mower', 'Red quadbike', 'Grandad's car', then bingo. 'Main garage'.

'Found it.' I couldn't resist bestowing a grateful kiss upon the key.

I glanced back again. Those figures in the murk were becoming clearer, and closer. They showed an interest in me now. Their body language revealed that, slowly, they were beginning to realize I was one of the guys they did not like. I was prey. I was a target for their murderous rage.

'Okay,' I told myself. 'You can do this – get the door open.'

In went the key – into the Yale lock on the side door of the 'Main garage'. The crunching of feet moving through snow became even louder...urgent, aggressive. The Creosotes had identified me and Tasmin as the ones they would love to kill.

I punched the door open. **CRASH!** By now, cramps had turned my body into a torture zone. Pains shot through my legs. I could hardly move.

'Jack,' murmured Tasmin as fatigue pulled her down into a fever-sleep. 'They're coming. Don't let them hurt us.'

Taking a huge breath, I grabbed Tasmin, and then the machine gun which I'd propped against the building. With a final volcanic eruption of energy, I slid Tasmin over the snow and inside.

As a mob of wild-eyed men and women, howling with homicidal rage, ran toward the open doorway, I slammed the door shut. Locked it from the inside, then I slithered down until I lay beside Tasmin on the concrete floor.

The truck stood just a dozen paces away from us. The thing was huge. A behemoth. A real mighty machine, clad in bright red paint. I would have kissed that truck, too. But I could not move. Paralysis had me in its cruel grip. Forcing me to remain flat on the floor, blasting white-hot flashes of pain through me. I lay there, not able to move, not even capable of reaching the machine gun lying on the floor by my feet, and I thought: *If they get in now. We won't stand a chance.*

CHAPTER THIRTY

'OVER MY DEAD BODY'

My body was as stiff as an iron slab. I lay beside Tasmin on the concrete floor. The fever made the woman drift in and out of consciousness. Even so, she managed to draw her body close to mine, positioning her head against my head, her mass of dark hair partly falling over my face, just as it had done when we lay together in the bedroom in the farmhouse.

I remained there, taken down hard by paralysis again. I felt the punch of my frightened heart against my ribcage. Above me, in the gloom of that massive warehouse of a place, steel rafters formed a grid pattern beneath two sloping halves of the roof. The dreariest of grey light oozed through windows that had been deliberately set high in the walls, above the reach of anyone intending to break into the building. Of course, this had been done back in the old world, when this was still a working farm. Vehicles filled the building – mainly, they were grimy agricultural machines: a couple of tractors, a bailer, three quadbikes that, years ago, farmworkers would have no doubt used to ride from field to field, when checking crops and cattle, perhaps carrying a dog on the pillion.

Picturing the dog on the back of a quadbike, ears and fur fluttering in the breeze as the bike trundled along, made me think of Piper. I shut my eyes, trying to crush guilt back down into the slimy hole that it had just slithered out of.

Instead of dwelling on those feelings of guilt, I opened my eyes again and forced myself to focus on our surroundings. There were no Creosotes in the shed, as far as I could tell. I listened hard for the worrying sound of footsteps scraping closer and closer toward us across the concrete floor – this vast expanse was lavishly decorated with dark patches of oil, cigarette butts, bits of string, a Wellington boot next to an inspection pit, and a dead mouse that was almost touching the side of my face.

The loudest sound was the fierce breeze. It was gusting against the building, conjuring a strange music all of its own: something like the sound you make when blowing across the top of an open bottle, yet much slower, much deeper. A profoundly mournful sound. I could imagine the god of love making that sound as it died of sorrow in a sea of hate...I clenched my fists, to help drive away those wayward, tormenting thoughts that preyed on me whenever this fucking awful paralysis trapped me in a prison of my own cramped-up muscles that hurt so much.

Focus on your surroundings, I told myself as I lay there, pressed close to Tasmin, endeavouring to warm her with my body heat – or what remained of it. And all the time, hearing the deep, booming sound of the river of cold air that had swept down from the savage north. Snowflakes darted past windows. Above the boom and drone of the ice wind, came the rhythmic *Tee-kuk* sound of the turbine blades, spinning round and around. *Tee-kuk...Tee-kuk* – a kind of backbeat rhythm from a phantom drummer, who accompanied the doom-laden flute sounds produced when winds surged against the metal structure of this cavernous mausoleum for dead machinery.

My neck muscles transmitted flashes of white-hot pain along my nervous system as I turned my head so I could see the small side door we'd entered by. The door was locked. A formidable steel slab of a thing, it was. Thank God for rural crime before civilization died. If it wasn't for the farmer's fear of being robbed, they wouldn't have gone to the huge expense of building this steel shed with thick metal doors.

Tee-kuk...Tee-kuk. How long had the wind turbine been loyally spinning in the breeze since the last time the farmer drew on the electricity its dynamo generated? Three years? No, closer to four years now, ever since one crazy night when the adult population of the world erupted into psychotic rage and went on a killing spree to end all killing sprees.

But were Creosotes emerging from insanity? Were they becoming well again? Myra insisted they had begun to regain their lucidity. She appeared sane...well, almost. Though there was something undeniably off-kilter about her in a psychological sense. She appeared to possess a near mystical belief that Del-Coffey knew the secret of repairing the minds of the Creosotes. Even the egotistical Martin Del-Coffey did not share her conviction that he could work miracles.

I told myself that we could not trust Myra. For all I knew, she might have a pretty collection of human heads on a shelf, and she desired to add our three heads to her display of trophies.

'Tasmin,' I whispered, 'are you awake?'

'Yes. How are you feeling?'

'Uh, muscles still in spasm. Cramping...I think it's passing.'

'I'll rest for ten minutes then I'll start work on the truck. Get the thing running. Hmm?'

'Yeah, sure.'

'It's so cold. Will you put your arm around me, please?'

The 'please' pulled at my heartstrings. A polite request in the midst of all this danger and absolute fucking dread, because, at any minute, Creosotes might find a way in here.

I repeated the words that had become a kind of prayer: 'We will live. We will not die. You and me, Tasmin, are going to survive.'

She shook her head. That cascade of hair softly caressed my face. A lovely sensation in that stark tomb of a building. 'No,' she murmured. 'Not survive.'

'We will survive.'

'No, Jack. If we do get out of this place alive, we must stop *merely surviving*. It's time we started living.'

'We do live. Back in my village, we had homes.'

'But have you been enjoying life since our parents went crazy? In the last three years, have your people been educating themselves, building lasting relationships, having babies, doing all the vital stuff you need to do to create a future for yourselves in a stable society?'

'Finding food took nearly all our time. And we were always worried that Creosotes would turn up in the village and start attacking us again.' I remembered my horrific return to New Home to find my friends scattered across the meadow. 'There isn't time to make a full and proper life. The best we can do is survive.'

'Well, Jack...' Tasmin sat up. Her eyes were bright again, her voice was strong. 'I have decided that hanging-on-by-my-fingernails isn't for me anymore. I shall begin living a life that is rewarding and will lead to a meaningful future. Can you help me?'

Her words echoed inside my skull. *Can you help me?* I stared at her. Was she inviting me to be part of her future?

She rose to her knees, unzipping her jacket as she did so. 'What do you think, Jack? Can you help me? With the truck? I'll need an extra pair of hands.'

'Oh...' My heart sank. No, that wasn't an invitation to be part of her life. 'Oh, right.' I nodded. 'Yep...the cramps are going. Just give me a couple of minutes to loosen up.' With a grunt of pain, I managed to sit up. 'Yep. It's easing.'

'While I've got the energy,' she told me, 'I'll find some tools. With luck, we'll get that old monster running in no time.' She shot me a beautiful smile.

I smiled back, while rubbing my shoulders until they felt as if they could move normally again.

And the cold winds blew – a long, mournful, heart-wrenching THROOOOM of a sound. Meanwhile, the wind turbine continued to play the sombre backbeat *Tee-kuk...Tee-kuk...*and the minutes were ticking relentlessly down to zero hour: the time when Tasmin and Del-Coffey must walk out into the snow and offer themselves to the Creosote Death Legion.

'Over my dead body, they will,' I whispered to myself as I finally succeeded in climbing to my feet. 'Over my dead body.'

CHAPTER THIRTY-ONE

TRUCKING HELL

Tasmin turned away from the truck, let out a yell of frustration, and then she threw the hammer across the interior of the building with enough force to produce a thunderous clang when the hammer slammed into the metal wall.

Her dark eyes glittered with rage. 'See for yourself, Jack. A chunk of the engine's missing – someone's taken the fuel injection pump along with the oil pan and most of the cabling.'

I stared at the truck with nothing less than absolute despair tearing my heart, and my hopes, to shreds. Tasmin had jacked up the cab, so it hinged forward to reveal the engine. Straight away, she'd realized that either before The Day, or just afterward, someone had stripped out some of the engine's vital components. It must have been a while ago, because mice had built a nest between the blades of the fan and the radiator, which would have once cooled the cylinder block assembly.

'It's dead,' she snarled. 'We are fucked. Going nowhere. Stranded.'

Grinding the heels of her palms into her eyes, she walked away across the cold concrete floor, her chest heaving as sobs threatened to overwhelm her.

The noisy drumbeat continued without pause as storm winds drove the turbine, which was fixed to its pylon that rose out of frozen dirt on the far side of the end wall of the shed. For a moment, I could not speak because whatever optimism I had harboured within me had been smashed into a million pieces. I could only stare at the useless, never-to-be-driven-again truck. A lifeless carcass of steel and plastic.

The turbine mocked us with *Tee-kuk...Tee-kuk.* A mechanical sound of metal on metal.

Tasmin let out a yell of frustration: 'That was to be our...our fucking lifeboat! We depended on that thing – it's just a pile of junk!'

I went across to Tasmin, intending to hug her, but when I got close, she put her hand against my chest, and shoved me back. Then she paced, arms folded, shaking her head.

'Tasmin,' I said. 'We'll think of something.'

'What? Dismantle those tractors and quadbikes, then make an aeroplane out of all the parts and fly out?' Her eyes were bleeding nothing less than despair.

Tee-kuk...Tee-kuk.

'Bloody thing,' she hissed. 'The sound is driving me bonkers.'

'At least, not everything's useless...sorry, that sounded crass, but come on. The wind turbine's working, so we'll treat that as a good omen. Eh?'

'Good omen. Wow. Bloody wow.' She shook her head with such an air of gloom my heart went out to her. 'We need more than good omens, Jack.'

'We've got a shed full of machines. Let's see if there's something we can use here.'

'The car is missing its two front wheels. Even if it did work, it's not powerful enough to drive through all those crazies out there. They'd pile onto the car and stop it dead. Same goes for the quadbikes.'

'What else do we have? Tractors?'

'Too vulnerable to attack. Their cabins aren't fully enclosed, see? We'd be overwhelmed in two minutes flat.'

'Well...that only leaves...' I pointed at the huge bulk of a combine harvester that lurked in the shadows. The machine was as massive as a dinosaur. It comprised several tons of steel and boasted a powerful motor. There was a drum-shaped arrangement of sharp steel blades at the front, which could harvest hundreds of acres of corn in a day, then bail the straw, which was pooped out at the other end.

'My God.' Tasmin let out a lungful of air. Her eyes glittered as she calculated what was possible. 'Oh my God. Jack...just imagine...'

'If we can get the engine started.'

'Oh, I'll breathe life into that monster.' Tasmin almost purred the words. 'Just you watch me work my magic.'

I found myself grinning. 'You know what we'll have, don't you? The Grim Reaper. A gigantic, mechanical Grim Reaper.'

'Jack, please retrieve the hammer. I think I might need it after all.' Then, once again, she smiled that beautiful smile.

CHAPTER THIRTY-TWO

RESURRECTIONIST

Tasmin got busy. Soon she had vanished into the gloomy recess of the combine harvester's engine bay. Its steel cover was held up by a pair of substantial rods.

From the depths of the metal beast, she called back to me: 'See if you can find oil – everything that moves should be lubricated, including linkages to the control pedals and steering.'

'Will do.'

'Also, find a foot-pump. These tyres'll need air in them.'

'Okay.'

Our mood had gone from misery to one of decidedly good cheer. I was energised now. The cramps had vanished from my body, I felt light on my feet, eager to get the job done, and hopeful that the fever-induced paralysis wouldn't come back. Tasmin, though still quite ill, moved quickly, every inch the professional mechanic – checking oil levels, the air filter, and all those greasy parts that would, when the motor started, make that big green monster of a machine move. Okay, we wouldn't break land-speed records, but the thing was built like a gargantuan battle tank. I reckoned it could crunch through brick walls without any problem whatsoever.

Before searching for the oil, I grabbed my rucksack. 'It'll be dark in twenty minutes; you'll need the torch.'

'Thanks.'

Even as I began to unzip the rucksack, I saw them. Three lanterns standing on a shelf fixed to the wall.

'Things are starting to break our way,' I called out.

'Uh?'

'Lanterns. Gas lanterns.' I picked one up, giving it a shake. 'There's plenty of gas in the cannister, too.'

Tasmin withdrew her head from the engine bay, revealing she'd acquired a picturesque streak of grime on one cheek from one of the motor's greasy components. Yeah, you guessed right: vehicle engineering does not fall even remotely within my area of expertise. Nevertheless, I enjoyed watching Tasmin work, her intelligent eyes shrewdly assessing what needed to be done to get the big green beauty up and running, her expert hands nimbly checking cable leads, plugs, alternators and whatever else the machine required to bring it back to glorious life.

Tasmin gave me a thumbs up. 'Nice one, Jack. The more light the better.'

The lantern simply required a tap turning on its brass neck beneath the glass vessel, which contained the mantle; this action opened up the gas glow. After that, I used my thumb to press an ignition button, fixed on the other side of the neck to the gas tap. A few firm presses of the button – *click, click, click!* – the bottled gas lit with a loud pop, and a brilliant light blazed from the mantle. I handed Tasmin the lantern and she positioned it on a strut inside the engine bay so that the engine, itself, would be flooded with that bright, white light.

Postponing the hunt for oil yet again, I decided to check on the bad guys. All windows in the shed were well above head height, so I had to climb a steel rack fixed to one of the walls. The racks' shelves were heaped with folded tarps, jars of nails and screws, lengths of chain, rope, spools of electrical cable – in fact, all the kinds of hardware required by people to maintain farm equipment and the buildings that contained it. Quickly, I climbed the racks as if they formed an oversize ladder.

Storm winds blew hard against the building, drawing that eerie THROOM from the metalwork. As always, the wind turbine spun, providing the backbeat of *Tee-kuk...Tee-kuk*...all in all, strange devil music that managed to be morbid and menacing in equal measure. I reached a high window that was grimy with fly splat, spiderwebs, years of dust, and oily particles, spewed out from when farm vehicles were revved up inside the building. Cautiously, because I didn't want to be spotted by those that would rip us to pieces, I rubbed a little corner of the window free of grime, before peering out.

I couldn't see a damn thing. The blizzard had returned with demonic vengeance. For all I knew, a thousand Creosotes had gathered out there to look up at me. However, billions of feathery white flakes created such a dense murk that I could see nothing but those snowflakes. I couldn't even see the ground immediately below the window. I listened hard, trying to pick up sounds that might indicate the Creosotes were trying to get into our behemoth of a shed. All I did hear was the ever-present Satanic flute music of those bitterly cold winds, which were accompanied by the *Tee-kuk* clank of the wind turbine. *Maybe our prospects are improving,* I told myself. *Those monsters aren't trying to break in. And if Tasmin gets the combine harvester started then we have our ride out of there.* A smile glued itself to my face as I clambered back down to the floor; a glow of optimism began to warm my spirits again.

After that, I found the oil Tasmin needed to lube the moving parts. Then Tasmin sent me in search of rags to wipe away old grease where it had formed dry crusts on the cable linkages that helped govern the running of the machine. At the far side of the shed, I happened upon a table with cups, an electric kettle, and what looked like the ancient remnants of a meat pie. The oblong of rock-hard crust had turned bone-white, while dry gravy had stuck to the plate in a smear of unwholesome brown. No doubt the owner of the pie had intended to dine on that, but then the tidal wave of madness had overwhelmed him or her, making them forget the pie, as a crazed lust for violence against their own young took hold. Hanging from a wall hook was a red T-shirt. Maybe left by the owner of the pie, should they ever require a change of clothing. In any event, that garment would be useful for scraping away caked-on grease from the engine.

As I lifted the T-shirt from the hook, I noticed a wooden board bolted to the wall nearby. Power switches were fixed to the board. Cables ran from it and up the wall. For a second, I stared at the board, paying close attention to a voltage meter fixed in the centre.

Above my head, the wind-turbine beat out its mechanical drum-beat.

'Jack...' Tasmin waved to attract my attention. 'Have you found something to wipe these linkages?'

'Coming.'

I trotted back to her.

'Thanks.' She set to work with the T-shirt, dislodging old gunk from parts that would pivot, thereby tightening and slackening linkage cables that controlled the running of the motor.

I asked, 'How's it going?'

'Not bad. Nearly there.'

'What about the battery?'

'Flat as roadkill.'

'Uh? How will you start the motor?'

'Old agricultural machines like this have a backup system. You can fire up the engine by manually cranking a handle.'

Above us, the *Tee-kuk* backbeat got louder as the wind blew harder. The rhythm quickened, too.

She leaned forwards into the engine bay, scrubbing hard with the red T-Shirt. 'Did you come across a foot pump?'

'Not yet.'

'Best find one, then, and make a start on getting some air into the tyres. It'll be a hell of job inflating them.'

Tee-kuk! Tee-kuk!

Then, a revelation – one that was a long time coming, and which finally ignited the relevant neurons inside my brain. Almost with a sense of wonder at why the idea had taken so long to occur to me,

I returned to the control board with its switches and voltmeter. There, I gazed at the switches for a moment. They were all labelled with phrases like: 'Lock Turbine' and 'Disengage Genny' and 'Yard Lights' and 'Primary House Router'.

A large switch drew my attention. This was fixed just above the voltmeter. Of course, I'd not seen electric house lights work in the last three years. There was no electricity these days. All the power stations would be falling into ruin and tenanted by bats and vermin.

With a detached feeling, as if afraid to hope for too much, I reached up and pulled the big switch down.

A clicking...a glimmer of light...then dazzling flashes. Lightning captured in a bottle flashes. The effect seemed so strange, because I hadn't seen this happen for such a long, long time.

What came from my lips was the tiniest whispered, 'Oh.'

Up above my head (above the roof), on top of its pylon, that windmill arrangement of blades. The rotating blades drove an axle, the axle drove the generator. The generator produced electricity – power.

Tasmin's voice rose in something close to a squeal of astonishment. 'Jack? What did you just do?'

Above me, the strip lights stopped their clicking and flashing as they came fully on, illuminating the big cavern of a place. The light evicted gloom and shadow, and annihilated those chilling ghostlands of darkness.

I grinned at her, while making shrugging gestures, which sort of announced that it wasn't a difficult achievement. Tasmin grinned back at me, the dark smudge of oil on her cheek, her eyes twinkling with joy. I made another expressive gesture with my hands, the kind a conjuror might make when they've just astonished the audience with a dazzling trick. You know, rabbits from a hat, or the Ace of Spades from a sealed up can of beans, or some such wizardry.

We both stared up at the illuminated tubes of glass fixed to ceiling struts. Electric light. For the first time in years, in this dark and dangerous world, actual electric light.

Tasmin saluted me. 'Well done, sir. You have the magic touch.'

Still grinning with such huge pleasure as doing something as simple as filling the place with light by pulling a switch, I walked across the floor toward her.

'Another omen,' I told her. 'A good omen. We've got electric light. We've got our escape vehicle. We're going to survive.'

'Correction, Jack. We're going to start living.'

We looked at each other. She was all smiles and bright eyes. Then we looked up at the light again. We started doing comically exaggerated shrugs. Then both of us paused, stared into one another's eyes, becoming serious – that didn't last long, however, and we burst out laughing like we'd just seen the funniest comedy in the world.

Laughing like that? It was the release of tension. After all we had been through today. Crossing the farmyard, having to thread our way through thousands of murderous individuals, then entering the big building to find the truck we needed was useless. All that stress and tension and absolute fucking terror. If Fate had dealt us a different hand of cards, we could have been sat in a corner, howling with misery, while pounding our fists against our heads as our own sanity crumbled, because we knew we had no means of escape.

But a twist of fate had brought us good fortune. We had electric light. And we had our big, oh-so beautiful green metal friend, the combine harvester. Many, many tons of diesel-powered muscle, complete with a cab set high about the ground, well above the reach of enraged Creosote hands. Also, add to that, the twenty-foot-wide arrangement of sharp cutting blades on the front – a mechanical reaper that could sever stalks of corn by the thousand every five seconds before gulping them into its steel throat where a conveyor belt would carry them to a threshing drum where grain would be stripped from stalk.

So – we laughed with sheer relief.

We still chuckled to ourselves, in a giddy, light-headed way, as we continued with our work. Tasmin finished checking out the engine. I stuck a bamboo cane down through the pipe in the combine harvester where the farmer would have pumped in fuel. The bamboo came back out all gooey and dripping with diesel. So, plenty of fuel to get us to safety.

I didn't even need to use the foot-pump. I found an electric powered compressor on wheels. The wind-turbine provided ample juice for the compressor's electric motor, so I simply plugged that little miracle of invention into a wall socket, then inflated the combine harvester's flat tyres. The big machine rose slowly as the huge tyres, which were almost as high as I am tall, inflated.

Tasmin watched me at work, and when I took my thumb off the air-hose trigger and the noisy compressor fell silent, she said, 'Keep them under-inflated. Better traction in the snow that way. Also, we don't want too much pressure in case the rubber's perished and they burst.'

'Don't put horror images into my mind, Tasmin. If one of these tyres rupture now, the blast will knock my head off.'

'Yep, it will.' Her smile vanished. 'And seeing as there are no replacement tyres, as far as I can see, our escape machine will be of no use to us whatsoever.'

Carefully now, I squirted air into the tyres...bit by bit...slowly inflating the tyres, doing my best not to overinflate the old rubber, which was showing plenty of surface cracks.

Ten minutes later, we were ready. Tasmin slotted a crank handle into a socket in the side of the engine. I took up my position by the building's steel roller doors. Those doors were as big as the side of a house. Initially, we'd thought we'd have to raise them manually, perhaps using a system of ropes, but a simple control panel at the side of the door with a 'Door Up' button and a 'Door Down' button happily indicated that, if the electric door motor still worked, I could raise the door just with a push of that 'up' button.

Tasmin took her place at the crank handle. 'Ready?'

Suddenly, I raised my hands. 'Wait. I'll be ten seconds.'

With that, I rushed back across the floor to the wind turbine's control panel. I'd remembered what one of the labels said alongside a switch.

Yep, and there it was: 'Yard Floodlights.'

I flicked the switch.

From outside, came a loud grunting noise – something I believed to be a verbal expression of astonishment from the Creosotes. Because the yard's floodlights had just burst into life with such dazzling power that they blazed light through the blizzard and through the windows of the building. The sheer intensity of the radiance was immense. The incandescent lagoon had even forced a reaction of amazement from those brutish individuals outside.

As I ran back past Tasmin to the roller door I called out, 'Now we can see the route! Not only back to the house, but away from here. Ready when you are!'

Tasmin began to turn the big handle. Cranking away at the steel guts of our monster machine.

CHAPTER THIRTY-THREE

THE COMING OF THE BEAST

Tasmin turned the steel handle that protruded from the combine harvester's motor. Cranking, cranking, cranking. Even from where I stood by the door, I could see her face begin to shine with perspiration. She panted hard. Gusts of white vapour were spurting from her lips into cold, cold air. The woman was still sick with fever. I could tell that she grew more exhausted with every crank of the handle that rattled as she tried to fire up the diesel engine.

'Tasmin,' I shouted. 'Let me do that!'

'No. Get ready to open the main door when the engine starts.'

'But will it start? You've been trying for the last two minutes.'

'Give it a chance.' She wiped her forehead with the back of her hand. 'The fuel pipe from the tank to the engine will be empty because any diesel in the pipe will have completely evaporated away. After all, it's stood idle for the last three years. So, I need to draw fuel into the fuel injection pump first.' She tightened her grip on the crank handle again. 'Then the pistons will fire. Trust me.'

So, as I waited, ready to push the button that would roll up the steel door, I watched as Tasmin worked the handle again, filling the building with a loud clanking that even drowned out the mournful drone of storm winds and the metallic heartbeat sound of the wind-turbine.

Tasmin's head tossed as she cranked the handle, flinging dark hair out. Carefully, I ran through our plan again. A simple plan, yet a downright dangerous one. A plan that would be busted to fuck if Tasmin couldn't start the engine, or if a tyre blew out as we trundled across the yard, because there was no way that machine could move forwards with a flat tyre...or, then again, the engine might fail as we tried to drive away. Or Creosotes might climb onto the vehicle in huge numbers, swamping it, their combined weight stopping it dead. Or what if...*No*, I told myself. *Stop imagining what might go wrong. Stop picturing us being dragged, screaming, from the cab by – no. STOP.*

Fear lubricates imagination. Slick images of your violent death begin to run so smoothly through your mind in a situation like this.

Focus on the plan. Yes, a straightforward plan. Tasmin starts the motor. Then she climbs into the cab. I press the button: the big door then starts to roll itself up into the roof space. I dash back to the cab before the Creosotes can flood in. When I'm in the cab, we drive across the yard and pick up Martin Del-Coffey from the house. And then we power away, leaving the Death Legion behind to freeze in the snow.

What about Piper? He can't climb up the ladder, which is fixed on the side of the combine harvester, to the cab. The cab door is over two metres above the ground. Piper can't jump that high. When Tasmin stops the harvester at the front door of the house, the Creosotes will rush forward. Del-Coffey will need all the luck in the universe to get from the house to the harvester before the Creosotes grab him. *So, what do we do about Piper?*

'DID IT!'

Tasmin's yell of triumph pierced right through my thoughts about the dog. Suddenly, blasting out great gusts of smoke, the green monster's engine woke up – it filled the shed with nothing less than thunder. That's when I punched the button beside the door, while hoping with all my heart the motor would still work.

Thank heaven. Clanking, rattling, the door began to slowly rise, as the roller turned above my head, winding all those hinged metal slats upward. Even when the bottom of the door was no higher than my ankles, flakes of snow shot through. They were carried by a skin-freezing rush of air.

Five seconds from now, the door would be high enough to allow the Creosotes to come storming into the building. I turned around and sprinted across the floor. Our weaponry and the rucksack were already onboard, so all I need do was get myself into the cabin.

Then the first problem reared its vile head. Tasmin sank to her knees – her head was drooping downward. The woman had exhausted herself to the point she could no longer stand, never mind climb up those eight rungs of the ladder to the cab.

Meanwhile, clanking and rumbling, the door continued upward, allowing a rush of snowflakes into the building where they swirled around me as I hoisted Tasmin to her feet.

'Don't worry,' I panted. 'I'll lift you up into the cabin.'

'Hurry, Jack. Creosotes are coming.'

A glance back over my shoulder confirmed what she'd said. Already hunched shapes were moving through the grey murk outside, getting closer to the massive doorway. With a heck of a lot of speed – violent speed, at that – and little in the way of gentleness, I hauled Tasmin bodily up the eight rungs fixed to the metalwork. Tasmin hung limply in my arms, yet she managed to help me by pulling open the cab door. I could tell the woman was wiped out, just tired to the bone, because she didn't even grunt when I shoved

137

her through the doorway into the cabin, then rammed her across the driving seat and into the passenger seat.

The massive engine throbbed, my nose was full of the stench of diesel fumes from the exhaust. The front of the machine faced the doorway, saving me from the difficulty of having to reverse out of the shed. Dear God, I hoped I could get the thing moving forward. I'd never driven a combine harvester before. There, in front of me, a conventional steering wheel (thank heaven for that, anyway), a control panel with an amber glow coming from dials. There was also a bunch of levers down by my side. What those levers did, I hadn't a clue.

I swung the door shut, then found the pedals with my feet. Again, pretty conventional layout: clutch, brake, gas. The gear lever was surprisingly stumpy for such a huge machine. I shuffled fully back into the seat, which had the comfortable dimensions of an armchair – an obvious requirement, I guess, for farm workers sitting there for a dozen hours or more, as they harvested vast fields of corn. Driver and passenger seats were side-by-side at the front of the cabin (I never even realized that some harvesters had a place for passengers; maybe this was specialist machinery, which required a crew of two to operate it). Behind the seats was a largish storage area, consisting of a simple open floor space, covered by rubber matting – no doubt this was to accommodate a toolkit and the like. Even two or three passengers could squat there if the farmer needed to take more people out into the fields during harvest time.

As I revved the engine, relishing that satisfying roar of power, a fist punched my forearm.

Tasmin had dragged herself sideways, to look down through the big glass panel in the door at her side of the cabin. Tasmin punched my arm again.

'No,' she shouted. 'You can't go yet.'

'What's wrong?'

'I never closed the engine bay cover. And the starting handle is still in place, too.' She turned her weary eyes to me. 'Sorry, Jack. I fucked up.'

I thought: *Leave the handle in there, and the cover open. What harm could it do?* Flakes of snow spat through the doorway, hitting the cab's windows. No...I had to shut the cover down, to keep the snow out. After all, what if all that snow, settling on the warm engine, turned into a flow of water that poured into the electrics. That would kill the motor for sure.

'Tasmin. Sit tight. I'm going to close the cover.'

I'd climbed halfway down those rungs before I realized I'd forgot to bring a gun with me. Shit! For a split-second, I considered going back for the machine gun. But already men and women were dragging their frostbitten feet across the threshold of the building as they headed toward the harvester. They had already seen me.

With time running out, I jumped the rest of the way to the ground, then raced around the vehicle to where the engine bay gaped open, exposing the oily workings within. A guy of around forty, with a halo of bristling dark hair, lumbered around the corner of the machine. Festering holes in his feet indicated where his toes had once protruded from flesh. Part of his nose had gone, exposing the raw gulf of his nasal passage. Though parts of his body had literally died from cold, his eyes were bright with hatred for me.

Even though the engine made a loud throbbing sound, I could hear the slap of his bare feet on concrete as he ran toward me. By this time, I had my hands on the starting handle – which was a formidable piece of steelwork, the length of my arm. I yanked the shaft from the socket in the engine. With a roar of fury, I swung the starting handle with all the savagery of a warrior hacking at their foe with a battle-axe. The greasy end of the starting handle whipped through the air before smashing into the side of the Creosote's head, crushing bone, and unlocking what must have been the equivalent of a mugful of crimson, which shot out before splashing onto the floor.

The guy didn't fall. Instead, with a bemused expression on his face, he simply walked away. No doubt, I'd pulped so much of his brain that his murderous intentions had leaked out of his skull on that copious stream of blood.

A pair of filthy arms appeared from behind me at either side of my neck. They crossed over, getting me in a headlock. I whipped my head back so viciously I felt a nose break against that solid head bone of mine. The backwards headbutt possessed enough force to knock my attacker away from me, whereupon I turned to see an extraordinary sight. A woman stood there, with hair that fell in soft curls down over her shoulders and chest, the very image of Aphrodite – that beautiful goddess who emerged from the shell. Blood began to pour from her nose into her mouth, turning her teeth bright red. Her green eyes regarded me with surprise, like she was an innocent person who had been attacked for no reason.

I hesitated, wondering if I'd attacked someone who wasn't actually a homicidal Creosote. I glanced down. Her feet were bare. What looked like rat bites had left dozens of small puncture wounds in the bare flesh of her shins, knees, and thighs.

The starting handle flashed through the air again. And the woman was no more.

When I glanced at the doorway, I saw perhaps twenty men and women coming this way...they had a purposeful walk, their hating eyes fixed on me. For a moment, I shoved ineffectually at the big metal cover that would seal the engine compartment.

'Come on, come on...close, you piece of shit!'

As I shouted and swore at the cover, which simply refused to budge, I finally saw that the cover had to be raised first, then the hinged supports would disengage in such a way the cover would close. I lifted, pushed the supports, they hinged backwards, folding in half. Thank God for that. I slammed the hatch shut.

Gripping the starting handle like a medieval warrior gripping a battle-axe, I ran around the vehicle to the rungs that would get me back into the cab. An old guy lumbered forward. I sidestepped him, gave him a shove. Down he went, his face slapping the concrete hard.

As I climbed the rungs, more Creosotes rushed forward. Anger was heating their blood – and fury was powering up their hearts, turning those creatures into dangerous predators. Three men darted at me with surprising speed to grab hold of my legs. The three heads, which belonged to the guys, were on the same level as my knees. The men pulled hard, trying to drag me down to the floor.

With a brutality generated by pure terror, I hacked at them with the long shaft connected to the starting handle. My blows opened rips in their faces, discharging blood. Another blow ruptured one man's eye. A clear, viscous liquid, looking pretty much like the white of an egg, came oozing out of the socket and then down his cheek into his wild-man-of-the-woods beard.

The men's nails were long, with splintered ends, and they hurt like hell when they scratched at my legs, even piercing the stout material of my waterproof bottoms.

As well as using the starting handle as a baton, I freely used my right boot. I kicked the clawing hands, then stomped on heads. The men grunted with sheer physical effort, their angry eyes flashed as they stared up at me, their damaged minds were pulsating with sheer bloodlust. However, they didn't cry out in pain when the starting handle snapped a jawbone, or my boot opened up another cut in a forehead. They simply focussed on what their perverse instinct commanded them to do, and that was: ATTACK, ATTACK, ATTACK. I was their entire world. They focussed on me, and me alone. Nothing else was important to them. Me. That's what they wanted.

Those thoughts renewed my own passion to get away from those crazed men. I stomped down hard on their heads. The moment all the hands had stopping gripping my ankles, I raced up the ladder into the cabin, slammed the door, then flung the starting handle into the rear storage area. After that, my own instinct took over. Without even rationally working out the process of how the machine worked, I'd released the handbrake, and then engaged first gear as my foot slammed down hard on the gas.

The harvester lurched forward. Beside me, Tasmin was fast asleep, her head lolling down, a fever-sweat shining on her upper lip. Almost at random, I hit switches, trying to find the headlamps. One switch fired up a flashing yellow light fixed to the superstructure behind the cab. A warning light, no doubt. You know, 'watch out monster machine at work, stay back, don't get chopped into pieces by the blades.' Though I knew the blades weren't working. When the harvester had been brought in from the fields, the last time it had gathered the wheat, the cutting-gear would have been disengaged from the driveshaft and raised so it would be high enough to stop sharp blades ripping out chunks of the road's surface.

Another haphazard stab of my finger finally triggered the headlamps. A wash of brilliant white light cut through the air to illuminate snowflakes falling beyond the entrance to the shed.

Creosotes, meanwhile, were hurrying through the doorway. To my disappointment, they had, this time at least, the sense to keep out of the path of a vehicle – a huge vehicle, granted, but one that moved slowly. The speedo revealed that I'd hit a less than breathtaking velocity of six miles per hour. But that's okay. What we needed was power and bulk, not some flighty, lightweight car that could do one hundred and fifty on the motorway. Believe me, a car wouldn't last two minutes out there, amid that swarm of Creosotes.

The blizzard was shitting it down. I can't come up with a better description than that. Absolutely shitting it down. White feathers spat out of the gloom, to stick on the windscreen. I pulled at stalks that protruded from the steering wheel column. Could I find the wiper control? Could I hell! The smeared glass granted me hardly any field of vision, whatsoever. I could not see any of that Death Legion of crazy folk. I couldn't see fences, or buildings, or even the fucking ground in front of me. Nothing. Zilch. Zero.

There may have been Creosotes getting knocked down during my six-mile-per-hour trundle, but the machine was so big I didn't feel any impact against the stationary blades at the front. This thing was so heavy that even if its massive wheels ran over a human body there wasn't so much as a judder – our vast weight would crush human flesh and bone flat. Consequently, our slow journey was astonishingly smooth.

Even though I could not see the farmhouse – nor ground, sky, or enemy – I knew that the house, containing Del-Coffey and Piper, stood around one hundred and fifty paces to my right. And though I could see no buildings, I did manage to make out the white glow of the yard's floodlights through the blizzard.

'We're making progress,' I told Tasmin, even though I knew she was sleeping.

The power steering made turning the wheels easy, so I quickly swung the machine's nose until it pointed in the direction of the where the house must surely lay. I knew, from memory, that there were no fences, abandoned vehicles or outbuildings in my way now. All I need do, was continue rumbling along at six miles per hour, through that snow globe effect, until I saw the house. And, hopefully, I would see the house in time to avoid crashing into the thing. I made slow, careful progress. The engine chugging with a reliable heartbeat of sound. My fingers randomly flicked switches, trying to locate the wiper control. Instead of wipers, however, a flick of a switch brough forth music from a CD in its player. A rousing orchestral symphony that I didn't know the title of. Music to drive battle tanks to war – that kind of military fanfare type of thing.

My heart pounded. Because, even though I felt safe now, the next phase of the plan was just about to begin. And that was anything but safe.

CHAPTER THIRTY-FOUR

THIS IS IT. DEATH OR GLORY

I never did find the wiper switch on the combine harvester. However, it dutifully lumbered across the farmyard, over frozen dirt, thick snow and, make no bones about it, over human bodies. The blizzard reduced visibility to nothing. Nevertheless, I had a good idea of the direction of the farmhouse – straight ahead. I could not see the house itself, because not only night had fallen, but clouds spat billions of snowflakes down onto my corner of the world.

Pretty quickly, snow covered the glass in front of me, and still I couldn't locate the damn wiper switch. The harvester must have been old when civilization collapsed, because symbols on the switches, which had once identified their function, had been worn away by the no doubt calloused fingers that belonged to farmworkers who'd once driven this thing. By chance, I hit the button that killed the jubilant fanfare of trumpets blaring from the speakers (believe me, muting that din was sweet relief, indeed). More haphazard flicking of switches and pressing of buttons, activated various lights inside and outside the machine, including an Anglepoise lamp fixed to the ceiling. This light shone down onto Tasmin as she slept, dead to the world, the fever adding a gloss of perspiration to her face, so it appeared as if her face had assumed a silvery glow. Her head rested against the side window as I drove.

'Tasmin?' I gently shook her. 'Tasmin. You okay?'

Her eyelids lifted to reveal exhausted eyes. She murmured something I couldn't make out. Her eyelids closed again.

Then – BANG!

A face appeared through the snowstorm outside to slam against the glass. BANG! BANG! A crazed man, with a huge beard and eyes blazing with total fury, tried to break the glass with his forehead.

The face lunged into view again, through the writhing torrent of snowflakes. BANG!

He struck the side window so hard with his forehead that the glass cracked, forming almost a spider shape – white spider legs radiating outward from a circular dot the size of a penny. The blow had been so severe that the Creosote had succeeded in opening up a huge cut in his own forehead. Blood gushed from the wound, a red cascade, steaming in the cold air. Whether the blow had concussed him or not, I can't say for sure. In any event, he rolled backwards, vanishing into the gloom, maybe falling the two metres or so to the ground below. He never came back.

I pushed on, careful not to increase the speed beyond six miles per hour. The last thing I needed right now was to drive this green monster into the house – a vehicle this size would smash in walls, bringing the front of the building down on top of us, no doubt crushing the cab, which was largely formed from glass anyway.

'Damn it, I can't see a thing.' I muttered the words as I leaned forward, my hands bunching into hard fists as I clung to the steering wheel. After straining my eyes, and seeing nothing through the accumulating crust on the windscreen, I knew what had to be done, considering I couldn't find the wiper switch. Steering one-handed, I used the other hand to grip the door handle. I lifted the handle upward, disengaging the lock, then pushing the door open. What looked like a white ghost monster rushed into the cab.

Creosote!

No, thank God, just a blast of snowflakes – though they almost felt like a solid body the way they struck me so hard.

Still driving, I half stood – then leaning sideways and forwards as much as I could, I reached outside and used my fingertips to scrape a small area of the windscreen, clearing it of that crust of snow that had forced me to drive blind. The moment I'd cleared an area, which was perhaps the size of a dinner plate, I suddenly caught sight of the house, massively filling my field of vision.

'Shit!!' I bounced back down into the seat.

Slamming my foot on the brake, I let go of the steering wheel and put my arm across Tasmin's chest to prevent her going face-first into the dashboard. The harvester wasn't moving fast, yet all those tons of metal don't stop easily on slippery ground. The vehicle slid onward, despite my savage pumping of the brake.

At last, the machine did stop. And it stopped no more than ten paces from the front of the farmhouse. Del-Coffey wouldn't have far to run (if he could run) to reach us.

The cab door swung and bumped in the wind. As I reached out to close the door, it swung wide open again. A woman of around forty had pulled it back. Red hair flapped in the breeze.

'Myra!'

No, this wasn't Myra, though there was a superficial resemblance. The cab lights revealed, horrifically, that her bottom jaw had been ripped away, leaving a tongue that appeared sickeningly long. It was a red tentacle of a thing, which appeared to flicker and taste the air like the sensitive, probing tongue of a serpent.

The abrupt appearance of this Creosote had taken me so much

144

by surprise that I just sat there staring at the terrifying apparition. The woman lunged inward. She grasped hold of my right arm, then she tried to heave me out from the cab. Through the swirling flakes, I could see more heads appearing as Creosotes began to scale the vehicle's metalwork.

I managed to turn in the seat until my legs were out through the door. The jawless woman thrust her face closer to mine – ugh, that stench of necrosis. Hoisting my knee up toward my chest, I managed to get the sole of my boot planted firmly in the centre of her torso that was clad in what looked like several layers of plastic sacks. Then I shoved her with my boot. Shoved as hard as I could. In fact, shoved so hard that my backside slipped completely across the driver's seat and partly onto the one occupied by Tasmin, making her grunt with pain as my back slammed into her side.

With a yell, I pushed the woman off the harvester. She fell backward, vanishing into falling snow. I never even saw her hit the ground.

BANG! I slammed the door shut. Locked it. That done, I slammed my fist into the horn button in the centre of the steering wheel.

'Del-Coffey!' I yelled, even though I knew he couldn't hear me, due to him being in the house, and me locked up here in my little fortress of steel and glass. 'Del-Coffey! Get your backside out of that house and over here!'

Just then, the blizzard stopped with an abruptness that was nigh on breathtaking. I could clearly see the house in front of me. And I could see Creosotes starting to gather around our big green beast that would, if luck was on our side, carry us away from the murder mob. So, I kept pounding the horn, sending out blasts of sound – an urgent salvo of noise that warned of danger. By now, those white feathers only fell in their twos and threes. Visibility had become perfect. Too perfect. All the fucking Creosotes could see our machine now. Soon they would come surging in over the snow, eager to rip youthful flesh.

Tasmin had woken up. Her eyes were bright again. Focussed. Intelligent. 'Jack...those yard lights. It's bright as day out there.'

'I know. I'm regretting switching the bloody things on. They're floodlighting us – every Creosote out there in the field knows we're here.' I shouted again, 'Del-Coffey! Where the hell are you?'

My fist punched the horn button, over and over.

Tasmin yelled so loudly my bones almost jumped out from their flesh. 'Jack! Look!'

I looked where she pointed forwards. A square of light appeared in the front of the house. Someone had opened the door.

Tasmin yelled again – a noise with the potential to scrape ears from skulls. 'Del-Coffey! He's carrying Piper!'

145

'Damn it. He should have left the dog behind. He needs to save himself. Now he can't use the gun.'

Del-Coffey carried my beautiful Border Collie in his arms. But he should have left Piper. When it's a case of choosing between human life and animal life, a human life must always come first. Now, Del-Coffey, the idiot – the fucking lovely, brave idiot – was going to die trying to save my dog from the Creosotes.

The plan had been for me to wait in the driver's seat while Del-Coffey rushed from the house and scaled the rungs to the cab.

The plan now lay broken and bloody in the great scheme of things.

I twisted around to grab the sub-machine gun from the storage area behind me. When the gun was resting across my lap, I stuffed four of those long, curving ammo magazines into the deep pockets of my jacket. Thirty bullets in each mag. So that meant one hundred and twenty in my pockets, with another thirty of those killer slugs loaded into the mag, which was already clipped into the underside of the gun.

'Tasmin, I'll get Del-Coffey. You move over behind the wheel.'

'Jack, you're crazy, there's thousands of Creosotes out there!'

'I can't think of another way, can you?'

She hesitated, for only a second, before giving a grim shake of her head.

Floodlights blazed as bright as a noonday sun in June. The snow reflected the lights skyward in a column of light – something like a spectral fire of Biblical enormity. A pillar of ice-cold flame, reaching up to kiss the belly of heaven.

Creosotes milled around the harvester. Even more of them were lumbering toward us.

Del-Coffey managed to move forward five or six paces, until he was halfway between the house and the harvester, then his feet sank into deep snow, the man lost his balance, falling forward with Piper in his arms. Piper immediately wriggled free before running under the harvester to escape the Creosotes (maybe he'd fought his own battles with them in the past and knew from experience that retreat was preferrable to violent confrontation). Del-Coffey, broken down by fever, was clearly too weak to get back up onto his feet again.

There were hundreds of Creosotes surrounding our green beast now. And they began closing in. A dozen of those psychotic killers stretched out their hands, reaching for Martin Del-Coffey as he lay there, helpless in the snow.

CHAPTER THIRTY-FIVE

LIKE AN AWFUL TIDE OF FLESH...

'Jack! You can't kill them all!'

With Tasmin's full-blooded yell shaking the bones of my skull, I all but hurled myself from the driver's seat onto a small platform, just outside the cab door. Tasmin, meanwhile, slid across to the driver's seat, where she grabbed the wheel, slammed her foot onto the gas pedal and pumped hard, making the engine bellow. At that moment, she did not engage the reverse gear. The machine, though it roared mightily, did not move. Would Tasmin stay? Or would she drive away from here, leaving me, Piper, and Del-Coffey to suffer hideously painful deaths? Of course, I believed she'd wait for us. I did truly believe that.

Like a flood, like an awful tide of flesh, Creosotes flowed across the snow until they swirled around our green monster of a farm vehicle. Hundreds of men and women tried to reach Del-Coffey, each one hellbent on being the one to rip his head from his shoulders. The thing is, there was so many of them, and their attack was so uncoordinated, and so violent, and lacking any logical coordination, they quickly became a swarming mob of chaos on the move. They got in each other's way. Some lashed out in frustration at one another instead of directing their punches at the enemy. Others stumbled in deep snow drifts where they were trampled underfoot by their own kind.

By now, there were so many of those killers I couldn't even see the ground. Come to that, I'd lost sight of Del-Coffey in that seething, chaotic movement of people – and Del-Coffey should just be five or six paces away from me. Then I saw him surface above the heads of the Creosotes. That high forehead of his gleamed in the savage glare of the floodlights. His blonde hair had been ruffled into a mess of upright stalks. A swiping hand cracked open the skin above an eyebrow, which released a trickle of glistening scarlet that ran down into his right eye. The reason I could see Del-Coffey so clearly now was that some of the mob down there had hoisted him from the ground, raising him above their shoulders – the way they used to do at music concerts, either to crowd surf a member of the audience, or remove someone who'd passed out in the crush of folk, then passing the individual at head height across the tightly packed mass of concertgoers. The Creosotes, by virtue of some spontaneous understanding, had decided to move Del-Coffey away from the harvester. They weren't gentle – no, not at all – grasping hands snatched out clumps of his blond hair, making him howl and writhe in agony.

The thought that blasted with lightning ferocity through my brain was: *The time's now...or not at all.* I flicked the switch on the side of the gun from full auto fire to single shot.

Aiming with as much precision as I could, I began to fire. Bullets crashed into the skulls of the men and women nearest Del-Coffey: they were the ones holding him above their heads at that moment. After I blasted six Creosotes from the world of life into the everlasting hereafter, Del-Coffey, like a submarine, slowly sank beneath the tightly packed crush of bodies again. Creosotes surged in from all directions, trying to locate their victim. I flicked the switch back to 'Full Auto', then I let those monsters have a long burst, which hurled bullets into faces, heads, arms, shoulders, chests, backs. At this short distance, each bullet punched through one body after another before the bullet's energy dissipated, and the metal slug then came to rest in a lung or heart or throat. The fact of the matter was, that each bullet I fired either killed or wounded three or four people.

White vapour formed dancing spectre shapes above the Creosotes I'd shot, as their hot blood gushed out to meet ice cold air.

The *chat-chat-chat* of the gun stung my ears again as I fired, hosing those killers with red hot slugs.

Of course, the Creosotes did not run away, or try and shield themselves from the bullets. Their blunted minds don't work like that. They merely surged back again, living bodies filling the vacuum left by those I'd killed or injured. I emptied the ammo magazine at more Creosotes surging forward to grab Del-Coffey. When the mag was empty, I unclipped it from the gun, flung it away, then I clicked in another one, which was full of those shining bringers of death.

After firing a short burst, to remove Creosotes that clung to the bottom rungs, I didn't even bother using the ladder and jumped down, landing on a soft mattress of dying flesh.

A fierce breeze tugged at my hair as I moved, blasting my enemy at point-blank range. The people in front of me, with their bright, glaring eyes, became objects. At that moment, they were not human to me. That's what I had to tell myself, because I fired into faces at such a short distance that it had a devastating effect on those heads that were full of blood and brain.

Tasmin was right, of course, I could not kill them all. There were thousands of Creosotes. Fortunately, there were so many they found it impossible to all attack at once, so only a relatively small number, a dozen or so at a time, confronted me. I moved over snow that turned from icy white to steaming crimson mush. My bullets were releasing blood by the bucket full. Figures toppled in front of me, some clawing violently at the bullet holes I'd put into their bodies. Soon, I didn't walk on snow. I walked on the dead.

A figure loomed from the chaos of arms, legs, torsos, snarling mouths. My finger curled around the trigger, ready to shoot.

Then I saw that the bloodstained forehead was an unusually high one. And the blue eyes were wide and scared.

'Del-Coffey!'

I grabbed hold of his arm. Then I dragged him hard...so hard he yelled with pain, but at least I'd got a firm grip on him. I could help him walk.

Despite his exhaustion, he managed to utter, 'Jack...thank God...'

'Del-Coffey, believe me, it's good to see you again.'

'Feeling's mutual, Jack,' he panted. 'I'm glad you came back for me.'

The return journey. Back over the gory dead. But the channel I'd opened up was now being filled by more Creosotes who clawed at each other in their furious lust to block our way. I fired the gun.

Rounds spat from the muzzle to smash the life out of individuals in front of me. An elderly man shrieked with a loud 'Eeeeee!' sound as the bullet ripped through a watery eye, and then erupted from the side of his skull in a spray of blood (however, by miraculous chance, not hitting his brain, not killing him, but it must have hurt so fucking much).

That's when the gun fell silent. No more bullets. And I couldn't reload because my other hand was busy hauling Del-Coffey after me.

With a scything motion, I slammed the gun into the side of the wounded man's head (the other side to where the bullet had emerged). He toppled to the ground where he still clawed at my legs. I simply stomped forward over him, bursting the flaccid sac of his bare belly, releasing blue snakes of intestine that were as slippery as they were wet.

Del-Coffey was on the brink of passing out. 'Leave me...leave me...'

'No way. Come on.'

I had to use the gun as if it was a machete to hack through a jungle of people. Though it had no cutting edge, as a machete blade would, I did succeed in inflicting gashes on faces. Hands clawed at me from the mob. I felt clumps of hair being ripped from my scalp – burning, hurting. Fingers gouged at my face, and I felt wetness trickle down from a split in the soft flesh of my nose where it met my left cheek.

My heart pounded. Massive gusts of air left my lungs in explosions of white vapour.

Then we were at the harvester. Tasmin leaned out through the cab's doorway. She began placing well-aimed shots from a revolver into the heads of Creosotes that lunged at me. That helped – believe me, that definitely helped.

I shoved Del-Coffey toward the rungs.

'Climb,' I yelled. 'Climb! I'll follow!'

Then he did the stupidest thing. He flung himself down onto the ground before crawling away, under the vehicle. Maybe this was a misguided attempt at both concealment and protection. Afterall, the Creosotes were bound to find him hiding under the machine soon enough.

'Del-Coffey!'

'I'm not leaving without Piper.'

So, I did the stupidest thing, too. I dropped down onto my knees.

The black and white Collie cowered under the harvester, his mouth part-open, revealing the soft flesh of his lips and mouth. His ears were flat, his head down – a posture of fear. His eyes were fixed on mine. He had the kind of look that mixed hope with dread. I sensed that he was terrified that I would abandon him.

When Piper was little more than a puppy, he wore that exact same expression when confronted by two fierce Pit Bull terriers that were intending to bite pieces out of him. I was nine years old. The sun shone in the park. Kids played on the swings and slide. Everything was happy and normal for them. And, in the corner of the football field, I ran to the dog I adored that was just about to be chewed to bloody shreds. Piper's ears were flat, his head down, his frightened eyes were fixed on me, rather than the two Pit Bulls. Those eyes of his...yep, scared, but hopeful that I'd save him. Of course, I ran over to him, then picked him up in my arms before those rage-filled Pit Bulls attacked. I carried Piper safely back home.

And, yes, the Pit Bulls vented their anger on me. I still have the scars on my legs. But they didn't hurt Piper.

As I crawled across churned-up slush, beneath that big machine, I knew I wouldn't leave Piper ever again. Even if it meant me getting more than scars on my legs this time.

I beckoned Piper. 'Here, boy.'

A flash of black and white fur and he was there, pressed up against my left side, as I lay belly down on the ground. Del-Coffey lay at the other side of me. Above our bodies was the grubby steelwork of the harvester's underbelly. While just beyond the edges of the vehicle, there were dozens of feet, tramping, shuffling, sliding through bloody snow – the Creosotes were making sure they tightly surrounded the harvester before they attacked.

I had three mags left full of bullets. Ninety in all.

Oh...how briefly they lasted. I emptied one mag after another into the forest of legs. As bullets slammed into shins and knees, dozens of Creosotes fell to the ground to flop about there like wounded seals. A few tried to crawl under the harvester to kill us. My gun spoke in my hands. They died in a heartbeat.

Then all the ammo was gone.

I glanced across at where Del-Coffey lay.

'I'm sorry,' I told him. 'We're out of bullets. We're going to have get into the cab before they overwhelm us.'

'Jack...I'm knackered. I can hardly move.'

'We'll do it,' I told him. 'You. Piper. Me. We will, you know.'

I wanted those words to give him hope, even though there was no hope. We'd never make that climb up the rungs to the cab. There were simply too many of those killers out there. I put my arm around Piper as I lay there and hugged his furry body. I could feel the beat of his heart through my fingertips. His pink tongue flickered out as he licked my face. To me, it felt like a kiss of absolute love. Yeah, I'm sentimental as anything, I know I am.

'Okay.' I took a deep breath. 'On the count of three, we crawl that way.' I pointed where the bottommost rung would be when we emerged from beneath the vehicle.

'"Into the valley of Death rode the six hundred."' Del-Coffey seemed to be quoting a line of poetry, rather than describing our decidedly hopeless situation. 'Yeah, pompous to the end, aren't I? Reciting a poem by Tennyson.' He gave a bleak smile. 'Indeed, Jack. On the count of three.'

I patted him on the shoulder. Then I said, 'One...two...'

I stopped counting, because that's when I heard the note of high-revving motors reaching us on the cold air. Motors? Who the hell was driving toward us? The din of motors quickly faded, before vanishing entirely. Had I imagined those engine sounds? Not that I had time to think about it. There were more brutal problems to deal with.

By now, ten or more Creosotes were on the ground, squirming toward us beneath the harvester. No way could we hide there any longer – not now that we had savage guests.

I took a deep breath. 'Three! Go! Go!'

Del-Coffey crawled across the ground. The way his eyes were huge and ablaze with terror told me that he was as frantic as a rat in a burning shed – hunting for escape and knowing that escape was as unlikely as being rescued by a UFO from fucking Mars. The Creosotes crawled under the steel guts of the harvester toward us. Del-Coffey's mind must have screamed to him that those crazies wanted to crack his bones and crush his skull to shit, because he froze in horror.

Del-Coffey still had the rifle, but there was little point in him firing off five single rounds (that's all the hunting rifle contained in its in-built magazine), because there were now at least a dozen Creosotes ramming their half-naked bodies through the gap between the ground and the harvester's underside. Yes, I had a couple of pistols in my pockets but no spare hands to start firing them, because I had my arm around Piper. I was pulling him toward the area where I'd find the rungs that would take us up to the cab. I also had to haul Del-Coffey by his collar – the guy was still downright feeble. And then...

Dear God. And then...

And then...damn it, no...the cramps started in my neck, arms, legs. Red-hot blades of steel being driven into my body: that's what the spasms felt like as paralysis returned.

'Not now,' I grunted, going frantic with the injustice of it all. 'Not now...my legs are cramping. Shit!'

Piper twisted his head, so we were nose-to-nose, eye-to-eye. Of course, I don't know what he was thinking. Who knows what really goes on in a dog's mind? But I really believed he was telling me, *You can do this, Jack. You can save us.*

With a howl of such power the sound even hurt my own ears, I dragged every atom of strength from where a residue of physical energy still lurked within the depths of my bones. That howl might also have been some instinctive call to my ancestors' spirits – for them to fly from their tombs and gather up their still alive descendent in their spectral arms and carry him to safety.

Maybe some magic of sorts did work. The dredging out of the last reserves of strength, or the helping ghost hands of long-departed ancestors. Whatever sorcery I managed to release that night, I succeed in dragging both Piper and Martin Del-Coffey out from under the harvester. Already fingers grasped at my feet, fingernails clawed at my legs. Piper opened his tooth-filled mouth – there was a white flash of incisors – and he bit into a hand that grabbed me by the throat – the dog bit deep and bit hard. The hand jerked away from my windpipe.

Then we were outside in the open. Floodlights cast a fierce glow of white on the snow and on the Creosotes and on the farm's outbuildings. The lights were so bright they even lit the underside of the clouds above us, like the clouds themselves had begun to burn with a silver flame.

I shoved Del-Coffey up onto the rungs. Above me, Tasmin leaned out of the cab.

Suddenly, engines screamed again. High-revving motors, driven to the limit of what they could achieve. Someone was intent on driving their machines beyond the edge of what was possible.

Though everything happened in a rush, with lots of events occurring in a blazing spate of thirty violent seconds, some mechanism in my brain slowed down the mad chaos of activity, until I saw many simultaneous events individually, and with a clarity that was nothing less than terrifying. Imagine standing on the trapdoor of the gallows, a noose around your neck, and seeing in slow-motion the executioner pull the lever, and the hatch swinging downward beneath your feet. You stare into the deep, dreary gloom of the void below into which you will lethally fall...yet you float, weightless, the noose still slack around your neck, the rope still to snap tight, then...and only then, do you begin that long, slow fall down toward your death...

Right at that moment, this fight for my life was like that. The world around me slowed down. Each event took an abundance of time to unfold. Above me was the pale form of an owl flying through the night sky, its cream-coloured wings lit by powerful floodlights that were fed electricity from the wind-turbine, which rose above the building at the far side of the yard.

Snowmobiles...

In the distance, six foxes sat on a hill, white snow behind their reddish coats of fur. Their bright eyes were fixed on the absolute shitstorm of events taking place at this farm in the middle of nowhere.

Three snowmobiles...

Creosotes fighting each other to be the first one to drag me off the rungs.

Tasmin leaning out: black hair, a banner that fluttered in the breeze.

Three snowmobiles getting closer. Me, doing the impossible... me, with a wolf-sized Border Collie under one arm...the other arm bent at the elbow, so my forearm formed a living seat under Del-Coffey's backside. I was using that living seat to push Del-Coffey up toward the cab where Tasmin leaned out, a pistol in one hand, the other hand reaching out, ready to hoist Del-Coffey aboard.

Three snowmobiles...weaving, turning, spitting fountains of white into the air, as the machines tried to chivvy Creosotes away from the harvester. Three people on snowmobiles, attempting to herd their flock of monsters into the fields – just as Piper's canine ancestors once herded flocks of sheep from farmyards to meadows.

'Try and climb,' I shouted to Del-Coffey. 'Put your feet on the fucking rungs...and fucking well climb!'

Tasmin leaned forwards, her top half clear of the cab. Her hand reached down, her fingertips almost touching Del-Coffey's fingertips, straining to catch hold of him, so she could pull him up to the cab – then we could drive out of here. The harvester's motor throbbed. I smelt exhaust fumes.

The snowmobiles pushed forward, forcing the Creosotes to step aside – though not all did, some fell beneath the skids and were crushed.

A muscular guy clambered up the back of the harvester. Within seconds, he was crawling over its steel body toward Tasmin.

'Look out,' I shouted. 'Behind you.'

Tasmin's hand whipped up, her arm straight out, perfectly horizontal. Her pistol blasted out smoke and sparks. The attacker, gripping his throat at the point where the bullet penetrated flesh, stood upright on the harvester's rear deck. And then the guy dropped sideways to splat down onto the heads of his own kind. Five or six of the attackers were knocked to the ground by the deadweight falling ten feet or so onto them.

The snowmobiles edged closer, pushing the Creosote mob, dividing the densely packed crowd into segments. Creosotes turned to watch the snowmobiles that roared with such an ear-shredding noise.

A hand gripped my thigh. Even though my muscles cramped painfully I succeeded in using my knee to break the guy's nose as he tried to climb up over me. He lost his grip on the rungs and slipped downward.

Myra.

I stared at the woman who piloted one of the snowmobiles, her thighs clamping hard onto the flanks of the machine, her hands gripping the handlebars, guiding the machine as it skimmed across the terrain.

'Del-Coffey!' This yell came from Tasmin. 'Grab my hand!'

All the events – the flight of the owl, the arrival of snowmobiles, the movement of a hundred thousand men and women – all that had been, for me, in slow-motion. Now, however, everything speeded up. And speeded up by a million miles an hour. The speed of lightning flashes.

Tasmin grabbing Del-Coffey.

Whoosh, he vanished into the cab.

Snowmobiles moving closer to the harvester. Pushing Crazies back. Stopping them attacking us.

Disaster erupted – triggering yet another tidal wave of chaos.

The Creosote-Plus Types, riding the snowmobiles, had once controlled the original Creosotes of old, but now the Creosotes turned on their controllers. Men and women surged over the snowmobiles. Fists swung through the air. The mouths of that unholy legion were yawning wide, ready to bite what had, essentially, been their own kind, albeit a much saner version. The old model of Creosote was destroying its leaders.

My limbs were stiffening as paralysis took control of me. Nevertheless, after sucking in a huge lungful of cold air, I scrambled up the rungs to the cabin. There I stood on the ledge, guarding the entrance to that flimsy glass box, where passengers and driver rode. Tasmin slid back over to the driver's seat, behind the wheel. Somehow, Del-Coffey managed to get himself into the back. There were no seats, but there was a generous space for storage. Piper sprang from my right arm into the passenger seat and, without being instructed to do so by me, squeezed between the two seatbacks to join Del-Coffey. The guy joyfully put both arms around my dog and hugged him.

I stood there. I was tightly gripping the frame of the cab to make sure I didn't topple into the vortex of madness below where Creosotes went berserk – attacking their former leaders, ripping bloody chunks from them, daubing their own faces with their victims' blood. The entire mass of bodies steamed like a hot bath. I could smell their pungent sweat. An odour mingled with the stench of decaying flesh, as necrosis and frostbite rotted away toes and fingers. Okay, they were dying – yet for the time being, their sheer numbers and their sheer hatred for us, still made them deadly.

Del-Coffey leaned forward over the backseats to grab Tasmin by the shoulder and shake her hard. 'Drive...get us out of here! Drive this fucker!'

Tasmin engaged reverse, pumped diesel into the motor – its pistons clattered as the mighty green beast roared and began to shudder as its four massive tyres slowly turned.

I looked back into the mob. A figure suddenly burst upwards. It was head and shoulders above that whirlpool of murderous rage.

'Myra!' I shouted her name in surprise.

By a miracle of sheer willpower, Myra ploughed through the mob toward me. Hands clutched at that mass of copper hair of hers, pulling out fiery red clumps. Still Myra breasted her way through the mob – the same way a strong person pushes through rolling surf, when heading away from the beach into a turbulent ocean. Creosotes clung to her. I saw arms wrap around her neck. Hands grabbed at the bright red survival suit she wore and gripped tight.

And those green eyes of hers were fixed on my face. Green eyes that blazed with an absolute desire to live. For a moment, I stood there, not moving, but this wasn't fever paralysis, this was me having the air knocked from my lungs by the power in those eyes – like nuclear fire they were. Simply amazing to see.

I turned around and thrust my head into the cab. 'Tasmin! Stop!'

'What's wrong?'

'Myra's out there.'

'Damn it, Jack. She's a Creosote!'

'Yeah,' shouted Del-Coffey. His eyes were massive in his head – blue lagoons of terror. 'Leave her. She wanted to hand us over to the mob.'

'No!' I banged the side window with my fist. 'Tasmin, stop. We're taking Myra with us.'

Del-Coffey howled like he was in pain. 'She'll slaughter us!'

'No, she won't!'

'She will!'

I shook my head. 'Don't you see? She is the key to our survival. Not just for tonight, but for the future. For all time. We need her!'

Quickly, I pulled a handgun from my pocket, then scrambled halfway down the rungs. From there I could see Myra, still struggling through the Death Legion. The woman had slowed down. Exhaustion robbed her of the ability to keep moving forward.

'Carefully aimed shots,' I murmured to myself.

Then I started picking off the Creosotes nearest to her, and those blocking her way. A bullet smacked into the back of a bald man's head. Down he went. Then I targeted a woman of around thirty. The bullet punched through a perfectly shaped nose, gelling her brains. With every Creosote I brought down, the obstacle between Myra and the harvester was being removed.

A massive guy tried to wrestle Myra to the ground. I slammed a bullet through the top of his skull, flipping out a handful of brain. As he tumbled downward, Myra broke free.

It took Myra just five seconds to reach our vehicle. Ten seconds after that, she was sitting in the back with Del-Coffey and Piper. Piper eyed her with deep suspicion.

'Okay, Tasmin,' I panted. 'Work your magic.'

Tasmin clunked the gear lever into reverse.

Behind me, Myra gazed into the back of my head (I could see her in the rear-view mirror). She was cold again...emotionally separated from the eruption of danger and slaughter of just moments ago. And, no, she did not say, 'thank you for saving my life'.

She said nothing.

CHAPTER THIRTY-SIX

UNLEASH THE BEAST

The harvester was a magnificent steel beast, indeed. One that possessed four massive tyres that were almost as tall as me – and it had a powerful engine that thundered like the God of War. That thunder grew even louder as Tasmin reversed away from the farmhouse, and back across the yard.

I remained in the doorway of the cab, riding ten feet above the ground – that cold, hard ground over which men and women swarmed. The Creosotes didn't want us to leave. They lusted for bloody murder. And they were not inclined to let their mission slip away through their frostbitten fingers.

Myra sat in the storage area of the cabin, her green eyes bright and intelligent – and oh-so knowing. Had she planned this all along? Had the woman's intention been to join us? But for what purpose? Did she have a secret agenda? The woman did not move and said nothing. Piper sat between Myra and Martin Del-Coffey. The dog appeared calm, taking this new adventure in his stride.

Above us, the night sky began to reveal a silvery array of stars. A meteor cut a steel-bright line across the sky before guttering out to mere sparks.

As Tasmin reversed the machine across the yard, Creosotes ran behind the vehicle. There they raised their arms, clearly intending to use their own strength to prevent it moving any further. How wrong they were in their hopes. The vehicle simply reversed over them, where they vanished under the chassis – such was the weight of the vehicle, I never felt so much as the faintest of judders as wheels rolled over living, yet soon-to-be-dead, bodies.

I reached into the back of the storage area to grab fresh mags for the machine gun. Cramps in my limbs and in my back still drove jabs of pain through the muscle there, but the paralysis never came. Maybe the sickness that had recently blighted my life was leaving me.

Creosotes began to climb onto the vehicle. Thumbing the gun's fire selector switch to single shot mode, I began to pick off individuals as they clambered onboard. As for those that climbed the rungs toward me, I simply kicked them when they were high enough. These Creosotes fell back onto their own kind. By now, I had become coolly detached from the violence that I dealt out to those people, who were once sane and compassionate members of society. But their minds had been mutilated by whatever befell them three years ago. To all intents and purposes, they were dead. Their bodies were husks that housed brutal instincts and stunted intelligence. I would not even describe Creosotes as being reduced to the level of an animal. They were like bacteria. They had no personality. No memories of what they once were (that is what I believed). So, I killed without guilt.

Del-Coffey grabbed a pistol and shuffled sideways behind the passenger seat, until he could lean out and help me with my slaughter chores. Using the snub-nosed .38, he swatted down Creosote after Creosote.

Tasmin sang out as she engaged first gear: 'Hang on! I'm going forward now! Let's see how fast this beauty will go!'

The powerful motor roared as she hit the gas. The harvester surged forwards across the yard. Acceleration was hardly fierce. I'd be lying if I stated that the G-force slung me backward. Nevertheless, our vehicle gradually accelerated to the point where Creosotes behind the vehicle couldn't run fast enough to catch up with us. A few on our flanks still tried to clamber on board, but such was even our modest trundle across the yard that those grasping hands failed to grip the metalwork properly. Either our vehicle slipped through their grasp, or it yanked them off their feet, where they bellyflopped in thick snow, some of them rolling under the massive tyres where they were mashed down into fatal oblivion.

Eventually, I gauged it safe enough to stop firing at the Creosotes (thus sparing precious and scarce ammo). I swung myself into that big glasshouse of a cab and took my seat beside Tasmin.

'How're we doing?' I asked.

'Fifteen miles an hour.' She flashed me a beautiful grin that was huge and showed lots of shining teeth – believe me, that grin almost sang a hymn of joy that we were leaving. 'And our fuel tank is three quarter's full.'

'Hallelujah.' This was Del-Coffey singing out from the back.

Fortunately, most of mine and Del-Coffey's wounds, which were inflicted upon us when we fought our way through the mob, were very minor. Snowmelt washed away most of the blood from our faces; the rest was easily dealt with by wiping our skin with tissues from a carton that had been left in the front of the cab by the farmer long ago.

Myra continued to stare at the back of my head. Her eyes were full of uncanny wisdom and understanding. Yes, she knew all about the secrets within her own heart, and her motives for joining us, and I had a powerful suspicion she would not candidly reveal what she intended to do in the future. Maybe I shouldn't have brought her with us? Would it have been safer for me and my friends to leave her behind?

But...

And the huge **BUT** was that I knew, deep down at some visceral level, that this redhaired Creosote Plus-Type was important to us. Vital. Of absolute value. But what was my instinct telling me? Why was she important? Right at that moment, I did not know.

I reached back to stroke the soft fur on Piper's head. For a moment, I just enjoyed that heart-pounding sense of relief which gushed through me. We had cheated death. We were safe in this cab – we were high about the ground, the door locked shut. Warm air from the heater embraced me, and it felt just so utterly wonderful. I leaned forward, looking out through the glass at the white ocean of snow that covered the fields. A fence to our left and another fence to our right indicated the line of the road in front of us, even though the actual tarmac had been buried under all that white stuff. Figures clumsily scrambled over the fences before lurching into the road in front of us. These were Creosotes trying to block our way. The harvester rumbled over them. They could have been nothing more than life-size cardboard cut-outs, with no meaningful substance to them at all.

'We're losing the glow from the yard's floodlights.' I spoke those words to Tasmin as darkness closed in ahead of us.

'Gotcha,' she replied. She twitched a stalk that branched out from the steering column. The headlights now switched to full beam, blazing out from the front of the vehicle. 'Light, beautiful light, is going to guide us home.'

Again, she flashed me that triumphant grin. However, her expression quickly turned to one of shock. The fences had ended and were replaced by a pair of parallel walls that flanked the road. This is where the Creosotes had clumped together in their hundreds, maybe even thousands.

Tasmin braked.

Del-Coffey leaned forward, staring thorough the glass. 'We'll never get through that lot. They're so tightly packed, they'll stop the harvester.'

Myra spoke in a cold, distant voice – as if she was observing what happened here from a faraway world: 'Then they will climb onto the vehicle...break its windows...and kill you all.'

Del-Coffey rounded on her, shouting with such violence that flecks of white shot from his lips. 'Shut up!' He aimed his pistol at her face. 'This bitch planned it! She's tricked us! She ordered those monsters to pack the road here, so we'd be forced to stop. And now we're trapped!'

Del-Coffey stabbed the gun muzzle against her forehead, held it there – his finger was tightening on the trigger.

'Del-Coffey.' I grabbed his wrist and forced his hand upward until the revolver pointed at the cab's ceiling. 'Stop. Del-Coffey... hey, stop. Don't make me have to thump you.'

'Jack, she planned this. Now those shit-brains out there will slaughter us.'

'No.' I spoke calmly. 'Myra did not plan this. I will not let you kill her.'

Tasmin shot me a worried look. 'Okay, we won't kill your...your new friend. But it's safer for us if we kick her out of the cab.'

I shook my head. 'The Creosotes will rip her apart. They don't identify her as one of their own now. She's become their enemy, too.' I looked Myra in the eye. 'Isn't that right?'

The woman gave a single nod. 'For a while, I could control them. That control has been lost to me now. If you make me leave this machine, they will kill me.'

'Okay,' I said. 'That means we're all going to get out of here in one piece.'

'Then what do you suggest?' Del-Coffey, for once, sounded menacing. 'What great fucking plan do you have, Jack? Because if you don't have a plan, we die. Piper dies.'

For a moment, we all sat there without speaking. The motor was softly throbbing in the heart of this mighty contraption. Stars conjured glints of silver across meadows of undulating white. Then it happened...the Creosotes began to move. They were tightly packed into a dense crowd in the roadway. And because they were hemmed in between the two walls they had become concentrated into a hard piston of flesh and bone.

Tasmin laid her hand upon my forearm, a tender gesture. My skin tingled at her touch.

'Well, Jack? What do we do now?'

Del-Coffey's voice oozed bitterness. 'You can't shoot your way out. There are thousands of the fuckers.'

I gazed at those faces in the headlights. Faces with ferocious stares, and blazing eyes – all framed by shaggy manes of hair. The figures were human in shape. They had beating hearts. Yet they did not have human souls anymore: that is what I believed. They were meat and bone and blood. And that is all.

At last, I licked my dry-as-grave-dust lips, and then asked in a voice that was little more than a whisper, 'Tasmin. How do you switch on the harvester's blades?'

Her sharp eyes darted as she studied the levers and switches in front of her. She took a deep breath. 'This lowers the blades to cutting height.' She pulled a lever.

A loud clunking was followed by the stuttering screech of a

mechanism that had remained dormant for a long time – then more clunks. A green light on the dashboard came on, suggesting that the blades had repositioned to the optimum cutting height.

Tasmin's finger hovered over a large switch on the dashboard. 'And this is what sets the blades turning.'

Because we were stationary on the road, Creosotes began to climb up onto the harvester.

'Okay.' I nodded at Tasmin. 'Fire the blades up.'

She pulled the switch down. A hum started in a low bass register before the note rose higher and higher as that long cylinder of blades, which was as broad as the vehicle was wide, began to revolve. Faster...faster...the entire vehicle started to vibrate as the drive-chain spun the blades.

Quickly, I pushed open the door, before blasting the trespassers on our vehicle with the submachine gun. Meanwhile, Tasmin engaged first gear, gunned the engine, then released the clutch, and we moved smoothly, and slowly, forward.

Del-Coffey howled with devilish pleasure. 'The Grim Reaper! This is what I call a harvest!'

Tasmin nailed the speed down to five miles per hour. Perhaps she was being cautious because she did not know what the effect on the vehicle's performance would be when its furiously spinning blades began cutting down those sad relics of human life. Our headlights caught hundreds of eyes in their dazzling beams – those eyes were glinting like bright diamonds in gaunt faces. Even though hundreds of men and women were pressed tightly together, that mass of flesh did not even slow the harvester. And, all the while, the blades rotated at high speed. The people in front of us were simply dragged down by the blades and chopped into tiny – very tiny – bloody pieces.

Del-Coffey was instantly on his feet in the rear storage area. He leaned over my seatback, his stomach pushing my head forward, as he excitedly watched the destruction of our enemy. A bloody and total destruction, at that. He was shouting and gleefully thumping me on the shoulder, and then doing the same to Tasmin.

'I knew you'd think of something, Jack!' That was Del-Coffey's surprising statement, considering he was saying pretty much the opposite just five minutes ago.

Del-Coffey turned around to look out through the back window of the cab. He could have been an over-excited kid in a car on the way to the seaside.

'My God,' he yelled. 'Just look at that! The bailer's working. Look! The harvester's discharging body parts out the back. It is actually pooping out arms and legs and heads. Shit! All that blood. All that fucking blood!' He ran his fingers through his hair; his eyes were bulging with amazement. The man was high on a combination

161

of exhilaration at the bloody violence and the fever raging in his body. 'Look! We're leaving a red stripe behind us in the snow! A juicy, fat red stripe!'

Myra did not share Del-Coffey's excitement. She sat there without moving so much as a finger. She did sigh, however, and then spoke in that oddly stilted way of hers: 'You exult because you are murdering all those men and women who, through no fault of their own, have had their mental function damaged.'

Tasmin glanced back over her shoulder as she harvested lives by the hundred. 'Myra, they would have slaughtered us if we hadn't done this to them.'

Del-Coffey agreed: 'They're savage. They are nothing more than murderous beasts!'

Myra responded in gentle tones. 'No, sir... think of them as frightened children. That is what they are like. Children who fear you.'

'What?' Del-Coffey shook his head in amazement. 'Frightened children? Is that how you see that...that Hell-brood?'

Yep, 'Hell-brood'...you can always rely on Mr Martin Del-Coffey for a vivid phrase to paint mind pictures inside your head.

Myra continued in that soft murmur of hers: 'Yes. Frightened children. That is what they are like to me. I tried to protect them.' She regarded Del-Coffey with her cool gaze. 'I invested all the faith that remained in my heart into believing that you, sir, could help them regain their humanity. Their dignity...' Her eyes glistened with tears. 'And regain their minds, so that they understood who they are again, and to remember who they loved.'

All this, while the machine rumbled forward, claiming all those souls...carving life away from living bodies and leaving only an ever-growing number of bloody dead – more accurately, bloody dead in tiny pieces, at that. If you believe in such things, our big green monster was a ghost maker. A maker of hundreds and hundreds of ghosts.

Ahead of us, Creosotes still crowded the road. Myra wept in silence. All those people, who she had conscientiously gathered and brought to this place to save, would either lose their lives quickly to the blade, or they would slowly die in the remorseless cold. The woman had gambled on Martin Del-Coffey saving her people. She had gambled everything – now she had lost everything.

Piper squirmed his furry body through the gap between the front seats until he could rest his chin on my thigh. Tasmin leaned forward. Both her hands were gripping the wheel, while she focussed on the route ahead. Ahead, in the distance, the hills gleamed coldly. They were ghostly shapes against the night sky.

We did not speak. Only the sound of the engine reached us now. I did not hear any of those men and women being taken by the blades cry out. Not a single one.

162

CHAPTER THIRTY-SEVEN

ANOTHER KIND OF REUNION

At that moment, how did I feel? What was my reaction to this entire sequence of events? It begins, I suppose, way back, all those many days ago, with my return to New Home to find my friends crippled with the virus and them crawling through the snow. Then the Creosotes attacked. After that, the escape to Sugar Island. In turn, that lead to travelling to the farmhouse and me being sick with fever myself. Then thousands and thousands of Creosotes had surrounded the place. Powerful memories surged through my brain, making me tremble. Memories of leaving Piper and Del-Coffey in the farmhouse. That dangerous trip across the yard with Tasmin, through a flesh and bone barrier of thousands of men and women who would, if they'd got the chance, torn us apart. And that marvellous moment when I fired up all those lights, powered by the wind-turbine. Tasmin had then managed to start the combine harvester. Following that, the drive from the shed to the farmhouse – all of it seemed sort of surreal now. A strange dream journey with Tasmin by my side.

Now, here we were. Tasmin driving. I was in the passenger seat. Del-Coffey and Myra sitting in the back. Piper still squeezed himself between the two seats so he could rest his chin on my leg, finding comfort in our close physical contact. Me, stroking the soft fur on top of his head, his pink tongue every now and then popping out to lick the bare skin of my hand. Piper was at ease now. The dog's serenity touched us all. Nobody spoke. After all that tension, all that drama, our bodies gradually sagged into a state of relaxation, even contentment. The trembling sensation soon vanished from my body. We'd fought the battle and we had won. Now we were leaving the scene of all that bloodshed. We were heading along a country road, which was covered with a smooth blanket of snow that, in the headlights, shone like glory.

Ever since we had left the vast swathe of Creosotes behind, there was no enemy to disturb the atmosphere of serenity as we sat in the glass cab, comfortably wrapped up in streams of warm air that came from the heater. Tasmin had switched off the cutting blades and raised them clear of the ground – she no longer needed them to cut a channel through a wall of flesh. The Creosotes were in poor physical shape. Even their murderous rage couldn't fuel their limbs sufficiently for them to run after us. Though the harvester's fifteen miles per hour was less than impressive, our speed was enough for us to outrun our enemy. Finally, we had left them behind to embrace their own slow death in the brutal chill of winter.

When I glanced back over my shoulder, I saw Myra and Del-Coffey sitting on the floor of the storage area. Del-Coffey's head was nodding as he dozed. Myra's eyes had a watching-and-waiting quality as she looked me in the eye.

What does she want from me? It's like she's expecting me to give her the answer to a question she hasn't even asked. What does she want me to say to her?

I broke eye-contact, because I wanted to look back the way we came. To make sure that we weren't being followed. However, all I could see were our tyre tracks, cutting two dark lines in the snow-covered road, which ran back toward the distant farmhouse. The yard and buildings were still illuminated by the fiercely bright floodlights. Snow on the ground reflected the lights upwards, so something like a dome of radiance formed a spectral shape over, and enclosing, the farmhouse. Without a scrap of doubt, those lights were the brightest things for miles and miles. I even imagined that the pool of brilliance would be visible from space.

The harvester continued to efficiently trundle along – its massive wheels, and weight of many tons, meant that snowdrifts proved to be no obstacle to our slow but relentless progress. Our vehicle devoured mile after mile of road. The cab was so pleasantly warm – the air possessed a sweetness all of its own, a kind of agreeable soap scent – perhaps that was imagination. Even so, I felt completely at ease sitting beside Tasmin.

I had begun to fall asleep. Piper was dozing with his head on my lap. At that moment, Tasmin braked hard enough to bring me back fully awake.

'Okay.' Tasmin spoke in a way that meant business. 'Jack. What are we going to do with her?' She turned her head, stabbing her gaze in the direction of Myra. 'Tell me why that woman is so important to you. And why, exactly, you had to bring her with you.'

Ahead of us was the white smoothness of the road. It formed a path of magic and hope, leading away from the carnage of the last few hours and toward the start of new days, new lives. Stars burned in the sky – diamonds embedded in all that cold darkness of a universe that did not care whether we lived or died. No. It's up to us to decide what our lives should be. We are the only ones who can make our time on Earth happy and worthwhile and meaningful. We should be the ones who decide the route our lives will take.

I glanced back at Myra and Del-Coffey. Del-Coffey was wide awake now – he clearly wanted to hear my response to Tasmin's question. As did Myra, no doubt. I turned back to meet Tasmin's steady gaze. Her dark eyes were magnetic. Drawing my focus toward her.

I spoke with absolute certainty: 'We need Myra.'

Tasmin's eyes narrowed, her mind processing those three words of mine. 'Jack. Do we need Myra? Or do you need Myra?'

Tasmin glanced at the woman, who sat absolutely still, saying nothing, but watching us with one hundred percent of her attention.

I repeated my statement. 'We need Myra.'

Del-Coffey's mighty forehead wrinkled as his eyes narrowed in such a way that let me know all too clearly that he was suspicious of what I'd just said. 'Why, Jack? Why is this woman important to us? She might be waiting for the opportunity to kill us all.'

I glanced back at her. 'You won't hurt us, will you, Myra?'

Her gaze fixed on my face. Those eyes were knowing. She had formulated her own complex plans inside her head. Her expression told me that she'd done exactly that.

When Myra answered me, her voice was quite gentle. Almost a purr. 'No. I won't harm you. But you must tell Tasmin and Del-Coffey what you are going to do with me.'

'Oh.' Tasmin's 'oh' suggested that she had interpreted Myra's statement in accordance with her own suspicions.

Piper shivered. He had picked up on the rising tension within the cab.

'Del-Coffey,' I began, 'you wanted to study the Creosote-Plus Types – the ones you'd locked in the cage, the ones that were half-sane.'

He shook his head with a great deal of bitterness. 'I was wrong about them. Okay? Yes, they were saner than the regular Creosotes, but I couldn't learn anything from them.'

'But here is your chance now,' I told him. 'Back on Day One, Myra lost her mind. She became as crazy and as murderous as the other adults, but something happened to her in the last few weeks. Look at her, Del-Coffey. You, too, Tasmin. Myra has almost recovered. She is virtually normal. Heck, she might have undergone some kind of psychological evolution and has now achieved a state of higher mental function. Maybe, at times, her behaviour appears bizarre. But what if her mind works better than ours do?'

Del-Coffey's face was grave. 'Myra could be just some aberration. A freak Creosote that appears to have recovered her sanity. You can't know anything about her true mental state.'

'You are exactly right, Del-Coffey. I don't know if Myra is

165

becoming a human being again. That's where you come in. Spend time with this woman. Become her friend. Discover how her mind works. I believe in you.'

Del-Coffey became thoughtful. 'Yes, I can study her...with your consent, Myra?'

Myra nodded. 'You have my consent, sir. All I ask is that I am not caged.'

'No, we won't put you in a cage. This is where we learn to trust each other.' I looked at Del-Coffey. I could tell he was becoming interested in this new challenge to his intellect. 'Del-Coffey, you can do this. I know you can.'

That's when Tasmin sighed. 'With reservations, I agree that we should at least try what you're suggesting, Jack. What we learn from Myra could save our lives. After all, if Myra has come out of that...that mind-storm. And she feels empathy again, and regains control of her thoughts, and can act like a human being that cares about other people, then there's every chance other Creosotes out there are undergoing the same change.'

Del-Coffey grabbed the baton of ideas and ran with it. 'Which means young people, who survived the apocalypse, will no longer fear those individuals who were once their enemy. We can rebuild civilization.'

'Amen to that,' I said with a hefty portion of feeling.

Myra did not smile. Yet I sensed that emotional ice wall between her and the three of us had started to melt.

Myra said: 'If you trust me, I will trust you. And that includes trusting you to protect me from your own people. Because they will hate me. They will want to kill me.'

'I promise to keep you safe.' I held out my hand for her to shake.

Myra inhaled deeply – then, gravely, she shook my hand, then she shook Del-Coffey's and, last of all, Tasmin's.

'Okay,' Myra said. 'Here comes your first opportunity to protect me.'

Myra looked forwards over my shoulder, out through the windscreen. I turned around to see a light approaching us along the road.

Tasmin narrowed her eyes as she stared out through the glass. 'Trucks,' she breathed. 'Those are trucks.'

Within seconds, we had opened the doors of the cab. As we climbed out, the sound of powerful motors reached us. By the time we'd reached the ground, the trucks were thirty paces away. There they stopped, and figures clad in Arctic survival gear began pouring from the vehicles.

A tall figure lurched through the snow toward us.

'Gorron,' I said in amazement. 'That's Gorron.'

My friend charged across to me, grabbed me in a fierce bearhug of absolute affection, and then started thumping me on the back.

His face was radiating sheer delight. 'Jack, we saw your floodlights! How did you make 'em work? Oh, what the heck, it doesn't matter how. But, my God, we could see the lights from ten miles away.'

I noticed that Myra had raised the hood of her jacket over her head. Not just to keep the cold out, either. Clearly, she was nervous of being identified as being above that certain age, which would reveal she was a Creosote. Something that would invite a salvo of bullets in her direction.

Tasmin quickly put her arm around Myra, which was a touching gesture of both reassurance and shielding her, should the newcomers identify her as Creosote.

Gorron still enthusiastically pounded me on the back with his massive fist. 'Hey, you found a dog. The Collie!'

'Yeah.' I smiled. 'I'll explain later.'

Gorron laughed with absolute happiness. 'Thank God, you're all safe. Hey, and you've found a new friend, too. The woman in the red suit.'

'I'll introduce you to Myra later. Like I said, I've a lot to explain.'

Gorron put his arm around my shoulders, so he could turn me to face more figures, which were walking toward us.

'Jack', he said, 'let me introduce you to my new friends. We found 'em up in the hills. They've got an entire settlement there. What an amazing place it is. Come and say "hello" to them.'

Del-Coffey pushed his hood back from his face as he stared in amazement at the people walking toward him. 'I don't believe it! That's Nick Aten! And there's Tug Slatter!'

The two men, who Del-Coffey had indicated, pushed back their hoods to reveal their faces.

Martin Del-Coffey began to laugh – a mixture of happiness and astonishment. 'Jack. That is the guy I told you about. Nick Aten. And that big brute is Tug Slatter.' He shot me a look, conveying a pile of meaning with his eyes, and murmured, 'Tug Slatter looks scary but don't let first impressions fool you. Tug Slatter is not scary...he is bloody terrifying. He is a monster. But the wonderful thing is...he is on our side.'

Del-Coffey ran forward to shake the hand of the man he'd identified as Nick Aten. They appeared to exchange warm greetings. Then Del-Coffey offered his hand to Tug Slatter. Tug Slatter did not shake Del-Coffey's hand – Slatter merely stared at him with eyes that could freeze fire.

Tasmin appeared at my side, where she watched Del-Coffey's reunion with his friends.

Then she turned to look at me. Her expression was as serious as I have ever seen it. 'Remember, Jack. The time has come to not just keep surviving.' She took my hand in hers. 'The time has come to start living.'

167

Above us, stars twinkled. I gazed up at their magnificence – at all those diamond-bright points of light – and it was as if I was seeing them in all their true glory for the first time. A star may live for ten billion years or more. We live for a hundred years or less. Though shouldn't our own lives shine just as bright? And shouldn't our love for those that we cherish shine brighter still?

I gently squeezed Tasmin's hand before lowering my face to hers, and we kissed.

That was the moment I caught sight of Myra's face beneath the cowl of her hood. Did I imagine what I just saw?

Was there a smile on Myra's lips? A sly and all-too knowing smile.

THE END

If you enjoyed BLOOD CRAZY BOOK TWO, you'll love the next in the series:

BOOK THREE: ATEN PRESENT

Nick Aten is back!

And this his story – in a world full of violence, danger, and sudden death.

Nick and his crew prepare to return to their settlement with Jack, Gorron and the others. But what happens next changes everything.

Nick finds himself on a ship with new friends – and with old enemies. To avoid being overrun by Creosotes, Nick cuts the mooring lines and the ship drifts downstream...Through a shattered land that is now the domain of human bones, and cities lying in ruin.

Nick searches for a car that still works, which will allow him to return to Sarah. When he explores a ghost town, he doesn't find the vehicle he needs, but he does find certain individuals who will force him to reassess his understanding of what the Creosotes are...and what transformation he might face in his own life.

Once again, murderous adults are getting closer. This time they just might be far more dangerous than he could have ever believed.

And not only are the adults dangerous. Not every young person is automatically an ally.

And, soon, it will be time to Carry the Can again. A game that is far from fun...and so often lethally explosive.

Here are the first three chapters to whet your appetite!

CHAPTER ONE

ONE HELL OF A REUNION
ONE HELL OF A DAY

My name is Nick Aten – yeah, Aten rhymes with Satan.

The day the world got much, much worse this happened...

Martin Del-Coffey trudged through the snow toward where I stood beside that big brute of a creature by the name of Tug Slatter. A cold wind was blowing – it felt like blades of ice cutting through our clothing to brutally dig into our flesh.

Del-Coffey brought his companions with him, the ones that had been riding on the blood-spattered combine harvester. This was a veritable monster of a machine, with a rotating blade arrangement on the front, which they used to harvest corn with in the old days, back before civilization died such a violent death – when everyone *over* the age of nineteen became murderous and attacked everyone *under* the age of nineteen.

Del-Coffey's gang comprised a couple of guys, two women, and a Border Collie that had to constantly jump as it moved, in order to free itself from the deep snow that came right up to the top of its legs and was no doubt icily scraping the poor mutt's undercarriage. Behind me, the members of my own band of survivors, numbering twenty-five in all, watched as the group approached. My people viewed the newcomers with a meaty portion of suspicion. Bitter experience taught us to be on our guard when we met anyone new. Because, so often, strangers who told us they wanted to be our friends sometimes turned out to be nothing more a bunch of murderous cutthroats that aimed to steal our guns and vehicles. You see, we were now at a universally wretched point, following the collapse of civilization, where working vehicles, fuel, ammunition, and food were in short supply. It had become a common occurrence that colonies of survivors would simply run out of food, then they'd starve. And, it's a fact, hunger is the engine that drives ordinary men and women to murder their fellow survivors for a mouthful of bread.

The people that plodded alongside Del-Coffey through the snow didn't carry guns (thank goodness for that) but (and there's always a 'but') they had the hoods of their Arctic survival suits and coats pulled up against the freezing blast of air. It's the little things, like a partially concealed face, that makes you wonder what else they're hiding – a pistol in a pocket? A grenade up a sleeve? A switchblade tucked in a boot?

Behind me, my own people moved slightly. It was a kind of bristling sensation, as they altered their stance, slightly raising their weapons, ready to fire, in case this was an ambush.

Del-Coffey held out his hands at either side as he approached, a clear gesture that he was being non-threatening. Then we all know that Martin Del-Coffey is the least threatening guy in the world, don't we? But his new friends? We couldn't be certain about them. Even though Del-Coffey had just trotted through the white stuff a few minutes ago to reassure us that his travelling companions were good guys how could we be certain? How could we be sure that they hadn't forced him to say exactly that? Afterall, they might have promised him a fuck-awful death if he didn't go along with their scheme to slaughter us.

Martin Del-Coffey's breath splurged from his mouth in huge gusts of vapour as he pulled down his hood so everyone could clearly see his face. 'Yes, it's me again. Del-Coffey. You all know me. Allow me to introduce you to these fine people. Next to me is Jack. That's Tasmin, and that's...Myra. Goodness me, it's cold, isn't it? Do you have a camp nearby where we can get some food and some warmth? Oh, the dog's called Piper. He's a lovely guy, very affectionate. And intelligent.'

Slatter turned his back on the group, so he could growl at me without the others hearing. 'Aten. You're not stupid enough to miss that, are you?' Huh, typical Slatter lack of tact. Then I know him well enough not to be offended by the way his lips punch out blunt statements in the same way he's quick to use his fists. Slatter continued in that low growl. 'Something's wrong. Del-Coffey's voice fucked off somewhere else before he used the woman's name "Myra".'

I whispered, 'So...there's something not right with Myra. Think she's packing a gun?'

'Aten. She's older than she looks.'

Slatter was so close we were almost eyeball-to-eyeball as he looked at me in a meaningful way. That psychopath stare of his blasted shivers of fear down my backbone.

Del-Coffey called out to us again. He sounded nervous. 'Anything wrong, guys?'

The one called Jack took a step forwards. *Click-click-click*...my people were thumbing off the safeties on their guns. Instinctively, my hand went to rest on the butt of a pistol strapped to my waist.

Gorron was the only one from my group that raised his hands clear of the machine gun that hung from a strap across his shoulder. He smiled, trying to ease the tension. 'Jack and Tasmin are my friends,' he said. 'I've known them for months. They're good people. You can trust them with your lives.'

Slatter pointed at Myra. 'What about her?'

I nodded. 'Gorron. Can you vouch for that one?'

'Never seen her before. If she's with Tasmin and Jack, though, she must be okay.'

Tug Slatter doesn't carry a gun. He hates guns. Which is strange for someone whose veins are filled with sheer brutal violence as much as blood. Slatter took a step toward Myra. He has a brutal glare that will freeze anyone's blood to ice. But the one called Myra didn't seem unnerved by him. A rare sight, indeed, because everyone is frightened of Tug Slatter.

'Del-Coffey,' rumbled Slatter. 'Tell that woman to pull her hood down. I want to take a good look at her face.'

Tasmin moved toward Myra and put an arm around her shoulders, like a sister ready to protect her own flesh and blood.

Tasmin said, 'I need to explain something to you about Myra.'

Myra stared back at us. Her eyes were peering out from the ring of fur that fringed the hood. At that moment, the woman's eyes were virtually all I could see of her face. They were large and green and glistening, and they stared coldly at us. I'll tell you one thing. She wasn't scared – she wasn't scared in the slightest. In fact, behind the cold stare I sensed a volcanic rage of murderous ferocity.

Slatter bunched those fists of his that were weapons of total devastation – believe me, I've seen him shatter skulls with those killer knuckles. Slatter's growl became more ominous. 'Tell her to take down the hood.'

Del-Coffey's reaction was one of nervy uncertainty. 'Guys, we can vouch for Myra. She's perfectly safe.'

'Safe?' I echoed. It was like he was claiming a bomb was safe, or a grizzly bear was safe.

'Nick, listen to me.' Del-Coffey was pleading now. 'Myra's okay. Nothing for you to worry about, whatsoever.'

Tasmin picked up the explanation. 'But we do need to tell you something that's really, *really* important.'

Jack tried to put us at ease by the way he spoke. 'Let's go to a place where we can talk. We can explain everything and put your minds at rest. Let's just get out of this cold, eh? The snow's coming down faster.'

Slatter erupted. His boots kicked through the snow as he violently charged toward the woman. 'Take down your hood!'

Tasmin tried to block his way. The big man simply shoved her aside.

Slatter grabbed hold of Myra, then yanked her toward himself as easily as if she was a lightweight doll. His massive hand slashed downward, dragging down her hood, revealing the head and face beneath.

One of our guys behind me yelled in shock. *'Creosote!'*

Slatter clutched Myra by the throat, while his other hand bunched into a massive fist. Which he drew back, ready to punch her so hard that arteries would rupture in her brain, killing her stone dead.

Then the light came.

Such a bright light. Everything seemed to slow down, which meant I had ample time to see my own people leaving the Earth.

Their feet were losing contact with the snowy ground...and I saw Piper, the Collie, shrink back, his fur rippling against his body. Del-Coffey levitated until he was lying flat on his back in the air. He was fully five feet above the road.

The light blazed with such power that I had to shield my eyes with my hand as my own feet rose from the Earth. After that, I began to glide away above the snow. There was no sound...there was only silence...one so intense it felt like my ears were packed tight by some soft material.

There was no sound at all...that is, until I heard the explosion. At the same moment, I felt the savage punch of the blast that had knocked me off my feet. Bizarrely, the sky was below me, and the ground above me. Three seconds later, my entire world went dark.

Of course, I was as ignorant of the calamity as a worm is as ignorant of its own death, as it is crushed beneath the heel of a boot. To put it bluntly, I was as ignorant as shit. Though it wouldn't be long before I looked back at that moment, when my world detonated, and I would realize that I'd once again experienced the end of an era.

And the day after that would be:

DAY ONE
THE AGE OF EXTINCTION

CHAPTER TWO

SOME BLOODY FACTS ABOUT THE EFFECT OF AN EXPLOSION ON THE HUMAN BODY

'Sore neck.' My eyes were closed when I said the words aloud. 'My neck is sore.'

Lying there, with my eyes shut, I touched the back of my neck. Pain smashed through my flesh so ferociously that I lurched upwards onto my feet.

'That was bloody agony,' I told myself before sucking air in through my teeth. Then, upon touching my throat, I realized that my neck had been bandaged. The pain...it was like someone had taken a potato peeler to the back of my neck to shave away chunks of skin...*the pain...the fucking pain*...that's all I could think about. My eyes were watering so much I couldn't tell whether I was indoors or outdoors. As I stood there, swaying, feeling nauseous, I tried to pull out from my fuzzy brain the most recent memories.

'I remember...' I licked my dry lips. 'An explosion.'

I'd been standing next to Slatter as he pulled down the hood of the woman called Myra. She was a Creosote: that's what we call the adults that became murderously insane and began killing their own children.

I used the back of my hand to wipe tears of agony from my eyes. For a moment, I could only make out blurred shapes around me. There was a fusty smell, however, suggesting a building that had its doors and windows shut tight long enough for the atmosphere to accrete that stale pong, so that you actually smell dust and old woodwork. Sounds? None that I could hear, but had the explosion ruptured my ear drums? I clicked my fingers near to my right ear. I heard that okay. Repeat with the left ear. *Click!*

'Yep, heard that. So, I've not been deafened.'

But it was a hell of an explosion. I remembered the blast of white light. How the shockwave had picked us up from the ground before flinging us across the snow. At last, memory was starting to flow again. I recalled Slatter pulling down the woman's hood, her red hair speckling white with snowflakes. A shout of 'Creosote!' Del-Coffey standing there, an expression of horror on his face; he was expecting Slatter to punch the woman. And my people were grouped behind me – they must have been...

I paused, not wanting to complete the awful thought.

I gulped before murmuring, 'They were closer to the explosion than me.'

Sarah, my girlfriend, had been sitting behind the steering wheel of one of the trucks. She would have been very close to the heart of the explosion. Using the back of my hand again, I roughly scraped tears away from my eyes, though this time they weren't purely tears of pain.

The floor moved slightly beneath me – or seemed to. I had to slide my feet to keep my balance and so prevent myself from falling over. Shit. The effects of the explosion must have damaged my sense of balance. Almost at the same time, I found I could see again. Immediately I saw that a nearby window was perfectly round. I turned my head to appraise my surroundings, a movement that made me grimace as nothing less than agony blazed through my neck again. Even so, I saw enough to realize where I was.

'A boat...I'm on a boat.'

Walking produced a jab of pain in every joint as I moved toward the porthole and looked out. Bird crap smeared the window. However, I could make out a broad river that reflected grey cloud above. The floor moved again, suggesting powerfully enough that the boat floated on water, and that it wasn't my sense of balance that had been wrecked during the blast.

The cabin I occupied was perhaps ten feet long, eight feet wide, and possessed two bunks, one above the other. It was distinctly utilitarian accommodation, with metal walls painted cream. Cupboards made from brown wood were fixed to the other wall, while a cubicle in the corner (its door was open) contained a lavatory and a sink. There were no bedsheets on the bunk. Only blankets had covered me as I'd slept for goodness knows how long.

At that moment, all I could think about was Sarah. Had she been hurt in the explosion? Hell, come to that, was she still alive? And what about my other friends? Vivid images of the huge blast of light kept rattling through my skull like train carriages rattling through a tunnel. In fact, I could not stop those flashbacks...seeing the flash of light...seeing my friends hurtling through the air...the shockwave punching me off my feet...

I tried to focus on something else. Anything other than those alarming flashbacks, which were making my heart pound faster and faster. So...what about me? Right now? I was dressed in jeans, sweater, socks – either I'd taken off my Artic survival suit or someone else had. What's more, someone must have bandaged my neck. It's unlikely I'd have managed to fix a bandage there by myself. All the cupboards were empty. There was no sign of either my boots or padded suit.

The floor moved again – this time a lot, though this wasn't due to the boat tilting because of a wave. This was because I felt so dizzy that I had to sit on the bunk before I fell over. My entire body had joined the pain shindig – my joints ached, my lungs felt burning hot, my tongue began to sting as if someone had just hammered a nail through it. A fingertip inspection of the tongue revealed a split in one side that stung so much my eyes began to water again. Evidently, I had accidently bitten my tongue during the violent impact of the explosion.

After waiting until the pain levels had dropped by at least a little, I managed to get to my feet again, before shuffling in my socks to the cabin door.

Whatever vague plans I entertained about getting off the boat and finding my friends were immediately thwarted.

I pounded my fist against the door. 'Hey. Open this this thing. Let me out.' I didn't so much shout as croak the words. My throat was rivalling the arid nature of desert sand. 'Hello? Unlock the door. You'll be sorry if you don't.'

Yeah, as threats go that was as feeble as I felt right at that moment. Standing there on wobbly legs, feeling like crap. Even if the door hadn't been locked, I was hardly in a fit state to erupt into action and beat up my gaolers. Because even after croaking out pleas to open the door, and issuing threats of retribution if they didn't, my legs could hardly support my own bodyweight. My neck hurt so much it was like a hungry wolf was munching away at my spine and my neck muscles. I barely managed a feeble slide-slide shuffle back to the bunk where I lay down.

My plan was to rest for a minute until I felt strong enough to break down the cabin door, then I'd rush out there, find whoever had locked me in the cabin, and then I'd break their jaw. The truth was, however, I didn't even have the strength to keep my eyelids from sliding down over my eyes. And though I realized I was drifting away to sleep I couldn't stay awake.

CHAPTER THREE

MANY QUESTIONS, SOME ANSWERS AND THOSE HIDEOUS THINGS IN THE RIVER

The click of the door opening was loud enough to wake me. Straight away, I was on my feet, my fists clenched, ready to fight for my life. Then, into the cabin, stepped the young women I recognised from the group that Martin Del-Coffey had introduced to us, just seconds before the explosion.

'Tasmin.'

My voice still came out as croak. However, I felt my survival instinct kicking in. Tasmin paused in the doorway. There was a bowl of something steaming in one hand and a mug in the other. Wonderful rich scents of coffee drifted on the air. Tasmin stared at me, no doubt wondering if I planned to attack her.

She then spoke in soft, pleasant tones. 'I brought you ravioli. It's from a can, but it's hot and tastes nice. There's coffee as well.' She paused. 'Are you going to hit me?'

I didn't reassure her that I wouldn't because there was a distinct likelihood that I might just launch myself at her.

I said, 'Why did you lock me in the cabin? Where are the others? Where's Del-Coffey?' Then I asked the most important question that burned so bright inside my head. 'Where's Sarah? She's my girlfriend.'

'Nick. Is it okay if I put the coffee and the bowl down on the table?'

'Answer my questions.'

'Okay.'

'Where's Sarah?'

'I don't know any Sarah.'

'Okay. Del-Coffey. Where is he?'

'Look, Nick...I'm sorry about what happened. If you let me, I'll explain. Just rest assured, we are your friends. We won't hurt you.'

'My friends have never locked me in a room before. Why are you keeping me here like a prisoner? Frightened I might knock you on the head?'

Tasmin gave a sympathetic sigh. 'You were delirious. We had to stop you jumping off the boat into the river. Don't you remember?'

I didn't remember trying to do anything as crazy as that.

'There was an explosion...' I had prompted her with the statement while still eying her with suspicion.

She nodded. 'There was. Someone must have planted a bomb on one of your trucks.'

'One of your people put it there.'

'No...listen, Nick. I don't know how much you remember because you were knocked unconscious by the blast. You've been asleep for two days.' Without asking again, she put the bowl and mug down on a little table bolted to the wall beneath the porthole. 'Del-Coffey had just introduced us to you when a bomb exploded. There's no easy way to tell you this – several of your people were killed. After the explosion, we were attacked by a group of young people, some little more than children – they had assault rifles, pistols, grenades. Myra and Jack managed to get you into a Jeep from your convoy. Then, along with other survivors from your group, we drove away. You see, we had to escape, because it was either that or get slaughtered by those kids. They must have been high on drugs – they were laughing as they were shooting at us. They even fired bullets into people that had already been killed by the explosion.'

'Where is everyone now?'

'The blizzard was so bad we got separated.'

'Or you gave them the slip?'

'You always this suspicious?'

'Damn right I'm suspicious. I'm bandaged up. I'm sore from head to toe but look at you. Not a mark on you. Not so much as a scratch.'

'We were further away from the explosion. So, we just got lucky, right?'

'Del-Coffey and Tug Slatter. Where are they?'

'I don't know. They got into one of the trucks that hadn't been damaged.'

'Then, here on this boat, there's you, me, Jack...Myra?'

'Yes.'

'Myra's a Creosote, isn't she?'

'Was a Creosote?'

'Once a Creosote always a Creosote. None have become sane again.'

'Myra has.'

'I don't believe you.'

After that statement, I picked up the bowl of ravioli. Maybe I was still dazed from the explosion, because after saying what I needed to say I decided the time had come to eat. Perhaps I wasn't being completely rational. However, feeding myself had become my priority. I looked into the bowl, at the yellow pasta parcels floating in spicy tomato sauce. I was hungry. Incredibly hungry. I figured if they'd wanted to kill me, they'd have done so by now, and not waited until I woke up before giving me hot food laced with poison.

The ravioli was delicious. The coffee revived me, too, so that I began to think more clearly. What's more, since moving around the cabin a bit, the aches began to ease in my joints. Though the back of my neck was as still sore as hell. And when I rubbed at where the bandage covered the wounds, I noticed smears of blood on my fingers where the red stuff of life had seeped through.

The boat rocked gently on the river. Because the scenery hadn't changed – and that scenery consisted of snow-covered fields on the far side of the water – I concluded that the boat was moored up and going nowhere.

When I'd started eating, Tasmin had silently glided backwards out of the cabin. This time she left the door open. I still couldn't hear anything, other than my spoon clinking against the bottom of the bowl as I scooped out the pasta parcels. After I'd finished eating, I sat on the bunk for a while, staring at the door, while trying to work out what to do for the best. One option: simply to creep off the boat without being noticed, then take the Jeep, which they'd used to bring me here, and drive back to my settlement. Though I still harboured suspicions about Tasmin and her friends, I told myself it was unlikely that they'd kidnapped me with sinister intent. Because, if they did consider me to be their enemy, they'd have dropped me overboard into the river while I was unconscious. Also, they had bandaged the wounds on my neck. All of which suggested they were trying their level best to take care of me.

After staring at the door for a good twenty minutes, I decided the time had come to ask more questions. I padded out through the door into a passageway, from which other doors led into other cabins (all unoccupied, apart from one, which contained several drums of coffee – clearly the kind of large containers that hotels and cafes would have in their stockrooms).

There were eight cabins on that deck. No doubt there was another deck with yet more cabins, which would be occupied by Tasmin, Jack and Myra. A stairwell led down to the gloomy guts of the boat. In the dim light, I could make out the shape of the boat's engine. Another stairwell took me up to a lounge area, complete with sofas and armchairs. A strong smell of coffee wafted from a coffee machine sitting on a table at the far end of the room.

'Hello?' I lobbed the greeting out into the air, hopeful that someone nearby, yet out of sight, would answer. No answering 'hello' came back at me.

A door led outside onto the open deck. Despite not wearing boots or a warm coat, suddenly the prospect of fresh air after the stale odours of the atmosphere belowdecks was distinctly attractive. Therefore, I opened the door and stepped out. My socks left their woven wool patterns embedded in the covering of snow. Instantly, a cold breeze sank its icy teeth through my sweater and into my skin.

'Hello, Nick. Feeling better?'

I turned toward the sound of the male voice. I immediately saw Jack, leaning back against the guardrail to my left. He had a cup of coffee in one hand.

'I feel fine.' My tone was defiant. I was aiming to sound strong enough for a fistfight if he decided now was the right moment to chuck me into the water. 'You're like Tasmin,' I pointed out. 'The explosion didn't leave a mark on you.'

'We were further away from the blast than you,' he said, basically repeating what Tasmin had told me down in the cabin.

'Where's the Jeep?'

'We got stuck in a snowdrift about a mile to the north, so we arrived here on foot. Dragging you on a tarp, though you're no lightweight.' He turned to look at the river. 'Have you seen what's in the water? I don't think I've seen anything as strange at that before.'

I stared down into the grey river. And suddenly it wasn't the cold breeze that was sending shivers down my backbone. For there, in the somehow greasy-looking water, and floating slowly along on the remorseless current, were terrible things.

I sucked in a lungful of air as the shocking sight met my eyes.

Down there, just twenty feet below me, were bodies – lots of human bodies – hundreds, possibly thousands, of men and women. Their apparent age was above twenty and, thereafter, heading northwards into old age, on account of lots of white hair and bald heads. There was no doubt in my mind. These were Creosotes.

The bodies weren't simply dead people floating individually in the water. No, they'd been connected together in a brutal and nightmarish way. The bodies had been threaded like beads on a string. Though in this case, the 'string' that had been used to connect them together were lengths of bright orange rope.

And that rope passed through the stomachs of some individuals to connect them to their neighbours. Others appeared to have had holes cut in the floor of their mouths to allow the roped to be threaded through their lower jaw to connect them with the next man or woman.

The process had been repeated thousands of times. Ropes fed through holes in jaws, or via a gash in their bellies, the rope penetrating flesh like a huge orange worm.

181

Jack's voice dropped to a murmur. 'There are hundreds and hundreds of people...all connected together. Who on Earth would do such a grotesque thing?'

'The really important question,' I said, 'is *why* would they do that?'

For more information about the *BLOOD CRAZY SERIES* and our other books, please visit:

Website: dv-publishing.com

Facebook: DarknessVisiblePublishing

Twitter: DV_Publishing

Instagram: dv_publishing

Printed in Great Britain
by Amazon

34491003R00106